THE
KEEP

THE
KEEP

the watchers

VERONICA WOLFF

NEW AMERICAN LIBRARY

Published by the Penguin Group
Penguin Group (USA) Inc., 375 Hudson Street,
New York, New York 10014, USA

USA | Canada | UK | Ireland | Australia | New Zealand | India | South Africa | China

Penguin Books Ltd., Registered Offices: 80 Strand, London WC2R 0RL, England
For more information about the Penguin Group visit penguin.com.

First published by New American Library,
a division of Penguin Group (USA) Inc.

First Printing, June 2013

 REGISTERED TRADEMARK—MARCA REGISTRADA

LIBRARY OF CONGRESS CATALOGING-IN-PUBLICATION DATA.

Wolff, Veronica.
The Keep: the Watchers/Veronica Wolff.
p. cm
ISBN 978-0-451-41636-0
1. Vampires—Fiction. I. Title.
PS3623.O575K44 2013
813'.6—dc23   2013002058

Printed in the United States of America
3 5 7 9 10 8 6 4 2

Set in Bembo
Designed by Ginger Legato

This one goes out to Rosanne Romanello,
with my warmest thanks.

ACKNOWLEDGMENTS

I'm grateful to my entire team at Penguin, especially my editor, Cindy Hwang. We've worked together for over six years, and my respect and admiration for her only continue to grow. I'd also like to give a shout-out to my publicist, Rosanne Romanello, who, quite simply, rocks. I'd also like to thank Robin Rue and Beth Miller at Writers House for such thoughtful support.

Thanks also go to Gudmundur Audunsson, for his continued help with Icelandic—any errors are mine alone. To Monica Mc-Carty and Jami Alden, for cheering this series from the sidelines. To my critique partner, Kate Perry, who makes me do the hard things that end up being good for me. To Tracy Grant, for all those many pep talks. To Martha Flynn, who's always game to discuss everything from three-act structure, to the tastiest local dim sum, to the latest constellation of CW actors. As always, thanks to Connie O'Donovan and Joey Wolff for being such enthusiastic (and honest) early readers. And finally, to Carlos "Sapão" Ban and the rest of my family at Ocean Beach Barra Brothers—they taught me everything Drew knows about grappling.

Last but not least, I'm most grateful for my miraculous family. They never complain, even though they know the simple act of getting into a car with me brings with it the distinct risk of enforced brainstorming. A lot of that went into this book . . . and who knew my husband and kids would be so brilliant at devising crazy vampire mythologies? Love you—couldn't do it without you.

THE
KEEP

CHAPTER ONE

⸻

I t was a new semester, and this term my combat class was a martial arts intensive. We were practicing some basic Brazilian jujitsu, doing sweeps. Half the girls were on their backs, whisking the feet out from under a partner who stood above. But, apparently, my partner had different ideas. Before I'd regained my footing, she clipped my heel out from under me, sending me toppling.

"What the hell?" I hopped up, giving a shake to my ringing head.

"What?" she asked, playing dumb.

"You're supposed to let me get into position before you sweep me." I approached again, taking a tone that was more ridicule than reprimand. "This is practice, Audra."

"It's *Frost*," she snarled, though I didn't need to be reminded of her ridiculous new name. I'd become acquainted with her when she was Emma's roommate and remembered the day she'd announced it, chosen in honor of her love of life on *Eyja næturinnar*.

I couldn't help it—I smirked. "Isn't that one of the X-Men?"

The girl was a nerd the caliber of which made me look cool. I mean, I might've been smart, but I wasn't a dork, thankyou-verymuch. But under that white-blond bob, she had a tiny heart and a brittle mean streak that, when combined with her slavish affection for everything the vamps represented, made her a shoo-in for the island.

She swatted at my leg, glaring at me with almost comically narrowed eyes, but I hopped out of her reach.

I stifled a giggle. "Are those your angry eyes?"

"I hate you."

"I'm sure there's a club." I began to step over her hips to straddle her where she lay on the floor, but before I got into position, she grabbed my ankle and whipped my foot from under me again. I toppled like a tree to the floor, cracking my head on the thin mat.

I rolled up more quickly than before, mad now. It was wrong of her to catch me unawares during a simple workout, but I hadn't tucked my chin, and falling incorrectly was definitely my bad. I hated when I messed up, especially in Priti's class.

"Stop it." I stepped over her and quickly bent my knees and found my balance positioned over her. "You're not even doing the move correctly."

She cupped her hands behind my ankles, but now I did all I could to make it difficult, imagining myself anchored to the floor, and this time it took her a few tries before she could topple me.

I felt Priti's eyes on me, so I finally let the girl sweep me. It was an exercise, after all. When I popped back to standing, I asked sweetly, "Do you need me to give you some pointers?"

Frost and I had been butting heads since we'd found out we

were to be placed together as roommates in the Initiate dorm. We both hated the situation—me because Frost was a kiss-ass with the vampires, and the last thing I needed was a snitch roomie, and she hated me. . . . Well . . . apparently there was a constellation of reasons I was still beginning to understand.

"I'm doing something right," she said. "You fell, didn't you?"

"This is class, not a fight to the death."

"Kill or be killed," she said, trying to sound cool.

I rolled my eyes. As if I hadn't learned that lesson already.

Honestly, I blamed much of her attitude on jealousy. Enamored of anything with fangs, the girl fancied herself a bit of a scholar on island matters. But here I was, someone who was considered a genius, who'd also attracted the attention of two of the island's most notable vampires.

First and foremost, there was Carden McCloud, the swoon-worthy Scottish vampire I'd bonded with. Nobody knew just how intense our relationship really was, but there was no hiding the fact that we spent a lot of time together. Increasingly, his eyes gleamed with desire and—somehow even more unsettling— fondness when he looked at me.

Then there was Hugo de Rosas Alcántara. I detested the ancient Spanish vampire, but I was undeniably obsessed with him, too. My best friend, Emma, was dead, and I blamed him. The dream of revenge had become the thing that spurred me out of bed in the morning. It was what drove my workouts. What kept me up at night. It might take me years to exact my vengeance, but I would have it.

"Look, I don't like the new room situation any more than you do." It was time to make peace. I'd already done the roomie-who-hates-me thing, but going to bed each night, wondering if

I'd wake up alive in the morning or not, well, it really wore on a girl. I raised my brows, decided. "Truce?"

"Fuck off, Drew."

"Alrighty then," I mumbled, rolling my shoulders for the long fight ahead of me. "Don't say I didn't try."

"Time for holds," Priti called, drawing our attention to the front of the mats. Her bell-like voice momentarily elevated the place into something more transcendent than just a stinky, sweat-stained gym. Her lithe grace promised a female power that I, too, might carry inside. "On the floor, little birds. Time to grapple."

Everyone dropped to their knees, awaiting the next instruction.

"Begin in the cross-side position. Five minutes. Go."

I moved quickly, pinning Frost on her back before she had a chance to get up. "I'll go first."

"This is such a joke," Frost snarled. She bucked her hips, and I lurched forward, releasing my grip to catch myself before my nose crunched into the mat. "I can't believe they put me with you."

I felt Priti standing close by but out of view. She chuckled. "Ladies, please don't kill one another."

"We won't," I said, but my eyes on Frost added a silent . . . *yet*. I stole a glimpse of the girls next to us, going through their moves in a way that rehearsed mechanics, not gave bloody noses.

I resumed my original position, lying across her body, putting her in a hold. "You just can't stand that the vampires like me"—I tilted my head, whispering for her ears alone—"more than you."

"No." She let out a feline snarl and grabbed my arm. Her nails dug into me as she wrenched my elbow to her chest, thrusting her hips and flipping me onto my back. She straddled me, pinning with her knees. "I can't stand you because you think you're better than everyone else. You think you know so much. But guess what, Drew? I know more."

Little bits of spittle flew from her mouth, and I squinted against the onslaught. The girl was making this more than just a practice fight, and it was pissing me off. I hooked a foot around hers, propelled my hips, and flipped her back under me. "You need to learn, Audra. All this posturing just smells desperate. Vampires hate desperate."

"Is that what you told Emma?" She wrapped her legs around my waist, hooking her feet at my back, but she was unable to get leverage.

"Screw you." We were grappling for real now, but our strength and size were well matched. She bucked and squirmed, but I held on, keeping her pinned. "Don't you dare mention Emma."

"You think you're the teacher's pet." She shifted her weight, and I just barely escaped a choke hold.

"There's always Master Dagursson," I said sweetly, referring to the remarkably unattractive ancient Viking vampire. "He loves you."

"You think you're better than everyone else."

"And you don't?"

"You think you're the vampires' little darling." She wrenched her legs up and cinched my neck. "But I know better."

I tried to tap out, swatting her repeatedly—the universal sparring language for *stop killing me*—but there was no stopping her.

"It's your fault Emma's gone," she said.

I rolled to my side, forcing her legs to unclench, and sucked in a breath. "It's a vampire's fault that Emma's gone."

But deep down, I worried she was right. Deep down, I tormented myself with thoughts that I should've done more to save my best friend. Could I have found a way to sacrifice myself to save her? *Two girls enter; only one will leave.* . . . So why had I been the one to emerge alive?

The memory of her body, limp in Alcántara's arms, brought fresh rage and anguish. Power shot through me, and I broke Frost's hold, flinging her away like she weighed nothing. "Get the hell off me."

"Your roommates are cursed." She crouched on hands and knees, and I could see her mind working furiously, looking for her chance to pounce. "I refuse to be tied up like Emma, taken to that castle just because you're some vampire's pet."

I froze. "What did you just say?"

But she'd frozen, too. "Nothing."

"What do you mean, *tied up like Emma*?" Maybe if she'd said *carried*, it would've implied Emma's body—her dead body. But she'd said *tied up*. Dead bodies weren't tied up. "Was she still alive when they took her?"

"You saw her," she replied, giving me a non-answer, but Frost's eyes betrayed the secret she'd spilled.

"They took Emma to the castle . . . and she was alive?" The words came out slowly, a chill creeping over my body.

"How should I know?"

I could tell she was lying. Frost didn't want to be forced to go to the castle . . . like Emma.

Emma was alive. Or she had been.

What happened to her after Alcántara slashed her down the middle? As with all the fallen girls, Tracers had come into the ring and taken her away. I thought of the vampires' castle, a hulking granite keep, looming silently beyond the standing stones. Was that where they took her body? For what purpose?

Oh God, Em. It was unthinkable. Was it possible Emma still lived, enduring Alcántara's tortures?

I needed to go, to find a way into the castle. I wouldn't rest until I found her. I would find out what happened. I'd save her.

And then I would have my revenge. I'd take Alcántara down.

CHAPTER TWO

B y the time I left the gym, I was shaking.

What happened in that hideous castle? What happened to all those girls, each one disappeared from under our noses? I'd wondered before, but now I was obsessed. Never had someone so close to me been taken.

Was she trapped in there, still alive? Were there other girls? What did the vampires do in there? The need to know—to have some image, however morbid, to hold on to in my mind—consumed me.

I tugged off a glove and jammed my hand deep into my coat pocket. Found the handkerchief.

Emma's handkerchief.

I'd snagged it from her room before they'd cleared out her stuff. It was a simple square of white fabric, one we'd all gotten in our standard-issue kit bags. Not many of us used them—I mean, *ew*, right?—except for Emma. It'd been just like Prairie Girl to use her hanky all the time. While mine was still folded crisply in my drawer, hers was stained, bearing a rusty brown patch of blood that'd never washed out completely. Blood where she'd wiped her hands after skinning a rabbit on that night we'd been left stranded in the dark to face punishment. We'd faced it together and had been friends ever since.

I took it out and folded it as I walked. Folded and smoothed and refolded. I'd stolen the handkerchief as a memento, but as I put it back in my pocket, it became something else. It was my pact. *Pinky swear, Em. If you're alive, I'll find you.*

Frost was ahead of me on the path, and I watched as she squared her shoulders and slung her small gym duffel over her shoulder. She was headed back to the dorm, and if I wanted to shower before lunch, I'd need to follow her. But I couldn't bear going straight back to the room, especially not with her. Did she know the secrets of the keep? Did she know the fates of all those girls and yet chose to side with vampires instead?

Our new Initiate housing only made things worse. The dorm was smaller, with a warren of oddly sized rooms that had more the feel of a giant converted house than the first-year Acari dorm had. And how I missed that old dorm now. These new irregular rooms lent a false impression of intimacy to our roommate situation—like we were all sisters sharing rooms in a house instead of strangers forced together by circumstance.

I couldn't bear to face it. Not just yet.

I stopped abruptly and turned, taking a detour to the boys' housing. To the castle. I had to see it. If Emma truly were alive, that was where she was probably being held.

Could it really be true? That she might've been enduring the vampires' keep, all this time . . . *My God, Em* . . . It was too much to consider. If she were alive, it meant I'd failed her even more than when I'd let Alcántara slash her down her belly. Because, truly, I couldn't decide which was the greater horror: to be killed by vampires, or to be imprisoned and kept alive by them.

I walked briskly, picking along the edge of the path, tromping through what remained of last night's snow. A thin rime had crystallized along its surface, making a satisfying crunch with every step. The January light was weak and gray, and it struck me that my one-year anniversary on the island had come and gone.

So many others had disappeared, and yet here I was, still alive. Cheers to me.

A heaviness beyond grief weighed on my shoulders, and I glanced up. Sure enough, the ancient keep had appeared, looming in the distance. It was a grim scene, several thousand pounds of gray-black stone. What secrets were hidden within? I peered hard, studying every line, every crag and crevice in the facade, like I might've perceived answers through the force of my will alone.

A familiar voice startled me from my thoughts. "You've got guts, showing up here like this."

I spun. It was Yasuo.

I knew that happy, relieved feeling of seeing a friend, but the sensation was instantly cut short by the look of him. So crushed. So pale and bleak.

"Yasuo." I realized I'd hoped to run into him. He'd forgive me. We were friends. We needed each other. We'd work through this together. I put on a brave, gentle face, hoping to convince myself—and him—that there was forgiveness to be had. "How are you doing?" I hoped he heard how the words had come from my heart.

"How am I doing?" A smirk contorted his face, and his words came sharp and cold. "How am I doing? Please tell me you didn't come here to ask *how'm I doin'*? Because I'll tell you, Drew. Here's how I'm doing: I suck. You killed my girlfriend, remember? Or wait. Maybe you don't, because you're . . . too . . . freaking . . . self-involved to care about anyone but yourself." Hatred glimmered in his eyes. Emma was gone, and he blamed me.

"No, wait," I blurted. "It's not like that. I have news. I think—"

"Screw what you think." He spun away from me, shutting me out, striding in the direction of the dining hall.

Friends were rare on this rock. I needed Yasuo and I thought he probably needed me, too. Undaunted, I did a quick jog to catch up. "I think there's a chance she's still alive," I said at his back. The words spilled from me in a rush. I needed to get his attention, to convince him there was hope. That I was still a worthy friend before he shut me out forever. "Emma. She was *alive*, Yas. After the fight. What if she's still alive?"

He froze utterly, but it wasn't an I'm-listening kind of pose that he'd assumed; rather, it was more like rage had finally frozen him, crackling him to ice. "She's not."

I refused to believe it. I was desperate. I had sunk my teeth into this new hope and wouldn't give it up so easily now. "Just hear me out," I begged. "Audra said something weird. She said they had to *tie* her—"

"She's gone."

"Wait. What do you mean? Do you know what happened?" Yasuo lived *inside* the castle. He was privy to many of its secrets. He got to peek behind that thick granite curtain every day. "What do you mean *gone*? Do you know what they—"

"I just know, all right?" He speared his fingers through his hair in what looked like a gesture of desperation, and I saw how his hands trembled.

"But how do you know?"

"I know," he said through clenched teeth.

"Did you actually see her?"

"Let it go."

He stormed away, and I followed at his heels. Until I knew exactly what'd happened, until I saw it with my own eyes or talked to someone who had, I wouldn't believe it.

"I just need to understand. Did you see her . . . after?" I shuddered. It was unthinkable.

"Leave it."

His long legs were striding down the path again, and I had to do a skip-hop to catch up. "What if I can't leave it? She might've been your girlfriend, but she was *my* best friend. And that's something."

It'd once been everything.

He stopped and met my gaze full-on, throwing me in the path of hundreds of tiny razor blades. He peeled his lips back, revealing shimmering fangs. They were longer than I'd realized.

"When'd your fangs grow?" I wished he'd look away again. A nervous laugh fizzed out of me. "The better to bite me with, right?"

"Listen . . . to . . . me," he said, enunciating slowly and with ice-cold fury. "She's gone. Forever. *Gone.*"

"No," I whispered in a voice like a child's. His words finally registered. I saw the truth in his expression. It'd cracked—he'd cracked. I clutched my head in my hands, experiencing her death all over again. Grief embraced me—so familiar, it felt like my natural state. It would never go away. I'd carry it forever. "No. No, no."

"Yes, Drew. She was ripped up the fucking middle, and it was *your* fault." He looked manic, anguish flowing from him like a torrent of acid. "She loved you," he said, his words like a slap. "Emma loved, but it always was all about you." He stepped forward, stabbing a finger in my chest. "You, you, you. And Em was too good—she was too goddamned *nice*—to do anything but humor you. And you turned around and let her . . . let that happen to her."

"Not a minute passes where I don't wish that'd been me." It took everything I had not to take a step back. I would not be afraid of Yasuo—he was once my close friend. He'd be my friend again. I refused to accept that he was done with me forever. "If I could've traded places with her, I would have. We need to stick together now, more than ever. Emma would want us to be there for each other. There's no reason we need to be grieving alone through this."

He gaped at me, aghast. "If you think you can show up here and say some shit and be all nice and I'm-so-sad and that it'll make it all better, think again, D. You just want *yourself* to feel better. This is you making it about *you,* all over again, as always."

"You're not the only one who gets to be sad," I snapped. I was the one who was angry now. "Don't think for one second that there's anything pretend about how totally and completely heartbroken I am. You're not the only one who gets to grieve. You're pissed, sure, but guess what? I'm pissed, too. I should've been the one Al sliced up the middle—I get that. But I wasn't, okay? And now we have a chance for revenge. Don't you want to know what happened to her?" It was knowledge that'd surely torment me for the rest of my life, but I had to know her exact fate. Had Alcántara tortured her? What happened to all those girls? "We can take them down, Yas. We can fight them together. Get our revenge."

"None of your stupid little games or plans is going to bring Emma back. I wish *you* were dead instead."

"Fine. Maybe you should just kill me right now. How about that?" I took a turn stabbing my finger into his chest. "You can have your revenge on me, and we can all slaughter one another until there's nobody left on this stupid island."

I let the dramatic pronouncement hang, then continued more calmly. "Or we can team up, Yas. We can be allies. We can fight this system. Approach it logically, systematically. We take our time, and we can have payback. For Emma. You're on the inside. Maybe we can't save *her*, but maybe we can save the next girl. She'd have wanted that. We could do it for her."

He stared at me for a moment, silently processing. His features softened, and hope filled my chest like a balloon.

But then he said, "You're right. I should just kill you now."

CHAPTER THREE

I couldn't bear to see if Yasuo would be true to his word. A tide of students appeared, and I turned from him and merged with the others heading to the dining hall. When I got there, I didn't wait to sit down. I just grabbed my drink and pounded it, standing right there at the fridge, black lunch tray dangling empty in my hand.

I swallowed, and a pleasant shiver rolled up my body. It sounded disgusting, consuming the blood of another, but how quickly we got used to it. Who could resist the rush of courage and power that came from consuming the lifeblood of a vampire? It was cumulative, too—the more we drank, the stronger we grew.

I peered into the glass-fronted refrigerator. Vampire blood glimmered in preposterously formal, cut-crystal tumblers, all lined up in neat rows. For one crazy moment, I contemplated stealing an extra.

I shook off the feeling. As with all good things, just enough was just right. But too much? Too much could make a girl powerful beyond imagining . . . or it might just make her nuts. Too much of a good thing could drive a weak mind mad.

And me, I had to be extra careful, bonded as I was to Carden. Already I got to drink straight from the source, from Carden's own powerfully beating heart, and that was infinitely more reckless than simply filching an extra shot glass at dinner.

An explosion of sound startled me from my thoughts. A cluster of guys coming into the dining hall. I tensed, hearing Yasuo's voice rise above the rest.

I stole a peek over my shoulder. His eyes were waiting for me, glaring so intensely, I wouldn't have been surprised if there were a couple of red laser-beam dots wavering on my forehead. I had to look away.

It was hopeless. Emma was well and truly dead. I wanted revenge, and apparently Yas did, too. Only he wanted revenge on *me*.

The rush of strength I'd felt from the drink evaporated. My bravery faded into bravado, leaving me feeling like a wispy paper-doll cutout of myself.

My head was buzzing. I needed to sit.

Despair and the ghosts of friends past scratched at a door in the back of my mind. Because I needed to sit . . . but *where?* Less than a year ago, I'd have been settling in at a table with Emma. Yasuo would've been there, too, cracking stupid jokes, goofing off. I'd watched as the two of them slowly began to crush on each other. Watched as it'd developed into more. My old Proctor, Amanda, would've been there, too, with her Cockney accent, calling her fries *chips* and her chips *crisps*. Tracer Judge might've stopped by, his friendly puppy-dog eyes meeting everyone's gaze but Amanda's. They'd been a couple, and their failed escape had been the death of them.

So few people in my life had gained my regard, and now most of them were dead.

I swayed. *Get to a chair.*

I made my feet walk to the first empty table, which was thankfully out of the fray, along the wall near the door. I just needed to eat. Not talk to anyone. Get in and get out. I didn't want to be there, but I needed my calories—proper nourishment could mean the difference between life and death on this island.

I wolfed down bread and soup. An awareness of my surroundings was even more critical than those calories, and I pretended to keep to myself while really I was reading the room. I could no longer see Yasuo, but still I felt his eyes boring into me. He was across the room, sitting with his fellow Trainees.

Emotion clenched my throat, making it hard to swallow. I hadn't known many friends in my life. Losing one hurt worse than any injury, and I'd had a lot of bad injuries.

I tried to focus on my breathing instead. I chewed and swallowed and chewed and swallowed. Chewed, swallowed, and tried to consider the fact that I did still have people in my corner.

Carden . . . Just the thought of him unspooled something in my chest. I tried to picture him, to remember his scent, his eyes. The taste of him. To recall the touch of his hand and the sound of his voice. Though I couldn't summon a complete snapshot, I clung to every thread of every memory as though I could weave it all together into a lifeline.

I longed to see him and consoled myself with the knowledge that I'd see him later. He would come for me—there was no question of it. It was something I knew in my bones. He always sensed when I needed him.

And there were other people I could rely on to cheer me up. Ronan was, well, Ronan—and oddly, he usually managed to make me feel not entirely alone. There was Josh—he always made me laugh, which was nice. And thinking of my old roommate Mei-Ling was always good for a smile, too. Even though she'd escaped and I'd probably never see her again, I liked to think of her out there somewhere, sending positive thoughts my way.

I tried to think of more.

I couldn't.

Grief seized my throat, and the fresh-baked bread stuck there, my mouth suddenly too dry. I dunked the last crusty heel of it into my soup, but that released a potato smell into the air, a bland, tepid, creamy sort of smell, like the puddle of milk leftover in my school thermos at the end of the day. My stomach turned.

I shivered and clenched my teeth against sudden chattering. I'd never warmed up after the run-in with Yasuo, and not even the dry blast of ancient, pinging radiators could touch the chill that cut to my bones.

The screech of a chair leg against the floor brought my head up. Three girls were settling in at the end of the table. They were Acari, *new* Acari, clearly green enough not to know that my blue catsuit was code for *stay away*. One nodded at me, but I only stared back, my face an even blank.

My training had been good for something, and in that brief instant, I managed to assess reams about them. One was petite— she looked about my height—with hair that would've been a boring shade of brown were it not for her mesmerizingly perfect ringlets. Another had dark hair and olive skin in a tone that suggested an uncommon lineage, the sort of thing involving an Irish grandfather and a Lebanese grandmother. The third was tall and lean, and her prettiness had an unremarkable quality to it, that brand of conventional uniformity that made a girl instantly popular in high school.

I had a surreal flashback. Me, sitting at a table almost exactly one year ago. I'd have looked short, just like Curly over there, sitting next to Miss Pretty, whose legginess summoned the ghost of my nemesis, Lilac.

Curly nodded at me like her friend had. I looked down, suddenly focused on my soup. It was early days for them, when the culling of new girls was fierce and daily, and I found it best not to be friendly with anybody who might disappear at any moment. Besides, I just didn't have the energy to enlighten new Acari about things like friendly nods and how they could get a girl's butt whipped.

My old Proctor, Amanda, would've nodded back. She probably would've had a kind word, too. But I wasn't Amanda. The realization bummed me out—though, in a weird way, it should've bolstered me, considering Amanda's behavior had gotten her killed. Besides, I might not have been friendly, but neither was I flashing around my throwing stars like any good Initiate should. So there was that.

"Yo. Curly." Yasuo had showed up to assess the new blood, and his words were a knife in my chest. He'd voiced a nickname—Curly—that I'd been thinking myself, and it crushed me to remember how things had been between us. All the old secret looks and private jokes, the stuff that two like-minded people—two *friends*—shared. All of that was gone. Then the knife twisted as I remembered how his first words to *me* hadn't been much different. *Hey. Blondie.* We'd sat next to each other in Phenomena class. He'd been my first real friend on this island.

No longer. Now he just studiously avoided eye contact with me.

Curly might've given me a nod, but the appearance of the boys had her intent on her bowl of soup. Was she right to be scared? Was Yasuo being friendly as he had been with me so long ago, or had his warmth all died with Emma? He had a little gang now, unlike when we'd first met. Sitting there, I'd dismissed them—all the guys blurred together as a mass of cocky attitudes and half-grown fangs—but when the skin on my neck prickled, I reassessed.

Scanning the group, I saw there was a pair of eyes trained on me. While the others were studying the fresh blood, Rob had been studying *me.*

Rob. He was the jerky Trainee who'd once made a move on me—if you could call attempted assault *a move*—and when I responded by slicing a giant hole in his pants with my throwing star, I'd made an enemy forever.

He'd sworn revenge, but at the time, my reaction had been a resounding *what-ever.* I knew I should've taken threats like that seriously, but I mean, *really.* We were surrounded by threats, and I had enough on my plate trying to make sure there weren't any real vampires trying to kill me. Teenagers like Rob tended to pale in comparison when someone like Master Alcántara had you in his sights.

And besides, I had an ancient and powerful vampire on my side to protect me. I wasn't sure whether or not I could call Carden McCloud something so mundane as "boyfriend," but he was my bonded vampire, and that seemed infinitely more powerful. So, I had Carden looking out for me, and though it was probably a false sense of security, it *was* security.

"Is she deaf?" one of the guys asked.

Curly hadn't responded to Yasuo's little greeting, and these were the sorts of guys who weren't used to being ignored. Yas leaned down to speak in her ear. "Hey, Shirley Temple. I'm talking to you."

The leggy, pretty girl went wide-eyed, making her look like a panicked woodland creature. Her gaze skittered over the Trainees. They'd closed in, standing behind the girls in a half circle, looming. Pretty Girl looked like she wanted to bolt, but then a redheaded Trainee named Danny came up from behind and planted his hands on her shoulders. I'd misread her. Unlike Lilac, this girl was scared. Easily intimidated.

She wouldn't last a day.

I had to look away. I tried to dismiss her from my mind.

It was past time for me to leave. I piled my cutlery neatly in my bowl. And yet . . . I didn't budge.

A strange, new light was burning in Yasuo's eyes, and it kept drawing my attention, mesmerizing me. I didn't know what that expression meant. I had to see what he'd do. Who he'd become.

He reached out and pulled one of Curly's ringlets straight. It sprang back into place as he let go. "Well? Do you have a name? Or are you mute *and* deaf?"

This wasn't the Yasuo who'd sat next to me that first day of class, the guy with the spiky mussed hair and the crooked smile. This Yasuo was unsmiling, bitter. His eyes had been drained of their warmth, and for an instant, he looked like a marble version of himself.

This Yasuo was becoming Vampire.

"My name's Regina." She gathered up every inch of what I estimated was her five-foot-zero frame and gave her best contemptuous smile.

I could tell it wasn't practiced, though—she hadn't been one of *those* girls in her high school—and I read her story in a flash. It was all in the way she held her shoulders, that flicker in her eye. She'd thought herself a loser back home. Maybe she'd been knocked around like I had, or maybe she just thought about things too much, seeing flaws where there were none, which was kind of like me, too. Either way, the whole thing gave me a painful pang.

"Regina!" Danny crowed. He'd rhymed Regina with vagina—*of course* he had—the joke exaggerated by his thick British accent.

No friends, I reminded myself. No pity. Just survival. I crumpled my napkin and tossed it on my tray. I wasn't getting involved this time.

Regina marshaled her expression and spun in her chair to face him. "Like I haven't heard *that* before."

So not the way to deal with this particular problem, Curly. With a quiet sigh, I couldn't help but pause and watch just a second longer.

Gangly boy bodies closed in, looming over her, blunting the fury in her eyes. But she had spunk, this one, and she snarled, "Go crawl back under your rocks."

I should've left then and there, but it was like watching a train wreck—one that I'd been on before myself. My feet were poised to leave, but my butt was glued to the seat. Here it came, in five, four, three . . .

"Aw, don't be like that." A Trainee named Colin plopped

down at the table. He was blond and cute, looking like the high school star quarterback.

I hated Colin.

"We're the welcoming committee," he added, and something about his lizardy grin morphed him from high-school-quarterback into high-school-quarterback-who-buried-victims-in-the-backyard.

Bingo. That was my cue. I scooted back my chair. Outta here.

I picked up my tray, but Rob had appeared at my shoulder. "Acari Drew," he said, using my official term of address. I might have ascended to Initiate, but I'd still be called Acari, at least until the time when—or rather, if—I survived to become Guidon. *Acari*—the word itself originally meant a subclass of bloodsucking arachnid, as though we girls were ticks, and Rob had enunciated it like he wanted to remind me of this fact.

He slammed my tray back down again. "Going so soon?"

CHAPTER FOUR

———∞———

"Actually," I said, "I was thinking I'd skip this particular party."

Keeping his hand planted where it was, Rob eased into the chair next to me. "But we're just getting started."

"And I was just finishing." I tried to tug my tray back, but his hand was splayed across the black fiberglass, my fork tilting up under the pressure of his palm. I gave up and let go—there'd be no battle of strength with these guys. *Ever.* I'd always be the weaker one, and I hated it.

He slid the tray away, grinning at me like he'd read my mind. "That's right. You're gonna stick around here with us for a little while instead."

I was in it now. I'd learned there were times to show fear, and this wasn't one of them. "What's your problem anyway?"

"We're just trying to talk to some pretty girls . . . and *you*." He guffawed, like he'd just made the funniest joke ever.

I rolled my eyes. "Whatever."

He scooted closer, grinning suggestively. "Though maybe we can work something out, you and me. If you're nice enough, I might forgive you for being such a bitch."

I scowled. "Thanks, but no, thanks, Romeo. Not in the mood."

"Hey," Colin called from the other end of the table. "El Trainee Roberto. A little focus here. Eyes on the prize. Isn't that right, ladies?" He gave a smooth grin to the dark-haired girl. But she was staring at her lunch like she was trying to bust out some telepathy and bend her cutlery with her eyeballs, so he turned his attentions to Pretty Girl instead. "You need to come to the castle," he told her. Then his eyes lit. "In fact," he added, "all you first-years have to."

The girl actually said, "Really?" She was studying him like she might find some good there if she peered hard enough, as if he might've been cute enough to look past his evil little soul.

I rolled my eyes. Don't pass go, Pretty Girl. Just go directly to the door to collect your Darwin award now.

"Oh, totally," Colin said, sensing her interest.

Redheaded Dan added, "You new girls get assigned what are kind of . . . buddies, like."

"The vampires in charge didn't tell us anything about that." Regina was more skeptical than her friend, and I gave her better odds.

"They sent us to tell you," Yasuo said.

Pretty Girl looked from one to the other. "You're not joking?"

Dan grinned and nodded. "You'll be ambassadors, like." He sure liked the word *like*. Maybe it was a London thing. He clarified, "You know, mates." That, I knew, was a Britishism, but still, the boys guffawed at the double entendre.

"Seriously?" I muttered to myself. I couldn't decide which angered me more: the girls for being blinded by a couple of cute faces, or the boys for taking advantage.

Colin scented Pretty Girl's weakness and had her cornered like the doe-eyed creature she was. "We take you on a tour," he told her with that creepy grin.

"Get real," I whispered.

But Yas had heard. His eyes instantly zoomed to mine. "What did you say?" He wasn't dumb. He knew me, and he'd know exactly what I thought about these clowns. It was what *he* used to think. So why was he hanging out with them?

"I said you're a real big deal," I lied.

Dan, the ginger moron, actually smiled. "Jealous?"

"In your dreams, Danny Boy."

Colin angled away from me, giving his full focus to the girls. "Don't you ladies listen to Drew. She's an Initiate—she's just trying to screw with you."

Dan was staring at me now, with a combination of macho bluster and flat-out stupidity. "Little D is messing with you. It's what the older girls do."

The new Acari looked like they were actually buying his story, and I told them, "*They're* the ones screwing with you. Not me."

"Not true," Dan protested. "We're supposed to explain things to you." The way he said *things* sounded like *fings*.

Colin added, "Show you around."

I shot a glance at Yasuo. He was silently watching the proceedings. The look on his face was unreadable, like a combination of amusement and scorn. Why was he even involved with these knuckleheads?

"But we can't go off the path," Regina said warily.

"Oh, you won't. You won't. We just need to . . ." Dan gave Colin a loaded look, uncertain how to finish what he'd started.

Colin caught the ball and ran. "You have to come with us so we can explain the curriculums that you're going to take while you're here."

I groaned. The guy had the IQ of a tennis ball. "The *curriculums?*"

"What?" Dan's glare was meant to challenge me, but I just thought it made him appear slack-jawed.

I sat forward, planting my elbows on the table, leaning forward, bracing for a fight. So much for leaving. Because, seriously, nothing made me madder than dumb *and* mean. "It's staggering."

"What?" the guys asked in unison.

"Your stupidity," I said, louder now, enunciating slowly and clearly as though speaking to a couple of deaf and doddering old men. "It's staggering."

I turned to the girls. "Don't listen to these idiots." The dark-haired Acari looked scared and confused, while Pretty Girl was acting like she wanted to trust the guys and not me. *Whatever.* "They've got nothing to show you." I pinned a look on Rob and added, "Trust me."

He looked like he was considering gutting me then and there. He could try. I knew for a fact I could give him a run for his money, and even if I couldn't, I could see in his eyes, *he* knew I had a vampire for backup.

I stood. "Your little joke is done, gentlemen. Take the clown act somewhere else."

Dan attempted a last-ditch effort. "But we have to take them to the castle."

"Yeah, D." Yasuo finally spoke. His eyes glittered at me from across the table. "Tell them how all good girls end up at the castle."

I felt his comment like a physical blow.

I locked my knees. I wouldn't show my pain. "All good girls get back to the dorm." I aimed the next words at Regina. Maybe it was because she'd reminded me of me, or maybe it was just because I could tell from the hormonal glow radiating off Pretty Girl that she was a goner. "And if they're smart, they'll go *now*."

I walked away, refusing to look back over my shoulder. But still, I felt Yasuo watching.

His comment had slashed like a knife, and I needed to stay alert. One of these days, there just might be a real blade and it would be aimed at my back.

I couldn't believe I had to go back only to find Audra—excuse me, *Frost*—in our room. I didn't bother to say hi. I simply slung my bag on my desk and flopped on my bed.

"You tracked in snow," she said, not turning around. She was sitting at her desk, acting completely entranced by what appeared to be some ancient primary text.

Did I look that smug when *I* studied? "How can you even tell?"

"Take off your shoes," she said impatiently.

I grumbled, but still, I leaned over to free myself from the knee-high winter boots. They looked cool, especially when paired with my new Initiate's uniform—most things would probably look cool paired with a navy blue catsuit—but all those laces were a supreme hassle, and it did feel good to slide the things off.

Wriggling my toes, I decided to annoy my roomie. "Whatcha reading?"

She gave a tormented sigh. "*The Poetic Edda*. You probably haven't heard of it."

As hard as I tried to break the ice, Frost insisted on being a little snot with me. Emma had been her roommate—Emma who'd been nice to everyone, including Frost—and Frost begrudged me her death. Did *anyone* not hate me for that?

Actually, there were two on this island who knew I'd done my best, who didn't think I was the raging homicidal teen I appeared to be. Ronan, and of course, Carden.

Where was Carden? I needed him, and it wasn't just the urge to feed. I needed to lean in to him. To shroud myself in the feeling I got when we were together, the sense that I could finally relax and stop looking over my shoulder for just . . . one . . . second.

"The *Edda* is the premier source for information on Norse myth and legend," Frost went on. I hadn't responded to her earlier ding, and apparently she was anxious to make sure I got how smart she was. "I'm currently working through the Niflung Cycle."

"Already read it." I couldn't resist my reply. Frost's real problem wasn't that Emma had been killed—it was that she wasn't the only smarty-pants on this island.

"You read it"—she deigned to turn in her chair to peer at me—"in *translation*. I'm working from the original Old Norse. I imagine that's too advanced for you."

I imagined I wanted to smack her upside the head. Instead, I mused, "Dagursson helping you with that?" The creepy old Viking vamp had chosen her as his teacher's pet, and I couldn't resist any opportunity to goad her about it.

"Master Dagursson says I'm the best student of Old Norse he's ever had."

"Master Dag would say anything for a little female attention," I snapped back. Fine, so maybe I didn't want to admit that possibly it killed me how she was better at the Norse stuff.

I swung my legs over and began to pull my damp boots back on. "I'm heading back out." If Carden wasn't going to come to me, I'd go in search of him.

"But it's almost curfew," she said.

I rolled my eyes. The girl really needed to learn to relax. "Don't worry, *Mom*. I'll be back."

Her body stiffened, freezing into a weird position in her chair. "Don't call me that."

It wasn't an easy task relacing wet, knee-high boots, and as I did, I wondered what nerve I'd just hit. "Not big on the family thing, huh?"

I thought of my own mother, as I so often did. She'd died when I was very young, leaving me with nothing but an abusive father and a tattered old photograph of her younger self. I'd fled the dad part of that equation but treasured my picture, currently hidden next to a rubbing I'd done of some old runic graffiti. The vampires had confiscated the photo once already, but somehow Ronan had stolen it back, giving it to me at the end of last term when I was at my lowest. I wouldn't lose it again. I had the feeling that neither the photo nor I would survive if the vampires were to realize it was back in my possession, not to mention its existence was probably a danger to Ronan. Enough people had suffered for their kind gestures on my account.

As for my graffiti rubbing, I didn't know how vampires felt about personal belongings, and I didn't want to test the notion, so I'd tucked that away, too, though I needed to do a better job of hiding my stash. I had plans to build a secret panel behind one of my dresser drawers. It was just a matter of getting Frost out of the room so I could construct it.

"I have a new family now," Frost said, pulling me from my thoughts.

"Good luck with that." I'd thought I could create a new family for myself, but my friends had all either died or, in the case of Yasuo, turned from me. So many people I cared for had disappeared from my life—one day there, the next . . . poof.

I stood. I needed a friendly face. I needed Carden. The wet suede of my boots was cold and uncomfortable, and I stomped my heels into place. I had to get out of there.

But then I flung open the door, and there he was. My glorious, beautiful vampire. White crystals glittered in his strawberry-blond hair, like he'd hiked through snow-covered trees to reach me. He wore a black wool peacoat that did epic things to showcase those strong shoulders, making him look extra manly, like he was ready for some action down by the docks.

I practically sagged with relief. Something I hadn't known was tensed, loosened. I shuddered in a sigh, realizing only then how shallow my breaths had been. How tense my chest and neck.

I breathed his name. "Carden."

CHAPTER FIVE

⚭

I stood frozen—how to react? I wanted to fling myself into his arms, but I felt Frost's presence vibrating at my back. I couldn't let her discover that Carden and I had bonded. I opened my mouth to say . . . *something*, when I heard my roommate's chair scrape along the floor.

"Master McCloud." She'd hopped to her feet, and the words snapped from her, crisp and formal. "How might we serve you?"

I snorted, then quickly covered my mouth to turn it into a cough. *How might we serve you?* Je-sus.

I looked to Carden, wanting to share a bemused eye roll, but his attention was pinned on Frost. The irises of his eyes had widened, and when he spoke, his voice was a hollow rumble. "You will don your coat."

Uh . . . okay. I was just about to ease this weird tension with some humorous crack when Frost got a peculiar look on her face.

"I'll don my coat," she repeated, and her tone of voice made it sound like this was a revelation, like she'd just had the brightest idea ever.

"You will run three laps around the quad," he instructed.

She gave a firm nod. "I will run three laps around the quad."

I gasped, then snapped my mouth shut when I realized my jaw was hanging open. Frost had set about donning sneakers and coat, her movements stiff and systematic like she was on autopilot. I knew vampires had power, but this Jedi-mind-trick stuff was something I'd never seen before.

"Acari Drew needs the use of this room," Carden said. "Privately."

The word gave me a shiver.

Frost's face was a blank. "Privately."

"This is awesome," I whispered. I'd automatically edged around to stand at his back, not wanting to get in the path of whatever mojo he was currently busting out. "I *like* Robot Roomie." I knotted my hands in the stiff wool of his coat and gave a playful jostle. "Tell her I'm smarter than she is," I added with a giggle. That's what Carden did to me—he made me do things like giggle and feel playful, like I was just a teenaged girl, not this cold, trained killer I'd become. "Tell her . . . tell her she should make my bed every day. That she serves *me*." I was really getting going. I could've gone all night.

"You will return two minutes prior to curfew," he said instead. He may not have told her any of my stuff, but I'd heard a smile in his voice, and that was better than anything. "If anyone inquires as to her whereabouts, you will inform them she is attending to work that is not of your concern."

My shoulders fell a little. I had work?

"Say good-bye to your roommate," Carden said.

Frost turned to me, her movements stiff. "Good-bye, Acari Drew."

I watched, mesmerized, as she made her way to the door. "I could get used to this," I muttered. But then, as the door clicked shut, I turned and gave him a deflated pout. "So, what's this work?"

"Hush, love." He tilted my chin up to face him. A slow grin spread across his face. "*I'm* the work, aye?"

"Oh." I gave him a tentative smile. I still didn't fully believe that there was a guy out there who'd seek me out simply for the purpose of spending time together. "Really?"

His low, husky laugh reverberated through me. "Really. I thought you'd have deduced it by now." He slipped his hand under my hair, sliding warm fingers along the back of my neck, cupping it gently. "I'm purely a man of sport and leisure."

I let my smile broaden. "That sounds"—he leaned down to nuzzle my neck, and my breath hitched—"good."

He nipped at my ear, his breath tickling along my tender skin. "I had to see you."

I shivered, contented. *Safe.* "I knew you'd come."

"Always." He tugged me closer. Tighter. "I felt you. Losing heart."

"Sounds serious." I tried to laugh it off, but it came off lame, so I began to confess. "I guess I've been kind of . . ." But I trailed off, not trusting my voice.

"Kind of . . . ?" he prompted.

This contact, this closeness, it made me feel raw, split open. As though I might finally let go, only I wasn't sure that I wanted to lose my armor—who knew what would happen if I ever did that, what feelings I might discover hiding beneath my shell?

He pulled from me and cupped my face. He was a creature of infinite power—as a man, he'd been a warrior, and as a vampire, who knew? I was still just beginning to grasp the full extent of his strength and abilities. And yet here he was, his hands cradling me tenderly, his touch so gentle on my skin. "Tell me, love."

There it was . . . the sound of my armor cracking.

"I can't stop thinking about Emma," I confessed. "I think not all is what it seems. Do you think it's possible she was alive when they took her?"

"Aye," he said quietly. "It's possible."

I gasped. I'd expected subterfuge. Backpedaling. Question dodging. What I hadn't expected was this honesty. Though that was the thing about Carden—he'd been honest with me from the start. Those times when there was something he couldn't share, he'd simply tell me he couldn't tell me. "What do you know?"

"I avoid Alcántara," he said, "and for the moment, he leaves me be as well. But I do know this: If your friend once lived, surely she lives no longer. That is the only thing I can say with certainty."

To have had such hope and then lose it again . . . I felt rudderless, at sea. I couldn't begin to imagine what a wreck I'd be if it weren't for Carden to lean on.

I told myself Emma was truly at peace. I thought it'd ease something in my mind, but instead it had the opposite effect. I needed to know what happened, exactly. What happened to all the girls. *Exactly.*

"But what . . . how—?" I couldn't finish. Yasuo knew something. Something that plagued him. Something that haunted him so much he wanted me to pay for it.

Carden took my chin and tilted my face to his, peering deeply at me. "What more troubles you?"

I couldn't explain about Yasuo, not completely. I wouldn't put it past Carden to seek out and snap the necks of every Trainee who'd ever crossed me, and I wasn't ready to give up on my friend yet. So instead I just shrugged.

"I must know," he pressed. "Why this despair?"

"Why not despair?"

"Ah, but I have a thousand reasons why not." He got that look in his eye—that hungry, wicked guy look that made my belly quiver. He brought his mouth a whisper away from mine, hovered for an exquisitely taut moment, then darted in to steal a hard, fast kiss. "There. That is one reason why not to despair. Shall I enumerate further?" He kissed along my cheek. "Work my way through the list?" He kissed the outer corner of one eye and then the other. "It's a long one."

His thousand possibilities exploded like a starburst in my mind, cascading down, setting my body alight, weakening my knees. I hadn't known *possibilities* until Carden.

My skin buzzed. For now, all else was forgotten. I reached up, standing on tiptoe, stretching my body along his, ready to make our way down this mysterious list, when I heard a door open down the hall. I froze. It was probably just some girl going to the bathroom, but still, instinct was strong, and I held my breath, waiting for our Proctor—lovingly nicknamed Killer Kenzie—to come and bang on the door and flay me for having a guy in the room.

He read my mind. "There's no need to fear when you're with me."

"But curfew." I mouthed the words almost silently. Because,

yeah, Kenzie was a Guidon and there probably wasn't that much to fear from her where Carden was concerned. It was the other vampires I worried about. "It's soon."

"Aye." He gently laced his fingers through the sensitive hair at the nape of my neck. "We have little time." His other hand took my waist. It felt broad and sure. "I'll not waste it." He pulled me closer.

Kissed me.

Vampires, curfew, old friends, and new enemies . . . it all fell away. When he parted from me, it took me a moment to gather myself. To catch my breath.

The guy could kiss.

He said nothing. Carden merely let those eyes bore into me, a promise of *more* and *later*.

The intensity made me oddly shy. I had to fill the silence. "So you could tell I was sad?"

"Indeed. Now will you tell me why?"

I remained wary of confessing my concerns about Yasuo, but I had no such qualms about his pals. Rob, in particular, flashed into my head, how he'd slammed my tray down. How stupid I'd felt tugging at the thing. He might as well have had *me* pinned to that table. I'd have been just as frozen in place.

"I'm weaker than the guys," I confessed. "I'll always be the weaker one."

He sighed, thinking. After a moment, he said, "There's a difference between strength and power."

My warm and fuzzy mood of a moment ago was fading fast. "Are we doing the speaking-in-riddles thing again?"

But he didn't take the bait. For once, Carden's expression remained dead serious as he met mine.

"All right," I said, considering his words in earnest. "I'll bite. Strength is different from power. I still don't have either."

"Don't you? Strength is physical. But power . . . power is strategy. Control. The capacity to act. Power is mental." He shot me a sly smile. "Aren't you the one who's always saying how your mental faculties are superior?"

"I do not." I gave him a little shove. But the lightbulb had gone off over my head. We'd discussed this once before. He'd told me how I wasn't helpless, but I thought he'd referred only to physical power. I'd listened, but I hadn't heard.

"Do they have power over you," he mused, "or is it merely that you allow it to be so? Power is a thing to be given or taken away. When, unthinking, you do as Hugo asks, you give him power."

"I can't just hop on the next boat out of here," I protested. I felt a stab, remembering my friend and former roommate, Mei-Ling. She had hopped on a boat out of here—I knew because I'd put her on it. "I need to play the game."

"I know," he said gently. "I'd be on that boat with you if I could. But trust me, love. I know better than anyone. Power *is* the game."

For a few minutes, he just held me. I became aware of his thumb rubbing circles along my side. "You do realize your melancholy isn't the only reason I'm here."

A switch flicked in my body, giving me that wiggly, lit-up feeling again. I tried my best womanly voice. "It's not?"

He pushed away from me with a grin. "No, dove. And it's not *that* either."

"Wait? What's the other reason?" It was a struggle to concentrate.

He pulled completely away now. "Do you truly not know?" He wore a bemused smile that made him look suddenly boyish. It gave me a pang of sadness for the innocent he'd once been, for the innocence in him I'd never see.

I stared, thinking hard, but pulled a total blank. Slowly, I shook my head.

"What day is it?" he asked.

"It's January. . . . *Oh*." My birthday. Suddenly my eyes burned and my vision blurred. I didn't blink. If there were tears in my eyes, I'd refuse to let them spill. I wouldn't cry in front of Carden like some mopey adolescent.

And yet.

I was touched beyond reason. Today was my eighteenth birthday, and somehow he'd known.

"You were born today, were you not?"

"How'd you know?"

He grinned, wicked Carden once more. "I have ways."

I gave a quick scrub to my eyes, anxious to put a chirpy face on it. "The whole all-powerful, omniscient thing really seems to work for you."

He barked a laugh, and I hushed him. The walls had ears. Maybe the other Initiates weren't a threat, but there were secret vampire sympathies that were.

"I simply make it my business to know about you," he added in a lowered voice.

"Eighteen. Hey, I can vote. Or be recruited. Oh wait," I added, fighting my returning melancholy with an attempt at humor. "I already was recruited. I'm boots-on-the-ground in the vampire army." I stepped away, blithely asking, "So what'd you get me?"

He pulled something from the pocket of his coat.

"Wait," I said, taken aback. "I was kidding. You really got me something?"

"Naturally." He waved the little parcel before me. It was rectangular and wrapped in plain paper.

"But you just gave me something. For Christmas." I stared at the package like he was offering me a bomb. I didn't get a lot of presents, and this marked the second one from Carden. The first had been the awesomest throwing star ever, with a bird's wing etched along the steel, though it was unsettling how I'd become the girl whom guys wooed with weaponry. "You've already given me so much," I added dumbly, my mind going to all those emotional places I didn't like to think about.

It appeared I was crushing pretty hard on my ancient Scottish vampire.

"Do you not want it?" He faked like he was going to tuck it back in his pocket.

"No." I snatched it from him. "I want. I want." The thing had some heft to it, and I could feel the spine of a book through the coarse paper. "Can I open it?"

He raised a brow, apparently an ancient Scottish way of saying *duh*. "Would you rather I did?"

I shot him a look that made him grin, and forget the gift, just the fact that I could make Carden McCloud grin sent warm tendrils of contentment through my veins. I sat on the bed, and he sat beside me, the bed sinking under his weight.

I carefully unfolded the paper. I'd keep it. I'd keep and treasure all of it.

"Oh. A dictionary." It was a basic Old Norse dictionary. Standard issue. In fact, I already had a copy, only mine was paperback, and this one was an awkward hardback in what looked like an older, outdated edition. I gave him a look that I feared was more like a mask than a smile. "Thanks."

He grinned. "For someone so lethal, you are remarkably polite." He took the book from my hands and turned to the back flap. Looking closer, I could see the binding wasn't paper; rather, it had more of a leathery sheen. He picked at the corner, and it took a moment for him to get purchase with his short nails. "When will you remember? Things aren't always as they seem."

He finally managed to loosen the top corner, and the binding peeled away to reveal a hiding spot.

I gasped. "Oh, wow. Cool."

"There is no more clever a hiding spot than in plain sight."

"Thank you. Just . . . thank you. I love it." To the naked eye, it would just seem like a musty old used book. The false cover was shallow, but just the right size to hide a key. *Or a photograph.* "It's perfect." I flung my arms around him. "Perfect."

In that moment, to me, *he* was perfect.

He chucked my chin. "For a woman with secrets."

Then it really struck me—I was eighteen today. I *was* a woman.

Raised voices echoed from down the hall, rumbling their way toward us. I picked out Kenzie in the din, giving the first warning—lights-out soon. I checked the clock on my bedside table. "Crap. Three minutes to curfew. Frost will be back any minute."

"In one minute, to be precise. That means it's time for me to leave you. But we'll pick this up again, sweet. And soon." He stole a kiss, pulling away just as I began to melt in to him. He felt my reluctance, and something in his eyes glinted in response. "I'm glad your gift pleases you. Though nothing could match how greatly you please me."

And with that, Carden disappeared.

I clutched my present to my chest. I'd ribbed him about it, but my vampire truly was all-powerful. I'd been on the brink of despair, but for the moment he'd made all that go away, and to me, there was no greater, no more awesome a gift than that.

CHAPTER SIX

I was sitting on the beach, stretching out my legs when I heard it. *What the—?* I tilted my head, straining to listen. Yep, there it was again . . . a whimper.

I hopped to my feet and dusted the sand from my hands. Today's martial arts class had been held at the shore. Priti had blindfolded us so we could take turns attacking one another. The sand broke our falls . . . or that was the theory, at least. In my experience, it remained precisely that—a theory.

It was pure coincidence that I was even still on the beach—everyone else had left long ago—but I kept having the same charley horse on the sole of my right foot, and though dehydration was probably to blame, I'd stayed after to work through a yoga series to stretch my legs.

I heard the sound again and froze. It was somewhere between a cry and a moan—if not for a trick of the wind bouncing off the rocks, amplifying it, I would've missed it. But now that I knew to listen for it, it was all I heard. It was more urgent now. A keening *hmmmm*, quiet, like someone out there was swallowing her pain.

I jogged up to the path to check it out. Once I was off the beach, the weird cries came to me loud and clear. Only now I heard another sound, too.

Snarling.

I broke into a run.

Potentially, it was a stupid thing to do—curiosity killed the cat and all. But I had to pass by here to get home anyway, I told myself. Plus, if there was some sort of attack happening, I'd much rather be on the offensive than be caught unawares. And so I pumped my legs and ignored my internal alarms.

I reached a part of the trail that wound through tall stones—prime hiding-place territory—so I opened my senses and, sure enough, as I rounded one of the larger boulders, I had to skid to a stop. The whimperer was Regina, aka Curly. The one I'd helped in the dining hall.

She was bloodied. Terrified. And hemmed in by three slavering Draug.

Their stench hit me instantly, the reek of decomposing flesh so fetid, so overpowering, it seared into my sinuses and throat. Eyes watering, I slapped a hand to my mouth—it was like I was tasting their foulness. I swallowed convulsively, fighting an instant gag reflex.

Regina was freaking out. I needed to catch her eye and calm her down—immediately.

I'd once been just as terrified of Draug—I knew girls who'd lost their lives to them in hideous and gruesome ways—but now I knew better. Now I knew Draug weren't the demon hell spawn they appeared; they were just kids, Trainees who hadn't survived their transition to Vampire. They were senseless, like rabid animals without reason or thought, questing for a meal. They thrived on blood, but their true craving was for the taste of others' fear.

Which meant Regina's panic was about to get her killed.

"Regina." I shouted at her while keeping an elbow over my mouth—anything to blunt the festering stench that stung my nose and pricked tears in my eyes. "Look at me."

What I should've done was back away slowly. But seriously, when did I ever do what I should?

I sized up the situation. One of the Draug was newly made, with bloated flesh so pale it looked lavender. The other two were older, in late stages of decay, their skin blackened and grizzled like jerky. No matter their age or condition, each had a pair of shining fangs, as lethal now as they'd ever been.

"Hey, you, Curly," I shouted mercilessly, but she just stood there frozen, making that keening, whimpery sound in the back of her throat. It was really beginning to grate. "You have *got* to calm down." I approached carefully. "Calm. The hell. Down."

The girl was obviously a trouble magnet, and with all that whining, she'd make herself a Draug magnet, too. The creatures might've fed on blood, but they were sustained by fear, and at the moment, Regina was radiating enough terror to power an entire continent of them.

"Hey, guys, over here." My shouts drew their attention. "Yeah, that's right." I waved my hands. "Look at me instead."

They tilted their heads. I didn't have the stink of fear, and it confused them. But the moment they'd glanced my way, stupid Regina snapped to life, spinning and running. A jolt moved through the beasts, and they snapped to life, too, their attention shooting back to her as though they were a trio of wild dogs and she were a rabbit bounding from long hiding.

"Wait!" I shrieked. Tom the Draug keeper had once told me to treat the monsters like dumb livestock, that terror was the thing that sparked their bloodlust. So I raced toward them, swatting and shoving at their backs, screaming at Curly to *calm the hell down*, all the while hoping Tom was right because otherwise I was tempting a world of hurt. Though, truly, fear wasn't my problem—*revulsion* was. I commanded the Draug over and over to stop, all the while trying to ignore the repellent feel of their rotted flesh squishing under my hands. "Regina, *stop* moving."

She did, finally. Panting hard, she stopped, frozen in terror, looking over her shoulder at me and the Draug who'd paused mere inches from her back. "Please," she whispered, pleading. "Run. We have to run."

The beasts' gazes shifted between the two of us, gaping and confused, like a macabre Three Stooges. Regina was bleeding profusely now, and they wanted that blood. The only thing holding them back was their dim fascination with me. Draug kept some vague set of memories in their addled brains, and I must've been a total anomaly in their little world.

"No," I said loud and clear. "*Don't* run." I stepped closer, putting my hands up, trying to look calming, to her, to them . . . to any other monsters who might be looking for a girl to snack on. "They're like wolves. If you run, instinct kicks in and they'll automatically follow."

She stared, her eyes wide as dinner plates, too terrified to speak. Her foot edged forward in the gravel. She was losing her nerve.

"Did you hear me?" I snapped. "You run, they chase. Get it?"
She gave a slow nod and that foot stilled. "Okay. Got it."

I approached slowly. "You've got to relax. They're thirsty, but mostly they get off on your fear."

I pushed my way through to stand by her, protecting her. I was shaking, but not because I was scared—mostly I was totally revolted by the smell of them.

Who were these strays anyway? Why were they even out here? Tom held them in a pen south of here. They were well fed. They had no need to wander.

But now, standing close to Regina, the answer became clear. She was soaked with blood—even I could smell it. It was her blood that'd called them.

"What happened to you?" Because it wasn't the Draug that'd done this to her. She wouldn't be standing if they had—once a Draug began to attack, it didn't stop. Only staking or fire stopped these monsters once they began to feed, a horrific fact I knew from personal experience.

"It was one of the guys." Her voice was slurry, her eyes blank, and I worried she might be going into shock.

I scanned the rest of her body, taking in the bloodied neck and collar. The knot of anger and resentment that'd permanently lodged in my chest cinched tighter. "What do you mean? Which guys?" But then the Draug moaned as one, jerking my attention back in time to see them take a few steps closer. "Oh shit."

I stepped in front of her. I needed a plan, and now. Personal experience told me this train was leaving the station.

"What?" Regina stiffened—I'd mumbled the wrong thing. "What's wrong? I thought you said it was okay. You told me not to run."

This close, I spotted a fire shimmering to life in the Draugs' eyes—it was hunger. Regina was getting hysterical, and the creatures were amping up right along with her.

"What are these things?" Her voice was tremulous, panicked.

"Draug." I felt her edging away and shot an arm back to snag her coat with my hand. "Don't move."

"What's a Draug?" she wailed, her voice cracking. "What should we do?"

"Relax. Lemme think." I wore my gym sweats and sneakers, which meant my stars were stashed in my pack. I had them out in seconds, pinched between fingertips, poised for throwing. Shuriken weren't stakes, but they'd create a decent distraction until I could figure something else out.

"What are those? What are you doing?" Terror washed off of her in waves, and it was whipping the Draug into a bloodthirsty frenzy.

"Hey, Curly." I shot her a look over my shoulder. "Calm down."

The Draug snarled and inched forward. She grabbed my shoulder and shrieked, "Throw them. You have to throw them."

I'd turned my entire focus from Regina to the monsters and was startled when she reached around me and ripped two of the stars right from my fingertips and whipped them at the Draug.

They swatted them away. Instead of being injured, they were even more riled.

"Don't you touch my stars. Ever." I had no choice. I had to throw the other two. A quick *thunk-thunk*, and the stars struck flesh—the neck of one of the older Draug and the chest of the younger. They swatted my shuriken away like they were mosquitoes.

We couldn't run, but I needed room to think. "Back up slowly."
I reached around and grabbed Regina's wrist to hold her close as I
edged us away. The only thing keeping away the Draug was my
tenacious grip on my own courage. *Not scared. Not scared. Not scared.*
I repeated the words in my head like a mantra. I tightened my
fingers around Regina's arm. "What's your weapon?"

"My weapon?" Her other hand found me, fingers curling into
my biceps. I doubted she'd really even heard me.

"Listen. Do you have your weapon?" I prayed it was something worthwhile, something *I* could use, unlike the flute that'd
been given to Mei-Ling, my roommate of last semester.

"My weapon?"

"You know. Your *weapon.*" Jesus. *This girl.* How had she survived her first day? "You did get a weapon, right?" The Draug
shifted from foot to foot now, edging closer, spreading out and
hemming us in. I let go of her wrist and shoved it away. "Whatever
it is, get it."

"Weapon." She dug frantically through her pack. "Weapon,
weapon."

"Not to stress you out or anything," I whispered tersely, "because, please stay calm . . . but really, any freaking day now."

"Got it." She pulled her hand out and shoved it toward me,
presenting what looked like some sort of esoteric kids' toy.

I peered closer. Two wooden handles with a cord strung
between them. I shot her an incredulous glance. "A garrote?"

She nodded, and the hopefulness in her eyes killed me. Because, really, what the hell good would that do? The garrote was
a weapon of elegance and subtlety that made me think of tuxedo-
wearing spies strangling their quarry silently and at close range.
"What the hell are we supposed to do with this?"

She unwound the wire, her hands shaking. "It's used to choke—"

"I know what it's for." Impatient now, I simply snatched her bag and dug through. "Not for these guys."

"Why not?"

I ignored her. There was no time to explain. I was getting scared, and that was a very bad thing to do with Draug around.

"Ah," I chirped as my hands met something cool and hard. I pulled out a glass bottle with a colorful *Irn-Bru* label. "Iron brew?" It was the toxic orange soda they served in the dining hall. "You drink this?"

The moment I'd taken to ask such a stupid question was one moment too long.

The rest happened fast.

Regina shrugged. The young Draug lunged. I acted instantly, instinctively smashing it on the head with the bottle.

Nothing. Just a dull clonking sound . . . The bottle didn't break and the Draug didn't blink.

All three of the monsters were facing me now. The young one lunged again, and I smashed again. The stupid glass still didn't break.

"Dammit." I planted myself more firmly in front of Regina. I wanted to protect her, but she was also a liability. She was small like me and scared out of her wits, whimpering again, making enough injured-puppy sounds to whip the Draug into madness. I elbowed her. "Seriously, shut up."

She nestled against my back, clawing my arms like I was her life raft. "What are they doing?"

They were about to attack. But I didn't tell her that.

She pressed closer, and as she did, I felt my bag dig into my hip. I nudged backward into her. "My bag," I said. "In my bag. Quick."

"What?" My bag jostled against me as she took it in her quavering hands. "What should I get?"

"Something. Anything." I spared a glance, pointing to my key chain. "That. My keys."

There were just two keys on my ring, one for the dorm front door—which was never locked anyway—and the other for my room. Both were antique-looking things with long shafts. Taking the soda bottle in my other hand, I threaded them between my fingers so they poked out like spikes from my fist.

Something about my movement catalyzed them. The Draug snapped. Like a pack of rabid wolves, they lunged on us at once. One of the older, grizzled ones was the first in my line of sight, and as he pounced toward me, I punched hard. Metal ground between the tendons of my palm with the impact, then a crunch and give as the keys punctured his heart. I flung him away.

I kept Regina safely behind me, and she was shouting in my ear, mingled screams and bizarre hysterical laughter, but the noise came at me as though from a distance. My sole focus was on the remaining two creatures. As the pale, bloated one came at me, he did an awkward amble over the body of his fallen buddy, and I used the half second to strike my keys against the neck of the bottle, and hairline cracks appeared in the glass. I hoped it'd be enough. I slammed the bottle down, hitting the Draug on the temple as he lurched at me. It dazed him for only a moment, but the neck of the bottle finally snapped off. I immediately slashed again, slicing his throat with the jagged glass.

I knelt, scooped up one of my stars, and whipped around to face the final Draug, but stopped short, needing a moment to understand what my eyes were seeing. A pencil stuck out of his chest—Curly had already dealt with him.

She gave me a weak smile. "Like a stake."

"Nice," I said, studying her in a new light. I realized she was trembling. I quickly gathered our stuff. "We need to get out of here."

We'd sprinted almost all the way back to the quad when she finally slowed and said, "Thanks for coming to my rescue."

I slowed to a jog then to a walk and looked back over my shoulder, still trying to make sense of the whole episode. "I don't even know what they're doing around here. The Draug, I mean. They never come this close to campus."

She stopped short. "You've seen those things before?"

I nodded. "Long story."

But I realized she was waiting, looking expectant, so I elaborated. "Yeah, I've seen them before. Well, maybe not those Draug in particular."

"What are they?"

"Like . . . Trainees gone wrong. They're attracted by the scent of blood." My eyes went to her neck. In all the uproar, I'd forgotten about her injury. "The wind off the water must've hit you just right and they picked up the scent. What happened to you, anyway? You said you were attacked?" I prayed we didn't have another rogue vampire on the loose.

Her face got pinched, and she turned from me and started to walk again. "Some guy jumped me."

I did a quick step to catch up. "You mean a vampire jumped you?"

"No, one of the *boys*."

"But Trainees don't attack Acari."

She shot me a look that could kill. "This one did."

"A *Trainee* jumped you?" At her nod, I pressed. "One of the guys just jumped from out of the blue and *bit* you?"

She nodded frantically now, looking pale and trembly like she was either about to cry or faint. Her adrenaline rush had faded, and shock was setting in.

"We need to take care of you." I slung my pack around to my chest, grabbed a towel, and held it out to her. First things first, we needed to staunch the blood flow. "Press this to your neck. When we get back, go straight to your dorm and clean it up as best you can."

She pressed the towel on her wound. It soaked red instantly, and she pulled it away, folded it to a clean section, and pressed again.

"That is seriously screwed up," I muttered, catching sight of the bite mark. "Like some Dracula shit." Carden had fed on me, but it was nothing like this carnage. "I can't imagine the vamps okayed this. You'd think they'd find it . . . I don't know . . . vulgar."

I needed to find out what those boys were up to. As if Emma's fate weren't mystery enough, now more than ever, I wanted to know what the hell went on in that castle.

She gave me an apologetic smile. "I'm really sorry about this."

"Sorry?" I gave Regina a probing look, trying to figure her out—for me, dispersing a pack of bloodthirsty Draug was child's play compared to the pain of bonding with strangers. "Why are you sorry?"

"Nothing like battling a couple of corpses to ruin your week."

I laughed. Her sense of humor was unexpected—and so much like something I'd say. "Actually," I found myself sharing, "it's my birthday week."

"That sucks."

I remembered my drunken, no-good father. "Believe it or not, this is far from my worst birthday ever. Pathetic, huh?" But then my mind went to Emma. My friend would've done something silly to commemorate the day. She would've written me a note, or stolen me an extra bagel, or something.

Regina gave me a sympathetic look that said more than any words would. "Well, at least this'll be the worst part of your week, right?"

"You'd be surprised." I didn't have a problem with optimism, but naïveté was a different story. I'd helped this girl a couple times now, and I was glad of it. But I had the dreadful suspicion I was wrong about one thing: Curly wasn't entirely like me. She'd need to toughen up if she was to survive her first month.

I sighed as I checked my watch. My next class was with Master Alcántara.

Regina had no idea how bad things could get.

CHAPTER SEVEN

It took everything I had to walk into Assassination and Elimination Techniques class, Alcántara's special Initiates-only seminar. I braced to find his cold, black eyes waiting for me as I entered the room—just like always. And like always, that stare unnerved me. Infuriated me. His creepy, unnatural interest in me had only intensified since Carden's arrival on the island.

Buzzing filled my head. Seeing him, I could think only:

1. Alcántara killed Emma.
2. I despised Alcántara.
3. Alcántara was the enemy.

My enemy.

Like downed power lines bucking and snapping inside my skull, my thoughts were wild, volatile, charged. Lethal. I would discover what he'd done to Emma. What *they'd* done to her. The decision was irrefutable. My goal, unignorable.

I glanced around, looking for a place to sit, but hostile faces were all around me. Girls in variations of tough and pretty, every one of them waiting for the opportunity to plunge a knife in my back.

It was Alcántara's fault I had no friends left. When Emma died, I'd also lost Yasuo. And if Master Al had his way, he'd take Carden from me, too.

It was unthinkable.

Memories flooded me. Unbearable memories. I flashed back to those days when I'd walk into a class to sit beside Emma or Yas. Our world had been fraught with terror, and yet who knew *those* had been my good old days?

Trembling now, I made my way to a seat, any seat, unable to meet anyone's eye. But even as I steered myself, going on auto-pilot, lurching toward an empty spot, I knew. I'd do what I always did: I'd survive.

And I'd uncover the truth of this hell.

I crumpled into a desk, and it was a pretty ungraceful landing, the chair leg squealing along the floor the moment my butt hit the seat. Some girl behind me muttered something. The girl next to her tittered.

I turned to see who they were. The mutterer was a silky-haired creature named Lissa whom I recognized from last year's Phenomena class, and her tittering pal was a pert-nosed thing from my dorm floor whose name I never bothered to get.

I had nothing to lose anymore, nobody to protect. I snapped, "Let me guess. . . . Is it my butt? My hair?" It was satisfying to give them a good, long, fearless glare. I'd been responsible for *the death of my best friend*. I was so beyond their meaningless middle school taunts. "Do you seriously think you're going to take me down with . . . what? Your snarky little comments? If that's how you roll, then you should probably give up now. I mean, how are you even alive?"

God, was I losing it? I needed to get it together. Keep to myself. Fly under the radar. Follow all those personal rules I'd once clung to.

"What the fuck?" Lissa muttered, and her friend added a whispered, "Freak."

But they'd averted their eyes. Two points to me.

I couldn't resist one last jab. "I'll bet you both just *ruled* seventh grade, didn't you?"

"Children, children." The sound of Alcántara's patronizing tone galvanized my annoyance into anger. He was studying them, and I imagined he didn't miss one little thing. He'd have noted who mocked whom, where they sat, and why.

I felt his attention zeroing in on me. Maybe it was my imagination, but I felt an anticipatory energy radiate from him, rippling over me. Like he'd been saving the best for last.

Hatred erupted from a place deep in my gut, churning through me with no place else to go. I had to look down, so strong was the bile burning my throat. I knew he kept his eyes on me, but I pretended not to notice and instead fumbled in my bag like I was looking for just the right pen.

He paused, a heavy moment of quiet, then made a noise in the back of his throat that sounded like amusement. "How I've missed your pretty faces."

The comment was aimed at me, and I felt it like a slapped cheek. He'd been staring at me, surely the only girl in the room who'd kept her *pretty face* averted. What I'd said to my classmates hadn't been entirely true: Snarky little comments could take me down in a second . . . if they came from Alcántara.

"I extend my greetings," he continued, "and my congratulations. It is an elite group who survives their first year on *Eyja nœturinnar*. You have been placed in Initiate-level Assassination and Elimination Techniques. Do you know what this means?"

"It's a survey of assassination theory and praxis?" Frost chimed from the front row. I hadn't seen her when I'd come in, but now my eyes followed her voice, and sure enough, there she was, sitting ramrod straight, looking her most kiss-assy self. And, by the way, did she not understand the concept of *rhetorical question*?

I scowled, then quickly smoothed my features before anyone saw. On this island, it was stupid to do anything other than play things close to the vest.

Nothing got past Alcántara, though. He probably knew how much tension there was between us, and he probably also relished every strained bit of it. Vampires liked things hard and fraught and dramatic. To them, we were just pawns in some screwed-up deadly chess game. I was sure Frost's and my mutual enmity was why we were placed together as roommates in the first place. Why we'd been put in so many classes together.

He gave her a bland smile. If his obsession with me—not to mention his bond with Masha before me—was any indication, he preferred his girls with an edge. "That is one answer, yes. But not the answer I sought."

Snap. I was right. Blatant brown-nosing wasn't Al's thing. He preferred his girls hard to get. Hard to kill.

He moved from behind the podium to glide around the room. "You are here, on this island, to recognize your potential, and the next phase of your journey begins in this very classroom. Assassination . . . elimination. You are here because soon you will be embarking on missions, and these are some of the skills you will require to stay alive."

More missions. I'd already had my first, rescuing Carden. I'd ended up with him as an ally—or was it boyfriend? I still couldn't wrap my head around the word, so out of place in the context of my superfierce Scottish vampire. When you shared a blood bond with an ancient, terms like *boyfriend* seemed a bit watered down. Either way, I adored Carden and so couldn't regret that particular mission.

And yet that assignment—discovering an island of enemy vampires, getting embroiled in long-standing Directorate politics—had almost been the death of me. I wasn't exactly anxious to set sail on another.

"But I get ahead of myself," Alcántara continued lightly, and instead of sounding frivolous, his silly-me tone made him seem all the more menacing. "We must begin at the beginning. With the basics." He wandered back to the front of the class, leaning on the edge of his desk. "The concept of assassination is not a new one. Though generally an affair conducted in secret, do not be fooled. Assassinations have changed the course of history for millennia. Assassinations have made and broken kings. It is the purview of the mighty. Of those with influence. With power. And now, dear Initiates, it is your purview as well."

Power.

There was that word again. I leaned forward in my seat. I had that feeling of a nascent idea dancing on the edge of my consciousness. Like, if I only peered harder at Alcántara, listened more closely, some essential truth would drift into my mind like a red balloon.

"The first lesson of assassination is discretion. The word has two meanings, does it not? The first is caution. On a mission, you rely on discretion to remain unseen, invisible to those around you. Hidden in plain sight."

I thought of the book Carden had given me and its secret hiding place. Unobserved, unnoticed . . . I was well acquainted with the concept, on all kinds of levels.

"And the second meaning?" He raised his brows as though one of us might like to pipe up with the answer, but we kept our mouths shut—we'd seen how Frost had been given the shutdown. "I will tell you. It is *choice*."

I bit my cheek, seriously doubting we'd ever have any choice in anything on this island, but sure, I'd give him the point for argument's sake. The elaborate wordplay was so like Master Al, who was scholarly to the point of aggravation.

"Discretion implies preference," he explained. "Inclination. Elements with which your future assignments will be rife. You will need to know the how of a job. When, where. And, sometimes, there is a choice . . . to act or not to act? These things you must answer for yourselves. Perhaps you'll make a decision your classmate does not; perhaps your subtle alteration will be the thing that keeps you alive and the thing that finds them dead.

"We will study a history of assassination and thus learn through example. Through the successes—and mistakes—of others. And I have a surprise, my dear Initiates." His lips curled into a smile, those coal-dark eyes dancing with a cruel bemusement that chilled me. "To make this more real, less of an academic endeavor, as a part of your curriculum, you will receive a top-secret assignment."

The classroom was so quiet, I could hear the breathing of the girl next to me. The silence told me I wasn't the only one who knew that, on this island, top-secret assignments were often a clever way to cut class size, generally resulting in a more favorable student-teacher ratio. Meaning: Acari who got special assign-ments often found themselves dead.

"Perhaps it will be a treat for some of you," he went on, and that chilling smile turned into an all-out grin. "You will each be assigned a Trainee, one of the young men from among our newest recruits. You will eliminate your Trainee, using skills learned in this class."

A hand shot up. "You mean, we have to kill someone? Like, for class credit?"

"You must kill someone," he confirmed. "An assassination . . . *like, for class credit*." His lip curled, speaking to his distaste for her diction. "Moreover, you will not disclose your target to anyone."

"We get to kill one of the guys?" A couple girls high-fived one another.

Wow. Did these girls have no clue? I'd killed before, and each time it stole a part of my soul. Maybe these girls simply lacked humanity altogether, and that was how they'd found themselves on this island in the first place.

"I ask that your project be thoughtfully executed. Extra credit is given for kills that move me. I appreciate the . . . poetic."

I shuddered. I wanted to drop my head, to cradle my forehead in my palm like the girl in front of me was doing. But I knew better than to show emotion and kept my face a cold blank, eyes glued to Alcántara.

His cold, black gaze shot to mine. His lips were a straight line, but somehow I could detect a smile in his eyes.

"What happens if we can't do it?" one of the other Initiates asked, and someone clarified, "Like, if the Trainee fights back?"

His eyes shuttered, head swinging to face her. "Then you have failed," he snapped. "The cost will be your life, presumably at the hands of your assigned Trainee." The way he'd said the words made it sound like she were dead already.

Great. Yet another semester wherein failure meant death. You could say I really missed the whole GPA system.

"However," he added, and my foreboding grew as he let the word hang, "there are rules. You are not to discuss this outside of class."

It took a moment for me to get the full implication of this statement. A chill settled over me. I didn't know what worried me more—that we weren't allowed to tell anyone what we were doing, or that at this very moment, other students in other classes were being given equally mysterious, equally deadly, tasks.

As though hearing my question, he elaborated. "The boys also have an assignment."

I thought of Regina and had a feeling I knew what was coming.

He gave us a patronizing smile. "A selection of Trainees have been told to catch one of you lovelies unawares. To catch you and bite you. So stand warned, *queridas.*"

Trainees dropping out of the sky to bite us. Well, that explained that. Regina had been on their list.

Had Yas and Josh had assignments like this last year? The Trainees and their secrets . . . and they were going to grow into *vampires* with secrets. Their whole world was shrouded with it, the secrets of men, hidden behind the iron gates of their keep.

Not if I had anything to say about it.

Not if I could infiltrate their world.

Finally, there it was, that red balloon floating into my consciousness, a thought popping into my head, impossible to ignore. I could use my training against them and simply break in. Spy on their secrets for myself.

Who killed Emma in the end, what happened to all the girls who'd disappeared . . . I'd get to the bottom of it all. I'd blow the roof off this island, these vampires and their secrets. And it all began with this bastard: Alcántara.

But I wasn't stupid. I thought back to Carden's words. Power was different from strength. Power was subtle. It was strategic. Power was planning and patience and smarts.

I could swing all those things. This was a game to be played slowly and very, very carefully.

There was another aspect of power that the average man didn't have access to, and giving Alcántara my most brilliant smile, I exercised it. In my attentions, I hoped he'd see excitement about the prospect of assassinating one of my classmates. That he'd see enthrallment for him and all this island stood for. I wanted him to see a smile rich with promise . . . for him.

I spotted the slightest flicker in his eye—there and gone so quickly, I wondered if I'd imagined it. Good. I'd surprised him, and it was remarkably satisfying. Step one, accomplished.

He was droning on, about methods, means. About considerations we'd have when the time came for our first hit.

And all the while, I poured everything I had into my rapt stare. I let my emotions simmer, let them darken my eyes. I thought of my lust for Carden, my longing for him. My longing for another life. My desire to go back and change history, wishing I'd had the courage to sacrifice myself in the ring with Emma. I drew on every last bit, all the while keeping my eyes trained on Alcántara as though I were just a poor, little, old moth while he was a bright, beautiful flame.

He noticed, too. Vampires might've been ancient, but in their hearts, they were guys, and guys could be so easy sometimes. I pretended enthrallment, and he and his oversized ego bought it hook, line, and sinker. His eyes kept flashing to me. They'd flit away, but they'd return again, pulled to me like I was a magnetic force.

He handed out the names of our "assignments," letting his fingers brush mine as he passed me my slip of paper. I braced myself to read the name of the boy I was supposed to kill. Toby Engel. I didn't recognize the name.

"Remember," Alcántara said, concluding his lecture. "This is an exercise in discretion. A lesson in secrecy and choice."

It was about choice. And I chose to fight.

CHAPTER EIGHT

The first thing I did was find out who Toby Engel was (using, of course, a good dose of that discretion Alcántara was so fond of). My "target" wasn't exactly Mr. Sociability, and I had to ask around a bit before I found someone who knew who he was.

Now that I did know, it was hard to notice anybody else. The guy was huge. Strapping. A great, big, freckly corn-fed boy with a whiff of the American farmland to him. Burly shoulders suggested a youth spent tossing hay bales and plowing things. I sat in the dining hall, pretending not to watch him.

God help the guy, he was dumb as a post. Even if I hadn't eavesdropped on snippets of his conversation, I could've seen it in the watery blankness of his blue eyes. Seriously, there were boxes of hammers sharper than this kid.

I tried not to panic. Because how was I supposed to kill *him*?

It wasn't his obvious strength that put me off. Brute strength didn't scare me—I was bright; I could outwit him blindfolded and on no sleep. It was that he struck me as a total innocent. He was like a character in a Steinbeck novel, a Lennie, some dumb and tragic brute whose greatest crime might've been accidentally petting someone's puppy to death.

This was Alcántara testing me. He wanted to challenge what little was left of my moral compass. He'd know I couldn't kill a Lennie.

A distinctly male body slid into the chair next to mine. My skin prickled, on instant alert. This body smelled of fresh air and salt water, his dinner tray held by hands I'd recognize anywhere.

Ronan. I didn't need to look to know it was him. He kicked back, munching on an apple.

I stiffened. He was acting casual. He never acted casual. "What are you doing?"

He took a big bite and made me wait while he chewed. "Sitting down."

"I can see that. I mean"—I flicked a glance right and left—"*why?*" There were Acari and Trainees all around. There were a couple Tracers, plus some Proctors and a handful of Watchers. Shouldn't he be socializing with one of them instead? He only came to me when there was bad news, stuff involving wetsuits and trials in deep water.

"I'm here to eat a meal. You were alone. So I sat down." He hooked his thumb along the edge of his tray, tugging it toward him like he might grab it and go. "Would you rather I left?"

"No. Of course not." That was Ronan—putting a fine point on the matter. He had a way of defusing me, making my drama seem silly. I felt a burst of vulnerability. . . . How I missed a rowdy table full of friends. "It's good to see you." And it was.

"Are you well? You look . . ."

The statement hung, so I finished it for him. "I look like I lost my best friend?"

"Aye," he said, instantly understanding. "So you do, and so you have."

Again with Ronan and his not-beating-around-the-bush thing. I felt his eyes heavy on me, searching for something. I ripped my dinner roll in half, trying to play it cool. "So," I asked stiffly, "are you here to drill me on what we learned in that wilderness workshop of yours?" I was in his Tuesday/Thursday elective, and he'd promised a semester of learning to live off the land, build fires, those sorts of things.

Emma things.

I had to sip water to wash down my bread.

"It's called a Primitive Skills Intensive," he said, but his voice had been taut. Too taut.

I let my gaze rise, finally daring to meet his, uncertain what I'd find. Would there be amusement? A scold? But what I saw instead surprised me. There was unmistakable tenderness in those forest-green eyes.

Scorn, discipline, mockery . . . those I could deal with. But tenderness? I was *so* not equipped to deal with tenderness right now. I had a plan. That plan didn't involve friends or kindness or vulnerability of any sort. I had to stay focused. *Resistance and revenge.*

I turned my full attention to my dinner, using my fork to push around a pile of cold, limp green beans, desperately racking my brain to come up with some random topic to chat about.

Emma wasn't the only thing bothering me. My eyes wandered back to Toby Engel. He sat at a table full of Trainees but was in his own world, busily shoveling food down his gullet like he might win a prize for it.

What was his story? Did he have a family who loved him? A mom who'd baked pies and cooked him breakfasts of eggs and bacon and biscuits and a dad who greeted every dawn from the back of an old tractor? Had they posted *Missing* signs? Was Toby's face at some post office, pinned up with thumbtacks, or on utility poles, shining from beneath layers of clear packing tape?

Then I realized the person to ask was sitting right next to me. Ronan would know Toby's story—hell, Ronan might even have been the Tracer who'd brought him in. "Is that Toby?" I asked, hoping against hope he'd divulge that the kid was actually a closet serial killer.

Ronan followed my line of sight, then looked back at me. I could see the cogs turning. Did he wonder why I was asking about some random new Trainee? Or maybe he already knew. Maybe Alcántara's "secret project" was actually part of the general curriculum.

Finally, he nodded. "Yes." The sudden stoicism in that single word said he understood a little something about my assignment.

I frowned, studying Toby, watching in awe as he polished off a dinner roll in two bites.

Alcántara wanted me to kill that boy *poetically*.

Poetic—what did that even mean? Like, was I supposed to go ironic with it? Maybe find some farm tool and get him good? *Farm Boy Trainee Slain! Rototiller-Wielding Initiate Reaped What He Sowed.*

I bit the inside of my cheek. Anything to keep myself from losing it. "He looks out of place."

"True."

I swung my gaze back to Ronan. "Then why is he even here?"

The question had been rhetorical. I hadn't expected him to

answer. But he surprised me, offering, "Perhaps the vampires believe he will be tractable."

Tractable. They'd bend this poor, dim boy to their will. And then they'd use his outsized physical strength against the rest of us.

Either I could do as I was assigned and kill Toby Engel now, while he was still an innocent, or I could kill him later, after he'd invariably gone bad, joining the other guys on this island who'd discovered just how fun it was to torment the girls.

My vision wavered. I had to flee. That Ronan could see how upset I was made my urge to escape all the more intense. I needed to bus my dishes and get the hell out of there. "Gotta go," I blurted, scooping up my tray and standing.

But Ronan wasn't going to let me go that easily. He snarfed down a last bite of his apple and hopped up to follow me to the dish cart, the majority of his dinner left untouched. "See you at *wilderness workshop*," he said, mimicking my earlier words.

Damned if it didn't bring a smile to my face.

In my time on the island, I'd known varying degrees of trust for him, but I guessed he really was a friend. I guessed I needed that.

The prospect of making my way through the sea of bodies back to the main entrance was too nightmarish to consider, so I headed to the service exit near the kitchens instead. I shoved open the metal door, leaving the cocoon of warmth and noise that was the dining hall, and was plunged into the cold, quiet air of the back hallway.

Alone again.

Until I heard the clip of shoes behind me.

I sped up a little, fighting the urge to turn around. If my follower were friendly, they'd call ahead to me. But they didn't speak. I told myself the person just happened to be using this same back exit at the same time as me, which meant I could speed up and their pace wouldn't change at all. To test the theory, I walked just the teensiest bit faster.

Their pace increased to match mine.

Crap. They *were* following. It was a menacing *clip-clip*, right behind me.

I burst into a little race walk, around the storage area, the outside door in sight. But they walked faster, and faster still until that *clip-clipping* burst into a jog. It definitely wasn't a benign, let-me-catch-up-so-we-can-chat sound.

I felt the person at my back—sensed it was a guy—and I began to turn, but before I could get into position, he'd pinned me from behind, my throat trapped in the crook of his arm. My body instinctively exploded to action, wriggling and bucking. "Get . . . off." My voice was a rasp as he choked the air from me.

I recognized the arm now. Long and leanly muscled, I'd seen it thousands of times, slung over the shoulders of my best friend. It was Yasuo. *Yasuo* was the person strangling me from behind. I clawed frantically at his forearm, but it was a steel band around my neck. "Enough," I croaked. "Stop."

"*You* didn't stop," he growled, and it was a feral sound, like he'd already made the full transformation from teenaged boy into something monstrous. He flexed his arm tighter. "Not when you fought *her*. This is for Emma."

My movements grew weaker, slower. I needed to think this through, but it was so hard. He'd choked off blood flow to my brain, and I was fading fast. If I didn't stop him, he would kill me.

No! a voice shrieked in my head. My own panic would be the thing that killed me. The first order of business was to calm the hell down. I'd held my breath for far longer than this. I grew utterly still, envisioning a self that didn't require oxygen to survive.

We'd practiced choke holds in Priti's class. I knew the move I had to do. Pictured the mechanics of my escape. I wasn't strong enough to pry my way out, but I could use leverage against Yasuo. The right twist, the right flex and angle . . . It was all physics.

Power, not strength.

The thing about grappling, it was counterintuitive. To get away, first you had to get closer.

I grabbed Yasuo's wrist and wrenched myself even more snugly into the crook of his elbow. The move opened the tiniest gap for me to shift, and I twisted in to him. Hugged him tightly around the waist. I ducked, bowed, and then was free.

I shoved off him at once and began to jog back and away, under no illusions that I could beat him if the fight got ugly. "Don't . . . say . . ." I coughed and clutched at my aching throat, catching my breath. "Don't talk . . . about Emma."

When he didn't pounce on me, I slowed. Stopped. And then I stared.

He was simply standing there, quaking, looking like a shell of the Yas he'd been. He was off his game. So much so, I wondered if I actually *might* have been able to beat him in a fight.

It gave me the courage to risk saying more. "This is the last thing . . ." My throat spasmed, coughs racking me, but I managed to catch my breath and swallow. "She wouldn't want this."

I paused to give my words meaning beyond this one tussle in this particular hallway. She wouldn't have wanted us to fight here, and more than that, she wouldn't have wanted this distance between us. We were becoming exactly what the vampires wanted us to become: scared, estranged, suspicious—things that made us need them.

"We don't have to do this," I said. It was a simple statement, and yet to believe it stole just the tiniest bit of power from them. I'd find ways to steal even more.

I'd convince Yasuo that I wasn't the enemy. Convince him that I wasn't the one to attack. If he channeled his anger at the real culprits instead, if we sided together against the vampires, we'd be stronger. Power could be ours for the taking.

Power, not strength . . . my new motto.

CHAPTER NINE

I was shivering in the bitter January night, trembling, race-walking back to the dorm. Yas had profoundly freaked me out. He was increasingly unstable, and I worried he was losing it, like in a fundamental about-to-snap sort of way.

I understood his anguish. His anger. But his fury went beyond grief or blame to something deeper. He felt horror, and he blamed me. If I found out what happened to Emma, maybe I could convince him that her death wasn't my fault. Maybe then he'd forgive me.

Carden had sensed my distress, and this time, he hadn't waited. He came right to me, catching up with me on the way back from dinner—right after my tussle with Yasuo. Like, *right* after.

He simply appeared beside me on the path, startling me. "Who hurt you?"

I put a hand to my chest, gasping a breathy half laugh. "Don't do that."

"I caught you unawares." His eyes hardened. "You must

always be on guard. It is a lesson you must learn if you are to survive." He softened, putting a fingertip beneath my chin. "And I'd prefer it if you survived, aye?"

"My guard is just fine." I couldn't help it—the fight with Yas had been too disturbing—and there was an edge to my voice that didn't usually come out when I was with Carden. "In case you haven't noticed, you vampires are a little on the stealthy side."

Vampires, and Yasuo was becoming one of them. I put a hand to my throat, feeling the ghost of his arm constricting around my neck. It was like he was still choking me. All those fragile bones ready to snap. And even worse than the physical sensation was the betrayal. That was what strangled me now. My loneliness, suffocating me.

"Have you been hurt?" He sounded ready to throttle someone. "Are you unwell? Speak to me."

I resumed walking, and Carden fell into step. "It's just . . ." I reminded myself I wasn't as alone as I felt. He'd sensed my distress and come to me at once. It should've been enough to improve my mood, and yet it was so hard to wrap my mind around. I still didn't completely trust the feelings between Carden and me. I mean, the guy was a *vampire*. I dared not tell him my concerns about Yasuo. I still held out hope that Yas and I could mend our friendship, and I didn't want him to be the one Carden throttled. "Let's just say the suck factor is particularly high today."

Carden was quiet for a moment, then said, "As you wish." He knew I was holding something back, and to his credit, he didn't push me on it.

Though . . .

Why *didn't* he push me on it? Only someone who had their

own secrets wouldn't demand the full story. *As you wish.* And didn't that just sum him up? Carden did as he wished.

I gave a shake to my head. I couldn't let myself spin out like this. What I needed was a refuge. A place where I could be safe, just for a little while. "Where do you stay?" I asked abruptly.

"Close by your side?" He raised a questioning brow, that jaunty grin of his firmly in place. Ever the smooth-talking flirt.

It was a great way to avoid the question.

For once, I didn't take the bait. "No, I mean when you sleep."

"I don't sleep."

"Okay, *rest*. Where do you stay *at night*?" Was it in the keep? Did he know the secret horrors of the island? Was he behind it, with the other vampires? The rapid-fire thoughts had me freaking out.

"It's no secret, dove." His features grew quiet, like he only now realized he was dealing with little miss crazypants. And how I hated the feeling that I was pulling the clichéd psycho girlfriend thing. But he tipped his head, looking off to the right, and gently said, "Northeast of here, there's an old hunting bothy. I use it when I need to come in from the light."

"Will you take me there?"

He paused. "Not tonight. But soon. Soon I will show you."

"Why don't you stay in the keep with the other vampires?"

"I avoid Hugo's lair at all costs, and I'd have you do the same."

"What goes on in there?" I needed to know the secret of that castle.

"Why the sudden interest?"

I couldn't stop now. Carden and I were close. If he truly cared about me, he wouldn't keep secrets. "If Emma was alive when they took her to the castle, what would've happened to her there?"

"This, I don't know." For once, he looked taken aback. This hadn't been the direction he'd expected our little chat to take.

"You don't know," I repeated flatly. But there was something in his eyes. Something distracted that told me he might have some idea. "You must know something. If not about Emma, then how about the other girls. You know, the ones who disappear *all the time*. You're a vampire. You say you're not one of *them*—"

"I'm not one of Alcántara's lackeys," he interrupted with a growl.

"Fine. Still, you must have some clue."

A heavy silence hung between us for a moment. "Your anger is misdirected. Trust me on this. Trust me, too, when I say I cannot tell you what occurs inside their keep."

"So you *do* know." Suddenly I was so tired. So sick of all these secrets. "Why won't you tell me more?"

"For your own safety." His answer was quick and sharp. "I know not what happened to your friend. Do I think she's dead? Yes. Do I know of dark doings at Alcántara's hand? Aye, this island is full of darkness. Would you have me secret you inside the castle, tour you around, introduce you to the one truth? I cannot, because there isn't one. There is no lone truth, no single secret revelation. Will I tell you more than this? Can I risk telling you everything? Take the risk that Alcántara might one day perceive the knowledge in your eyes? Can I give him any suspicions of any kind? No, and no, and no again."

"Sorry, Carden, but that's just ridiculous. It's dangerous enough just being here. Wouldn't knowing the Directorate's secrets be a good thing? Like, forewarned is forearmed?"

"There is some knowledge that is difficult even for me to bear. I would guard you against it. Against them." He had such a pained look on his face as he said it, like he truly did want to protect me, from everything, even the bad thoughts. "If there was one truth to share that would help you, one thing I could say that would safeguard you, believe me, I would enlighten you. I wouldn't hesitate; I would risk my existence to arm you with that knowledge. But there are only secrets and horrors in that castle, and I beg you to stay away."

"Then why don't you leave?"

"I'm bound to you," he said with a quick smile. But then he paused and looked blindly into the distance. "Aye, we could flee this island together, but . . . other things hold me here. Other allegiances. Too dangerous for you," he added before I could interrupt. "And there is no running from those. Some truths you cannot escape."

I understood a little something about allegiances. And he was right. Alcántara and his cronies were powerful—there would be no disappearing where they were concerned, only death. "I guess we could run, but we'll never be able to hide, huh?"

His eyes met mine again, and their light had returned once more. "Something like that."

He was so old-fashioned. I believed he truly did earnestly wish to guard me. It made it hard to be angry. I studied him for a moment, my seventeenth-century sort-of boyfriend. "Protecting me from the bad guys—is that you being chivalrous?"

A grin threatened along the hard line of his mouth. I'd surprised him. "That is one word for it."

I smiled then. "And I'd thought chivalry was dead."

"You cannot blame me if I wish to keep you safe," he said, growing serious again. "When I can."

"You do realize I've done a pretty decent job of protecting myself, right?"

"Call it my weakness, but the need to defend you is strong." Then he quickly added, "As you need it, of course." His expression grew panicked, scrambling to express his true thoughts to the modern girl. "That is, if you allow it."

His fear of making a conversational gaffe with *me* was the most endearing thing I'd ever seen. I leaned in to him, nudging him with my shoulder as we walked. "You're such an antique."

He laughed then, loudly, and his burst of good humor was irresistible. It broke the tension for good. "A man could do worse than to be your knight."

It was full dark, and I looked up, studying his strong profile. The white moonlight etched a line along his jaw, and his smile seemed to glow in the darkness. He was all-powerful and yet he was there, with me, walking me back to my dorm, ever the gentleman, while he could've been . . . what? Ravaging helpless villagers? Drinking the blood of innocents? Who knew what they did in the keep. All I knew was that Carden McCloud wasn't in there doing it with them.

So who was he really? I fantasized about taking down the Vampire Directorate, but maybe he did, too. "Why aren't you like them?"

"To be Vampire . . . it should not demand that one be evil."

Evil. Was it possible to require blood to survive and *not* be evil? I couldn't help but think of myself. Me, who now craved the blood of vampires.

It stayed on my mind all night and all through the next afternoon. I was still contemplating the meaning of it all, sitting there on the beach, waiting for Ronan's arrival.

I checked the time on my watch—it was a fugly digital model well suited to geeks and Navy SEALs everywhere. Thursday. 13:47. Getting close to Primitive Skills time . . . aka Ronan's *wilderness camp.*

Unlike the academic subjects, many of these survival classes were girls only. I supposed it was because the guys were going Vampire, and if you were a vamp, why learn to survive off the land when you could survive off the landowners, right?

Shudder.

How would Ronan act when he saw me? I'd headed over early, wanting to get our initial interaction over with before the other girls showed up. He'd been so kind the other night in the dining hall. The fact that I might've looked so sad, so raw, as to make *Ronan* feel sorry for me made me feel pathetic. And, frankly, a little embarrassed, too.

I wanted him to think I was okay. I wanted to say hi, to exchange a meaningful look that said *I'm cool; it's all good* before the start of his class. Usually he showed up early to prepare, but he still hadn't arrived.

Unfortunately, many of my classmates had. They trickled in, wearing parkas and boots over their navy blue catsuits, managing to look like they were slinking down a catwalk instead of simply walking across the cold, damp sand.

Did I look like that? Was I that graceful and just didn't realize it? I'd had a year of brutal physical training by now. It was possible.

"Imagine that you're alone," Ronan said, startling me from behind. He'd strolled up and was diving right in to his lecture.

So much for my meaningful look. "You find yourself on a beach such as this. You're hungry. Growing weaker." He walked to the water's edge, and we hopped into step behind him. The waves were calm today, a rhythmic crash and whoosh along the shore. "What do you eat? How do you quench your burning thirst?"

One girl volunteered, "I'd have water in my pack."

He brushed that off. "Your water is long gone."

An auburn-haired Initiate named Isabella rolled her eyes. "Isn't that why we're taking this class? So you can tell us what to do?"

"Nice," I muttered, giving her a critical eye. She'd never survive her first mission.

It made me want to do better. To excel. I forgot Yasuo and the nature of evil, and for the moment, I even forgot Carden. I wanted to be the one with the answers. "There are shells," I said. "For food, I mean."

Isabella chuffed a bitchy little laugh. "A little crunchy, don't you think?"

I gave her my best side-eye. "Where there're shells, there're shellfish."

"Very good," Ronan said with a firm nod. He gave me a pleased look, and Isabella looked like her head might explode. "Acari Drew is absolutely correct."

He walked to the water's edge. The tide pulsed and swirled around his combat boots, slowly soaking the cuffs of his black cargo pants. Even though it couldn't have been much past two thirty, the sky was a flat gray, the sun already threatening to dip below the horizon. A cloud shifted, shooting a beam of weak sunlight wavering and glimmering along the packed sand. Ronan squatted, peering closer.

"The light will fade quickly now." His voice was low, making him sound deep in his own thoughts. He raked his fingers along the wet sand, and for a moment, I lost myself to the image of it. That hand was strong, a man's hand, with close-clipped nails and skin that was lightly tanned from his time outside, doing things like surfing and teaching us how to survive. He traced his fingers along the shoreline, and it was a slow, languorous movement, almost dreamy, like he was stroking the long hair of a woman.

I gave a sharp shake to my head. What the hell had *that* thought been? I reminded myself it was that very hand and its hypnotic touch that'd tricked me onto this island in the first place.

"Simply use your senses," he said. "Even in the moonlight, you can find shells. You can see, and if you can't see, you can feel the irregularities in the sand. See there." He pointed to a spot I hadn't noticed before, where the sand dimpled. He used his fingers to dig a well around it, revealing the tip of a shell. "Razor shells are common in this part of the world. If you had salt, you could sprinkle it and the shell would pop right up. But"—he dug deeper, till he could snag it with his fingertips and jiggle it free— "you're clever girls. You need only to pry it up."

He held up the shell. It looked like a long, golden-brown fingernail. "There's meat in here. Not much. But I know from experience—if you're hungry, it'll seem a meal, right enough." He whipped it back into the water, lobbing it past the breakers, where it landed with a hollow *plunk*.

He wandered again, scanning the shoreline. Each wave left behind a delicate ruffle of foam and a patchwork of shells and rocks and seaweed. "There is also the limpet," he said, and it took him no time to find and pluck one of the bumpy gray shells from the sand. "These are even more plentiful. You can't take two steps on these beaches without stepping on one."

He handed it around. It resembled a tiny conical hat and fit nicely in my palm. Whatever creature had lived inside was long gone, and shards of broken white barnacles covered the surface.

"Technically, the limpet is a snail," he said. "A bit chewy for my taste." He'd added the last comment with a shrug and a half smile, briefly catching my eye as he did so. I had the strange—and probably incorrect—thought that he'd said it for my benefit.

"Now it's your turn," he said. "*You* walk the beach, imagining yourself hungry and alone. Search for items you think could give you sustenance. You might be surprised at what you find."

A couple of the girls—mostly Isabella and her friends—began complaining at once. "I can hardly see," one of them griped.

I didn't bother to check who'd spoken. I just walked away, anxious for a little space to prove myself even further, finding my own selection of awesome foodstuffs.

"Why does this class have to be *now*?" Isabella asked, closer to me than I'd realized. She'd probably decided to follow me in the hopes that I knew what was going on.

"Yeah, wouldn't it be better, like, in daylight?" one of her friends said.

"We can hardly see."

Ronan spoke as if to a child. "If you are alone, stranded, on a mission, if you've risked coming out of hiding, chances are it's because night has fallen. You must prepare for the worst of circumstances. Were it in my power, I'd hold class in the raining pitch-darkness to make it even more difficult for you."

We split up, wandering our separate ways along the beach. I turned my focus to the plentiful and varied detritus that'd been spat from the sea. There were tons of shells, mostly broken, but I managed to scavenge a couple whole ones from ankle-deep in the breakers.

I thought of survival scenarios. If I were weak, starving, and unarmed, how on earth was I supposed to crack these suckers open? It was a good question, but I'd become very competitive and wasn't about to risk being overheard. You never knew when something like opening a shell bare-handed would be the skill that saved you over someone else. I made a note to ask Ronan later.

I heard girls' splashing footsteps near me. "Drew's finding shells," Isabella said. All her friends but one had wandered off, so it was just her and a tall, skinny, brown-haired girl whose gangly legs made me think of a spider. Her name always escaped me—it was something that sounded wealthy, Tiffany or Whitney maybe—but I just thought of her as some variation of Spidergirl in my head. "Hey," Izzy told her, "help me look here."

I smirked. Fine. They could have the breakers. I had a better idea.

High tide had left a line of debris farther up the sand, like some giant had come and spread a scalloped frill of lace along the length of the beach. Bits of greenery popped here and there, little poofs like tiny bright pom-poms. It was kelp. That stuff wasn't just edible; it was probably even healthy.

I race-walked toward it and scooped up the first bit I found. It was slimy and yellow-green, looking like nothing I'd ever want to put in my mouth. But it was nutrient rich.

I clutched my prize close, making a beeline for Ronan. I wanted props for this before any other girl copied me and got credit for the idea. It meant I was distracted when the hands grabbed me.

CHAPTER TEN

I flinched, but it did no good. Isabella and her pal had me, one on either side. Their hands were steel bands around my arms. Girlie Long Legs leaned close, whispering at my cheek, "Wanna play?"

"Back off." I took a sharp step back but couldn't break their hold.

Isabella tightened her grip and wrenched me forward. "Or what?"

Her friend grinned, and it wasn't a friendly one. She dug her fingers deep into my flesh. "She's all talk, Izzy. Ignore her—she can't do anything. Isn't that right, Drew? You're just a little girl." This close, she towered over me. She leaned down enough to tuck her arm snugly into mine. "And like all good little girls, we're going to play."

I twisted, but she was so close, too close for me to get any leverage. I gave a last tug, even though I knew it wouldn't do any good. "I had no idea you cared. Shouldn't you buy me dinner first?"

"Freak." Isabella gave a hard shove, steering me back toward the shore.

"Seriously." I wriggled and dragged my feet. Near the water with these two was the last place I wanted to find myself, but they had me sandwiched between them, heading closer to the breakers. "Get . . . off."

I looked right and left, suppressing the frantic sensation jangling its way up my legs to my brain. Steady, I told myself. I assessed. Ronan was no longer in sight. A few girls were beachcombing in the distance, and even if they had been nearby, they'd probably just watch anyway, cheering on Isabella and her friend.

"Looking for someone?"

"Yeah." I gave a sharp twist to my shoulder. My arms were going to have some major bruises. "Someone else for you to bother."

Isabella leaned disturbingly close. "But we want to bother *you*." The smell of her breath, like stale coffee, turned my stomach.

Revulsion gave me a burst of strength, and I managed to slip my arm from her hand. "Get off me."

But her grip found me again, and I felt the pop of my skin as her nails sliced into my hand. I was stronger since my arrival on the island, but they'd been drinking the same blood I had. They were stronger, too.

The tide lapped at our feet now. I'd forgotten I had the kelp clutched in my hand and dropped it, quickly grinding it into the wet sand with my foot. If I couldn't have it, they couldn't either.

But Spidergirl had spotted it. "Whatcha got?" She let go of me to lean down and scoop it up.

I kicked at her head, but Isabella hauled me back before I could connect. "What is it?" Izzy demanded.

"Give me a sec." Spiderlegs shook off the largest clumps of grit. The kelp was mangled, all squashed and covered in sand. She held it up, pinning a look on me like she was accusing me of something. "What the hell is this?"

"I bet you can eat it," Isabella said, one part of her mind still focused on our assignment.

Her friend stood and shoved it close to my face, demanding, "Can you eat this?"

I did my best not to flinch away. "How the hell should I know?"

"Oh, I think you know."

A catty smile curled onto Isabella's face. "Let's find out."

Spidergirl's jaw dropped with concentration, making her look like one long, stretched-out crazy person. She grabbed the back of my head, and her eyes were manic and laser focused as she shoved the kelp at me, grinding it into my face.

I was certain it was edible. It didn't mean I wanted to eat it. I clamped my lips shut.

"Make her open her mouth." Isabella sounded positively gleeful. Their hands were all over me, and my body exploded into action, struggling to get free.

The other girl barked, "Help me," and they tried to shove it between my lips, but I swung my head from side to side, evading them.

I felt a foot hooking mine. Isabella tripping me. I went to my knees in the water and felt my eyes bug wide. The freezing water stole my breath instantly. She leapt onto my back. "Push her in."

I panted through my nostrils, acclimating. I made my body grow still—not because I was giving up, but because I needed a plan. The cold would sap my energy. When I acted, it needed to be for good.

Izzy stood over me, trying to wrench my head down, riding me like a kid on a pony. She singsonged, "Drowning will make you open your mouth."

They shoved at me, and the water drew closer to my face. It was too hard to fight both of them at once. I was furious at myself. What a screwup. I knew better than to let my guard down for a second. If I got out of this, I'd never be taken by surprise again.

I was soaked, but Missy Long Legs was in the breakers with me, and with a sharp twist of my arm, I managed to slide from her wet grip and flopped forward. I knew a breathtakingly searing pain as a huge clump of my hair ripped out. "Gross," she cried, and I saw scattered blond hair drifting on the waves, gliding along the shoreline, before being sucked out to sea.

My elbows had stopped me from landing on my belly, and I rolled sideways, scanning for some help or inspiration.

Isabella's fingers raked along my scalp, grabbing another fistful of hair. "Looking for teacher?"

A wave crashed over my head, and as it receded, foam whooshed up my nose, the salt water searing into my sinuses. I fought, but they had me pinned again, shoving my face lower until sand scraped my cheek. Screams tore from my throat even though my mouth was sealed tight. I stole wild looks right and left. Where the hell was everyone? Where was Ronan?

"He can't help you," Izzy said, guessing who I was looking for.

"Teacher's pet," the other one spat.

"Bitch."

"He's gone. I saw him walk back to his truck."

"Maybe he can't stand the sight of you."

"I know I can't."

"You stink too much." Isabella's fingers curled into my shoulders, shoving down. "You need a wash."

I had to fight smarter. How could I survive on this rock if I couldn't even fight a couple of Initiates?

I let their voices dull in my head, focusing only on how I was going to get out of this. Spidergirl was squatting in front of me now, and she looked off balance. It was the chance I'd been waiting for.

I'd been trying to push her away, but now I pulled her closer instead. My arms crisscrossed in front of her neck as I slid my hands beneath her collar and yanked. A basic choke . . . Thank you, Priti.

I rolled backward, pulling her with me, on top of me. My head was in the breakers, but I had her. The sky was a dull gray overhead, the sun gone for the day. I was freezing, but I pushed all those thoughts to a distant spot in the back of my mind. I jerked my elbows out, tightening her collar. She began to gag.

"What are you girls about?" It was Ronan.

Finally.

Isabella popped to her feet. "Tracer Ronan."

Her friend had been trying to pull away from me, and the moment I let her go, she flew backward, flopping into the shallow waves.

I skittered away like a crab, and as I did, I spotted my bit of kelp. It was a mauled tangle of brownish green bobbing limply in the shallow water, but I grabbed it anyway, just as it was about to be washed away by a wave. I raised it over my head like a trophy. "I was getting this. Kelp. This is edible." The words came out rapid fire. I was sure I sounded like a madwoman.

He looked at me for a moment. His expression was hard to read, but I thought I saw strains of worry, anger, exasperation, and just the slightest bit of amusement. His gaze went to the other two. "And you? What did you find while you were mucking about in the breakers?"

Isabella was silent, her face a total blank as she returned Ronan's stare. It was her innocent look, and I couldn't help but let out a puff of a laugh at the sight of it.

"Nothing?" He checked his watch. "It's been over an hour and you've nothing to show for it?"

"No," Izzy said quietly.

He looked to Spidergirl. "You, too, Aubrey?"

So *that* was her name. Rather than looking at Ronan, she was glaring at Isabella, staring daggers. I noticed how she was soaked while Izzy was mostly dry. Clearly this hadn't been Aubrey's idea.

"Fine," Ronan said. "You have fifteen minutes left in class. There are tiny fish swimming in schools. See there." He pointed. "Just past the break. You won't return to the dorm until you catch one and bring it to me."

Isabella shrieked, her silent innocent act gone. "We have to get in the water?"

"You seem adept at getting wet," he said. "You figure it out."

Aubrey stabbed a finger in my direction. "Why doesn't *she* have to get a fish?"

"Acari Drew has her kelp. You, however, must retrieve a fish. Now. Unless you wish me to make it two."

He headed back up the beach, and I followed. It wasn't like we were walking *together*, just walking in the same direction. He called instructions to the other girls, telling them to wrap it up, to bring their finds to him at the truck, but I stayed silent. I dared not thank him. The exchange with Izzy and Aubrey could've easily been interpreted as him playing favorites, and I didn't know which would be more dangerous—for him to have a teacher's pet, or for me to be labeled as one.

Though he ignored me, he slowed until we were nearly side by side. He'd seen my kelp—did that mean class was done for me? When his Range Rover came into view, I gritted my chattering teeth and said, "S-so, does this mean I can go?"

He gave a steely nod, and I peeled off in the other direction, but then he surprised me by calling out, "Wait. Annelise."

I stopped, peering at him. It was almost completely dark now, and I tried to make sense of his expression in the twilight. Was I about to get it? Would he tear into me about needing to come to my aid? Had he changed his mind—would he make me return to the beach to gather my own fish after all?

"You're cold," he said instead. "You know I can't drive you back . . ."

For a surreal moment, I thought I heard regret. I was shivering, but my cheeks flamed hot. "That's cool," I said quickly. "I can walk. I want to walk." I tried to sound casual. Normal. At this point, I just wanted to get out of there.

"I've a towel in the car." His eyes were so solemn as he said it. Like he was offering me not just a towel but something more.

I was shivering now, my body seizing and shaking. I'd have *killed* for a towel, but I also had the gut sense that I needed to get away. I'd been alone with Ronan tons of times. I reminded myself we were cool. This was normal. He was kind of on my side.

And yet we'd always maintained complete formality in front of other people. So what was with the towel? It was such a simple thing, but might it be construed as preferential treatment? He wouldn't offer Izzy and Aubrey a towel—I'd have bet on it. What would the other girls think?

What would *Carden* think? I had a feeling Ronan knew about my relationship with the vampire, so why was he even acting like this? Did he suspect our bond and worry for me? Was this his way of looking out for me?

I didn't know what to do. I didn't know what the rules were. So instead I just stared dumbly.

"You're being foolish," he said, and his sudden coldness snapped me out of it.

I'd just been imagining things. I *was* being foolish.

"Sorry. You're right." I laughed and shook my head. "I think I must be, like, hypothermic or something."

He opened the back of the SUV and pulled out something that looked more like a blanket than an item you'd use after a swim. "Take it."

I did, shivering with relief as it absorbed the excess water from my clothes. It was a dark color—green maybe?—though hard to tell for sure in the moonlight. The edges were frayed, and errant threads tickled my hands. It was an old towel, not some standard-issue thing. Ronan's personal towel. I imagined it was the one he used after he surfed.

I had the weirdest urge, and as I brought it to my face to scrub my cheeks and eyes, I inhaled deeply, seeking some Ronan scent.

I smelled the brine of seawater, and sniffed again, trying to detect the other scent that lingered just on the edge of my senses.

The squawk of girls cut through the air—the other Initiates returning.

I abruptly wadded up the towel and tossed it back to him, hoping he couldn't read my expression in the dark. "Thanks." My voice came out way more earnestly than I'd intended.

"Annelise, it's merely a towel."

"No, I mean for earlier." I realized that was what I'd been wanting to say the whole time. "Thanks for what you did on the beach." That hadn't just been him being a teacher—he'd been looking out for me. I may not have known why, but I knew. I'd seen it on his face.

I expected him to deny it, to blow me off in his usual way, but instead he shrugged it off. "It wasn't entirely on your account. The leggy one had it coming."

He gave me a quirky grin that made me trust him. Made me want to take a risk. I strained my ears, making sure the other Initiates were still far off. I had a minute. Maybe two. Before I could chicken out, I asked the one question on my mind. "What happened to Emma?"

His face shuttered instantly, but his voice was kind. "Emma is gone. Let her go."

"She was alive." I knew it now, knew it in my bones. "They took her to the keep. What happened to her there?"

"You have enough to concern you without thoughts of the vampires' keep. It's my understanding that Alcántara has given you this term's assignment. Is that correct?"

"Yes, but—"

"Then *that* is what you must focus on." His tone was stern, relentless. "Alcántara's assassination class is infamous. Many girls have lost their lives not taking it seriously."

"But I—"

"Let . . . it . . . go." He paused between words, drawing it out, trying to make me hear. "You must. Unless, perhaps, you want to find yourself in the same situation." His words gave me a chill—and not for the reasons he would've thought. Did I want to find myself taken to the keep? He didn't know just how close to the mark he was—I was desperate to see inside.

"Well . . ." I gave him a sheepish look. "Actually, I was kind of thinking I *might* want to. Break in, I mean."

"To the vampires' castle?"

At my nod, he laughed. He actually *laughed*.

"It's not funny. I mean it, Ronan."

The smile lingered on his face, but his eyes hardened. "If you think you can simply *break in*, you're more foolish than I took you for."

"I'll figure out a way. What if I threw a fight? I could lose on purpose, and—"

"Don't even think it. Don't even say it." He stepped closer, lowering his voice to a menacing whisper. "You go into that castle, you'll never come out again." Pain bled onto his features, until he looked genuinely distressed by the thought.

"Don't tell me you care, Ronan."

He blew out a shaky breath. "Good Christ, Annelise."

I couldn't help the smile that popped onto my face. Maybe I wasn't as alone as I thought. Not nearly. "You do care, don't you?"

His upper lip twitched—a smile he didn't want to give me just then. "For one so smart, you're quite clueless."

It was a clear night, the moonlight vibrating on my skin, so I sensed the veil of shadow the moment it fell over my shoulder. Carden, standing behind me. I'd been so focused on how close the girls were, I'd forgotten how likely it was that he'd appear. I was still getting used to our connection. He'd probably set out to find me the moment he sensed my distress on the beach.

"Clueless." My vampire repeated Ronan's last word, and he didn't sound too pleased. *Great.* It wasn't that I didn't want to see Carden, or that I kept secrets from him. On the contrary, I've confided so much more to him than I've ever told Ronan. I just wanted to chat with Ronan without Carden misunderstanding . . . like he was clearly doing now.

I couldn't see his face, but if Ronan's utterly blank expression was any indication, Carden was giving him his best death glare.

"Master McCloud," Ronan said. "We were just finishing up class. To what do we owe this honor?"

Ronan would wonder what Carden was doing there, and sure enough, I heard his thought process in the shifting tone of his voice . . . at first surprise, then skepticism, and finally the sound of a suspicion confirmed. And of course it was—showing up like this was a pretty bold move on Carden's part. If Ronan had had a hunch about our relationship before, Carden appearing like this would be enough to confirm it.

"Perhaps you can explain," the vampire pressed, "about what, exactly, do you find our Annelise to be clueless?"

Oh hell. There it was. Final confirmation, if any had been needed.

"Clueless?" I interjected quickly. I didn't like the wrath I sensed in my vampire's voice, and I was so not ready for any *I-know-you-know* sort of showdowns. I cared about both of them too much. "I'm not *clueless*," I added, trying to break the tension with humor. "I've always thought I was more, you know, like a scattered-professor type."

Silence.

My mind raced for the conversational pleasantries that might break this level of tension, but I was pulling a blank. I decided on some version of the truth. "I was asking Ronan about the keep."

Carden's expression shuttered. "This again?"

I nodded sheepishly. *Caught.*

"I told you to think not on such things." My vampire paused briefly, an unreadable look crossing his face. "Nor should this Tracer allow you to entertain such questions."

"I was in the process of telling her as much," a steely-eyed Ronan said.

Great. Now they were both on me. Meanwhile, I'd begun shivering again, both from the confrontation and the dropping temperature, and Carden fully registered my condition. He shot a quick glare Ronan's way, then turned his full attention back to me. "You're drenched," he said, with an accusing edge in his voice. He adjusted himself beside me, sheltering me from the January wind. Feeling his body close was a relief.

Affection for him swelled in me, but I tried to hide it. He was being pretty blatant about his interest in me, and it was making me nervous. I gave his arm a discreet squeeze. "I'm fine."

He ignored this to glare at Ronan some more. "She will become ill."

Ronan bristled. Gathered himself. Then he dropped a bomb. "Acari Drew," he said slowly, meaningfully, "is stronger than any of us realize."

I gaped. What a statement. It shocked me into silence. I wasn't the only one, either. We stood there, awkwardly, for what felt like an eternity, and I imagined each of us was weighing all the various things those words could imply.

It was my stomach that saved the day. It grumbled, and I breathed a sigh of relief. Hunger, so ordinary and yet so undeniable. Cheerily, I announced, "Hey, dinnertime." Chirpy didn't come naturally to me, and I was sure I sounded like a complete moron, but it did the trick.

Reluctantly, Carden nodded. "I will escort you back." He was in full knight-in-shining-armor mode, his grim expression suggesting we were heading to battle instead of just the dining hall.

I realized he never gave his reason for seeking me out. Wasn't he worried the Tracer would figure out what was between us? Ronan was obviously beginning to put two and two together. Though Carden wasn't stupid—maybe that was what he'd wanted.

As we made our way back, I considered the good news and the bad news. First, I wasn't nearly as alone as I'd feared. I did, in fact, have friends on this island. All good.

But the bad news? Apparently, my allies were incapable of standing within ten feet of each other without looking like they wanted to draw blood.

CHAPTER ELEVEN

I didn't get a warning. Just a tug on my hand, then *boom*. Carden swept me off the path, behind a rock. And then he kissed me. Hard.

His body pressed mine against the cool granite. I'd been shivering before—the night was freezing and flurries had begun to drift down from the night sky—but no more. He was as cool and solid as the rock at my back, and yet heat blazed through me. My body—my blood—hummed in perfect recognition. This was where I belonged. With Carden.

He pulled from me finally, and I drew in a shaky breath. I'd been nervous what he might say. Nervous he'd be mad to have found me with Ronan. Our conversation surely had looked like more than just a chat between student and teacher. It *had been* more than a simple chat. But this intense kiss? I hadn't expected *this*.

"Carden . . . what was . . . wow . . ." I gasped a laugh, trying to get ahold of my senses. Was this his way of taking my mind off the keep? Because it was working. "What was that for?"

I couldn't see him clearly, but I felt his eyes bore into me through the darkness. He swept the hair from my neck and leaned close, whispering, "To remind you."

His words were a hot tickle in my ear, and I shivered with pleasure. If this was Carden being jealous, bring it on. "Remind me?"

"That you're mine," he growled.

Ronan was my friend. He gave my belly the occasional flutter. But that was where it stopped. In our time together, I'd known Ronan to steal my nerves. My will.

But Carden. He stole my breath.

I swallowed hard, gathering my senses. "Ronan is the last person you need to worry about."

Recent concerns about my safety—about Yasuo—invaded my mind. Carden must've sensed it, because he asked, "And who should give me cause for concern?"

"Nobody." I forced the thoughts from my mind. "I didn't mean it like that." Anxiety was a constant on the Isle of Night—I wouldn't let it come between us. Instead, I considered the powerful creature in front of me. Just the thought that this ancient vampire might've been jealous . . . because of *me* . . . It exhilarated me. Made me feel bold.

I cupped his face in my hands and drew him down for a slow kiss . . . one that I led. "I don't need any reminders," I told him as I pulled away. How could I ever forget *this*?

"I appreciate a woman who knows her mind," he said with a smile, then darted in for one last quick, hard kiss. "Perhaps I simply enjoy reminding you." His words were confident, but I heard a hint of relief in his voice.

I'd never been much of a flirter, but seeing his smile gleam in the darkness gave me the guts. Using my best coy voice, I told him, "Hey, feel free to jog my memory anytime."

He laughed, grabbed my hand, and tugged me around the other side of the rock. Leading us *away* from the path.

I stopped short, looking back to where we'd been. "Wait. The dining hall is that way."

"Ah, but you won't be eating in the dining hall this evening."

"I won't?"

"You wanted to know where I stay," he said.

As much as I longed to see where he spent his time, I truly was starving. My stomach grumbled again. "I'm afraid I need more than just . . . to drink. Do you think I could grab some food first? It'll just take a minute. I can just snag a—"

"Och." He *tsk-tsk*ed me. "Have faith, wee dove. I may no longer be human, but I haven't forgotten how to be a man. I have prepared you food."

He sounded so proud saying it, I felt bad doubting him. But seriously, what passed for a meal in his world? It'd been hundreds of years since he'd needed food to survive. Did he remember what tasted good? Plus there was the whole ancient Scottish thing. Delicacies in his day were probably things like blood pudding served in sheep's entrails. "What kind of food?" I tried not to sound too wary, but I probably failed.

He grinned at me, like he'd read my mind. "A good kind," he said firmly. "Trust me." He took my hand in his.

I did, and it was. Good, I mean. Like, all kinds of good.

His refuge was a modest, one-room cottage. I'd have called it a shack, except there was nothing shacky about the heavy stone and mortar walls. It was nestled on the bank of a lake that was small enough to have demanded only a few breaths to swim across to the other side. Though the general location was inland, it wasn't so far from the coast that I didn't get a visceral sense of the horizon, gray and empty in the distance.

"What is this place?" I ran a finger along the butcher-block table that punctuated the middle of the room. It was dinged up from generations of things like chopping turnips and deboning fish and yet it was spotlessly clean.

He came up behind me, resting his hands on my shoulders. "Such places are called bothies. Though I've staked my claim on this one, it would once have been open for any to use. Mostly hunters or fishermen. What do you think?"

I didn't know what I'd expected, and though it wasn't *this*, this didn't surprise me. Everything about the place was solid—much like Carden. "I like it. It seems . . . right."

My eyes went to the corner of the room and the sturdy wood platform that was the largest item of furniture in the place. It was covered in quilts and pillows—a bed.

His bed.

Oh God. His *bed*.

I was a virgin, obviously. And obviously, I was nowhere near ready to have sex with a vampire. But that big bed seemed so masculine. So . . . demanding.

"I thought . . . I thought you vampires didn't really sleep." So what did he use it for? I reminded myself that I was here because I'd asked him to bring me. I wasn't ready for sex. But I trusted Carden. He probably already knew I wasn't ready. This could be as innocent—or as not-innocent—as I wanted.

"Aye, it's true. I no longer sleep as you know it. But vampire or no, a man likes to rest." He seemed to read my mood, and with a light squeeze to my shoulders, he walked to the fire and, like that, changed the subject. "Here I stand like an unschooled lad, and yet you're hungry."

I sighed. Carden always knew how to put me at my ease. "I am," I said, happy to have the topic of food normalize this otherwise completely bizarro situation.

I smelled the food now and meandered over to stand with him at the fireplace. Taking up the whole back wall, the thing struck me as overly large for such a small cottage, but I supposed when it was originally built, that hearth would've provided heat, stove, and a gathering place all in one.

The cottage was dark, but the fire cast dancing orange light along the walls. "What is that?" I asked, studying the oddly shaped burning coals.

He went to stoke the fire higher. "Peat," he explained, "burns longer than wood."

"Handy." I gave him a teasing smile. "Seeing as there aren't exactly many trees on this rock you call an island."

He laughed. "Precisely." He sounded pleased, and that pleased *me* . . . more than it should have.

I looked away, self-conscious again. What was my problem? I was tripping out. I needed to relax. To let go. I was there, which meant he trusted me. What better way to relax, I decided, than by getting to know him better? I scanned the room, looking for the real Carden. The cottage was a bit on the Spartan side, lacking things like pictures or paintings. I realized what else was missing. "You don't have any appliances," I said suddenly.

"I'm not exactly in need of a refrigerator." He cocked his head my way, flashing me his fangs in a playful smile.

"No, I guess not."

He took a large fork from the hearthstone to spear and flip a piece of fish the size of my hand. He'd settled an iron grate over the coals, and the fish hit it with a sizzle.

I inhaled, taking in the aroma of butter and wild onions. I'd thought I was sick of seafood, but my watering mouth was currently disagreeing. "Wow, that smells *good*."

"Aye. It's fresh." He nodded to the window. Moonlight sparkled on the lake, shimmering and lapping mere feet from the door. "From the loch just outside."

He put down his fork, clapped the soot from his hands, and in one swift movement, I was in his arms. "I told you, love. I've not forgotten what it is to be a man."

If knowing how to kiss me till I was dizzy or cook the heck out of a piece of fish was a sign of being a man, then Carden was one with a capital *M*.

CHAPTER TWELVE

"I should go," I told him later. We lounged on his bed, and though he'd nestled me close, he must've sensed I wasn't ready for too much more. I loved kissing Carden, but feeding from him, too, added a whole extra layer of intensity. I wasn't ready for much more than that . . . not yet. I felt close to him, intimate, yet not put-upon. I was safe, utterly. He wouldn't demand anything from me that I didn't willingly offer.

It was just right—*he* was just right.

"Not yet, love." He flexed his large arm, snugging me more tightly to him. "First you must drink."

"But I drank already." We'd kissed, and I'd tasted Carden's lifeblood pumping power through me. I felt the effects of him more than ever now, the change in me, from his blood.

"Was it enough?"

"Yes . . ." I paused to turn inward, checking in with my body. I was stronger, and lately I needed less blood to feel this way. "I feel different from before."

He pulled away to meet my eye. "Good different?"

"Yeah." I smiled and flexed my hands and shoulders. "Really good, actually."

"It's as I hoped," he said. "As our bond grows deeper, you will grow stronger. Able to part from me for longer."

"No blood fever, you mean?" When we'd first bonded, my first impulse had been to break our bond and I'd experimented with being apart from him. Let's just say, the experiment didn't go so well. I'd felt itchy and achy and just plain crazy.

"The risk never completely goes away, but aye, you are stronger." He rolled onto his back, lifting me so I straddled him. "You are stronger," he repeated in a voice gone hoarse. He squeezed my thighs as though he'd test that strength then and there. "And will become stronger still." Then he pulled me down and took me in a fierce kiss.

I tasted him and thought of the fever. Even if I didn't fear it, I'd still want this. Want him. And yet it was a relief to know it was possible to get past that feeling—that I wasn't dependent on Carden every single day to function. Not that I wanted to part from him, but the fever had made me jittery, helpless. Girls died from it, driven insane by their dependence on the blood.

When we parted, I asked, "So does this mean the day will come when I won't need to feed from you at all?"

He gave me a hard, narrow-eyed stare that I could tell was playful . . . mostly. "Is that what you wish?"

I nudged his shoulder. "No, that's not *what I wish*," I said, mimicking his grim tone. "It's just . . . ironic, I guess."

"Ironic?"

"That the closer we get, the farther from you I can be."

"I don't know of ironic. But I do know, the closer we get"—

in a blindingly swift movement, he swept me beneath him on the bed and was kissing along my neck—"the closer I want you."

I totally lost my train of thought for a while, melting under Carden's touch. He was so strong and solid over me. How amazing that to drink his blood was to share that strength.

Finally, I pulled away, unable to push aside a nagging thought that'd entered my head. "Carden?"

He held my hands over my head and began to kiss his way down my arm. Distractedly, he mumbled, "Hmm?"

I unlaced my fingers from his and slipped my hand around the firm column of his neck. My thumb found his pulse, pounding. Beckoning. "If I were to drink more, would I get even stronger?"

He stilled and met my eyes, giving my question consideration. "Is that what you desire?"

If drinking from Carden made me stronger than the un-bonded Initiates, if I drank even more, would it make me stronger than a Guidon? Stronger than a Trainee even? "Maybe," I hedged. "Maybe I do."

"There are no guarantees." He genuinely considered my question. That was the thing about Carden—he was never dis-missive of me, and I appreciated it. "It could as soon harm as help you," he said. "There are risks."

"Aren't there always?" I thought of the castle. Even if I never found a way to spy inside, that kind of strength would come in handy with Alcántara's recent assignment. I was still waiting for a Trainee to jump out of the bushes in an attempt to bite me. It would happen any day.

Whatever came, I told myself I'd survive it. Just as I'd survived all the rest.

But I also knew that, until now, I owed part of that survival to Carden himself. He'd been my secret weapon, helping me escape from my first mission, saving me from the rogue vampire. More than that, his very presence kept the other students—not to mention other vampires—at bay. He felt like the last guard, the emergency reserve. My Plan B.

But what if I didn't need so much protection? I was getting the most advanced, the most lethal training in the world. And with extra doses of Carden's blood, I was getting stronger. Would the day come when I could truly look out for myself completely, even against the vampires?

"I'd like to try." I curled up toward him, nibbling at his neck. But strong as I was, I was still just a human girl, and my teeth were useless.

He pulled away, and for a moment, I thought he was angry or that he'd deny me. But he bit his wrist and held it out to me. "Then I'm yours to take, *mo chridhe*."

I took, and took some more. It surged into my mouth, warm and rich and so much more exciting than simply drinking from a glass. I took his blood until I grew woozy from it. Drunk with it. My head spun from the rush of his blood in my veins. It spun with possibilities.

I felt closer to him than ever. I knew I'd never be immortal like Carden, but if I drank enough, would the day come where I'd age more slowly? What would happen the next time I faced down a vampire? I knew there was information Carden had kept from me out of concern that too much knowledge might put me in danger. But what if my strength made that moot? There was so much to know and learn . . . about the island, about Carden.

"Tell me," I said suddenly.

The fire had died down, casting us in deep shadows, but his laugh was quiet and close. "Tell you what, dove?"

"About you." I was feeling buzzed and easy, and it loosened my words. "About your childhood. Your family."

"My family?" he asked warily.

I could tell I'd caught him by surprise. "Yeah," I said. "You know . . . Did you have siblings? What was your father like? That sort of thing."

"I . . . I didn't much know my father," he said quietly.

I adjusted to see him more clearly. The topic was clearly an uncomfortable one.

Before I could probe further, he changed the subject. "What of you? What of *your* home?"

"My home?" I brushed that one right off. "I don't have a home. My father used to knock me around."

"You mean to say he hit you?" His lips peeled back to reveal his fangs. "I'll find him and—"

I hitched up on my elbow to kiss his cheek, cutting him off. "Thank you for that." The sentiment warmed me. He looked so fiercely protective—I think that was even a hissing noise he'd made. "But I promise you, it's not necessary. I'm sure I'll beat you to it anyway." I thought for a moment about my dad. Would I kick his ass if I ever saw him again? Was he even still out there, or had he already drunk himself to death? Did he ever think of me? I realized I didn't care. "I'm over it," I said, feeling my outer shell harden that much more. "What doesn't kill you makes you stronger, right?"

But he wouldn't let it go. "Your mother allowed this to happen?"

Sadness sideswiped me, welling from some hidden place, clenching my heart. "My mom died when I was a kid."

He murmured some tender but unintelligible thing to me. I thought it must've been Gaelic, but it didn't matter. All that mattered was him, how he cared. How he tucked my head in his hand, comforting me with his sure and gentle caresses.

Between the blood and his touch, I grew drowsy. It made me oddly philosophical. I wouldn't press Carden on his father but made a mental note to try again someday. There was still one thing I didn't understand, though, that I did want an answer to: Why was I the one here, in his bed, being touched like this? "Why me?" I asked groggily. "Why are you with me, Carden?"

"Why am I with you?" The words came out sounding amused and perplexed.

I mustered energy enough to pull clear of his embrace, though his fingers remained tangled in my hair. "I'm serious. I'm not the prettiest girl on the island. I'm smart, but hell, that Audra-Frost girl isn't exactly a dummy. I'm . . . I don't know . . . I'm just me."

He used a single finger to trace the hair from my brow. "That's it precisely. You're just you." He let that sink in; then, growing quiet, he added, "Perhaps you help me to remember." At my questioning look, he elaborated. "You are an innocent. You are so steadfast. So true."

"An innocent, huh?" So how come I didn't feel so innocent? I considered his other words—steadfast. True. Ronan had called me loyal once. I'd never really thought about it, but maybe they were right. After all, I felt ready to risk it all to discover what'd happened to Emma.

So then why wasn't Yasuo recognizing any of this steadfast trueness?

I zoned out, thinking all this, and he must've mistaken my silence for bewilderment because he went on. "You have a sort of nobility. And when we're together . . . it's as though I, too, reclaim some part of that."

I angled away to get a better look at him. He was trying to explain, but he'd actually made it worse. "So the reason you like me is that I'm Miss Dependable? And because I'm innocent—a fragile and ennobled human?" Was that all? I shifted to let the moonlight hit him, peering for the truth on his face. "You were one of those guys who went for the broken birds, weren't you?"

"Broken birds?"

"You know. The kind of guy who likes to save the ones with the broken wings."

"You intentionally misunderstand." He pinched my chin. "Aye, it's true. I've spent long years seeking a wee dove to adore. But not because I wished for one to tend. I've wanted one with whom I could soar."

I leaned back with a sigh. Was it Carden's words or that amazing accent that made it sound so fantastic?

I couldn't think anymore and snuggled close, suddenly so tired. The extra-intense feeding had finally gotten to me, like I'd consumed three consecutive Thanksgiving dinners. I must've fallen asleep because I felt his arms slide under my legs, under my shoulders, and I had the sensation of the ground rushing away from me as he lifted me up. I wrapped an arm around his neck, curling into him.

Something happened as he slipped through the doors of the dorm. It was the middle of the night, but still, deep-seated instinct woke me. I tensed, suddenly on alert, aware of every creak and rustle.

"Quiet yourself," he whispered in my ear. "Nobody will hear us."

We reached my room. Still holding me, he leaned down and turned the knob. Miraculously, the door opened without its usual moan.

My eyes went to Frost, sound asleep in her bed. "Don't wake her."

He paused, his breathing low and even. He looked like he was sending his consciousness into the universe, if that made any sense. "She will not wake," he said with surety.

"Okayyy." I slid from his arms. "Someday you'll need to explain that."

I stood, but was still woozy, and I lurched, grabbing one hand to his chest and one on my bureau to steady me.

His laugh was a low rumble in the darkness. "You must rest."

My fingers curled on the top of the dresser, palm sliding instinctively along the front. "Wait," I said, deciding there was one last thing I'd share. "I need to show you something. A picture."

The picture. The one of my mom that I'd treasured my whole life. Old and yellowed, the paper had begun to separate at one of the corners.

I went to my desk and retrieved the gift Carden had given me. Our eyes met as I pulled it from my bookshelf. He grinned at me, obviously pleased.

But as I peeled back the false binding, I knew a flare of panic. I was showing Carden everything now. The photo. Its very existence could get me killed.

Not to mention Ronan—he'd risked much getting that picture back for me. We'd never discussed it again. If the vampires found out, he'd be dead meat.

"This is her. My mom." I handed him the photo. It was the ultimate show of trust. But still, I couldn't help but plead, "You can't tell."

The look he gave me put me instantly at ease. "Your secrets follow me to the grave."

I sighed, watching him as he studied it. I'd expected him to warm to it. Or maybe to look from her to me and back again, catching the resemblances. We had the same wide eyes. The same mouth. But instead his reaction was the last one I expected.

His eyes dimmed. He was cold, handing it back to me. He gave me a sharp nod.

What the hell?

Did he realize how much of a leap of trust this was and decide we'd gotten too close? Did he know this was completely illegal for me to have? Or worse, had he guessed that Ronan was the one who'd stolen it back for me?

But in an instant he was Carden again, leading me to my bed, tucking me in. "You must drink, my love." He held his wrist before my lips.

So I must've just imagined his reaction. It made sense—I was really out of it, like I'd been drugged. "Drink again?" I asked groggily.

"You must. Just a wee bit. Just once more."

I fought to keep my eyes open. "I'm too tired."

He rubbed his skin against my lips, and instinctively I opened my mouth. Instinctively, I suckled. I couldn't help it—as sated as I was, my body still longed for it. He was whispering odd things to me, mesmerizing me, things I only half heard in my stupor. About how strong I was. How strong I would be.

How strong I'd need to be.

He stroked a slow hand up and down my side, and I moaned with contentment. I wanted to open my eyes to get a last peek at him for the night, but I was so tired. So full.

"You must take care, my love. Do naught that is foolish."

"I'm just going to bed, dumb-dumb. Do you think I even *sleep* recklessly?" I gave a muzzy chuckle. "Don't go all Ronan on me, okay?"

He was silent for a second, long enough for me to hold my breath and wonder if I'd made a misstep mentioning Ronan. But then he spoke again, his tone oddly pensive. "He looks out for you, Ronan does. You believe he has your interests at heart?"

I sighed, relieved at his soothing tone, and nestled deeper in my blankets, sleep beckoning me. It was an effort to parse his question, and I shrugged drowsily.

"Annelise? Ronan. He looks out for you?"

"Yeah. Sure." Part of my brain cried that I should be paying more attention, that something else was being asked here. But I was so very tired, the lure of sweet sleep pulling me down and down. "I remind him of his sister."

I faded then and was drawn back to consciousness one last time as he tucked the sheets tightly around my shoulders. He leaned down and whispered in my ear, "Good-bye, sweet love."

Be strong? Good-bye? Why was he sounding so intense?

I wanted to ask him. I meant to ask him, but before I could form the words, I slid into unconsciousness.

CHAPTER THIRTEEN

⟨⟨⟨⟨⟩⟩⟩⟩

It didn't surprise me that I didn't see Carden the next day or even the day after that. He was always so quick to come when I felt alone or afraid, but since our night together, I'd felt *awesome*.

I felt empowered. Fierce. While extra doses of blood could be dangerous to some, to me it was like medicine. Like vitamins. Like pure . . . liquid . . . bliss. I breathed more deeply. My senses were more acute. My muscles were limber and taut. I felt like a machine. A Ferrari.

I was determined to use that strength. To hone it. To take advantage. I'd be the strongest girl on this island. I'd show Alcántara he couldn't control me. I'd use everything this place had to offer; then I'd blow the roof off.

Which meant I had to destroy all my weaknesses. Banish *all* my fears. And there was one nagging fear that lingered above all others: water.

I hadn't known how to swim when I'd arrived, but Ronan had taken me under his wing. Taught me to float. Then to swim.

Later, to surf. But I still hadn't gotten past my fear of it, not completely. When Izzy and Aubrey had held my face in the surf, it'd all rushed back—that panic I felt underwater, feeling it whoosh up my nose and gurgle into my ears.

I was only as strong as my greatest shortcoming, and my lingering fear of water was one pretty ginormous shortcoming. I mean, we were on an *island* in the middle of the sea, right?

I needed to get past it once and for all.

I checked my watch as I jogged from the dining hall to the pool. I had a good hour till curfew forced me back to the room. The task I'd set for myself was simple—do some laps, then practice my breath-holding exercises. Ever since I'd learned that people could train themselves to hold their breath for fifteen minutes or longer, I'd been dying to work on it. But I'd also learned that immersion in water triggered something in the brain, meaning it did no good to practice unless you were actually underwater.

With my increased feedings with Carden, I needed to discover what else my body might be capable of. So far, my underwater record was two minutes. It wasn't much, but it sure beat my original fifteen-second attempts.

The natatorium glowed from across the campus in the bitter darkness, its bright interior lights shooting from windows high overhead. It always amazed me to find people working out at this hour. I was never a gym rat myself, especially not after dinner. Yuck. Yawn. No thanks.

On those rare times I *had* needed to venture to the gym outside of class, it was like how I imagined visiting a foreign country might be—you knew these people existed, knew they had different customs from you, but still, opening that door, walking from darkness into the bright hum of fluorescent lights and the chatter of sweating kids was always a shock. I tried to avoid it as much as possible.

Heading to the pool at this hour was no different. The natatorium was a large, hollow building, and with its Olympic-sized pool, mazes of locker rooms, showers, and hot tubs, its sole purpose was aquatics-related activities. I hadn't even made it inside before I heard those unmistakable pool sounds and stopped to take it all in. The splashes. Distant voices calling to one another, reverberating in the cavernous space.

Even from outside, the smell of chlorine hit me, eliciting strong gut reactions—fear, hate, panic. I fisted my hands, forcing myself to associate new things with the smell. Mastery. Ability. Vigor. Enjoyment.

Okay, so that last one went a little too far.

Even though I was distracted, I felt the presence behind me instantly. I smiled—it was the effect of Carden's blood. I sensed my attacker, sensed his threat. I stood still, pretending ignorance. Innocence. All the while I watched his shadow approach. I could tell by the width of it, by the gait, that my attacker was Rob.

When he leapt for me, I was ready. I braced my feet, and as his arm wrapped around my neck, I grabbed him at his wrist and elbow and twisted. "Hey, Rob," I said lightly. "What's up?"

He flexed, ignoring what must've been sharp pain in his arm, and jutted his chin through my hair, fumbling to reach my skin. A hiss spilled across my neck, hot in the cold night air. "I've been waiting for this."

"Funny," I said, gritting my teeth. "Me too." I tensed my neck—it wouldn't do me any good to accidentally choke myself—then dug my hands into his arm and doubled over at the waist.

The flip was a simple one, textbook beginner stuff, but so, so perfect. I flipped him over my head, then landed on him, pinning him. My body splayed over his chest, and though I was light compared to him, I aimed the full force of my weight through two points: my left elbow jabbing his sternum and my right forearm crushing his throat. "Cool," I said. "I always wondered if this martial arts stuff worked for real."

He darted his head side to side, trying to get air.

"Whoops." I gave him my brightest, my most feminine smile. "Am I hurting you?"

He was unable to speak, but his eyes narrowed to slits, glaring hard. In a quick burst of action, he kicked his feet, trying to wriggle out from under me.

"One question." I inched my hand up, sneaking for a grip on his collar. "Were you trying to *bite me*?"

He tried to buck me off.

I slid a knee to his groin, and he froze. I *tsk*ed. "You *were* trying to bite me. And I bet the moment I let go, you'll try again. You won't even pretend to negotiate. That's the problem with you boys. You lack subtlety."

It was time to speak his language. If he wasn't going to be reasonable with me, then I wouldn't be reasonable with him. But how to send a message without actually strangling him?—which, honestly, was also under active consideration. I'd already humiliated him once when I'd slashed a giant hole in his pants.

I'd broken out in a sweat, my hands aching where they fisted his jacket collar, but still, he was unable to break free. I *was* stronger than before. It was time to up my game.

He thought he could bite me, but I knew what would stop him. He could patch a tear in his pants. It was time to do some damage he wouldn't be able to hide.

I shifted, and he shifted with me, gasping in a breath of air and hissing it out. Hissing in my face, his mouth wide open. His baby fangs sparkled. Taunting me.

He thought he was so badass. Time to show him what badass was.

"You know what, Rob?" In a single, swift movement, I let go, reeled my right arm back, and punched as hard as I could, smashing my fist against his jaw. "Bite *this*."

Pain exploded up my arm, so complete it stole my breath. Punching wasn't like in the movies at all. Punching *hurt*. But I'd gotten good at compartmentalizing pain, and I tucked it away, a distant thrum in the back of my head. Something to deal with later. I was savoring this moment too much to bother with pain.

Clouds drifted overhead, sending a splash of moonlight over us. It glimmered over a ribbon of blood dribbling down the side of his cheek. He turned his face and spat. A small object landed on the gravel, gray in the darkness.

Both our eyes widened, realizing at the same moment.

I'd knocked out a fang.

He let loose some primal, nonsensical yell, and I pulled back as he popped to his feet. Holding an arm in front of his mouth, he stared at me. Our eyes held and locked for a weird, long moment, both of us panting for breath. He looked confused, unable to make sense of what'd just happened. At that moment, I couldn't either.

What became of a Trainee bested like this? What was a vampire without both his fangs?

He stepped backward, faded into the night. Disappeared.

Carden was right. I was stronger. Even stronger than I'd realized. I was supersized.

By the time I went inside, dumped my stuff in the locker room, rinsed off, and hit the pool, I was in a grand mood. I felt expansive, filled with a sense of anticipation. What would happen next? Would I tell anyone about it? Would people just find out? I'd need to ask Carden if he'd ever seen anything like this.

It fed my workout. I glided through the water. I was a missile. A great aquatic mammal. I surpassed my record, holding my breath for a whole 147 seconds. I was on the deck toweling off, still riding my high, when Josh appeared.

"Heya, nerd bird," he said in that cute Aussie accent of his. He stole a glance at the clock—we were closing in on curfew. "Never thought I'd see you here this time of day." He scanned the deck and pool, which was emptying out as students began to hit the showers. "I don't see Ronan, which means you're here . . . of your own . . . choice? Hold on. Is apocalypse nigh?"

"Shut up." I nudged him with my shoulder.

Unfortunately, this reminded me how scantily clad we both were.

Josh wore the standard-issue swimsuit, which for the guys was a pair of supertight boxer briefs—emphasis on *super*. Those things probably outlined more than I needed to see, but I couldn't say because there was no way in hell I was looking down. And besides, my eyes had snagged on his upper body. He was lean but muscled, walking that line guys tread at our age—almost a man yet still almost a boy, too—though Josh was definitely tipping over into the almost-man side of that equation.

I tore my eyes away, pointing my gaze in the direction he was looking. Kenzie, my Proctor, was the last one in the water, still doing her laps. She had this trick of gliding all the way across the Olympic-sized pool and back again. Without taking a breath.

"She's amazing," he said.

I nodded. She was a blur of blond hair and navy blue Speedo. Her hair was a perfect bob to match her perfectly proportioned body. "She's always reminded me of one of those American Girl dolls."

"Yeah, if there were an MMA version."

"MM . . . ohh, mixed martial arts?" I watched her, all sleek perfection. She was solid, but not buff like I imagined those MMA women would be. "Nah. More like . . . American Ninja Girl."

"That's it," he exclaimed, clapping his hand on my shoulder, a naked slap that made me self-conscious. "You seen her weapons? Those sai knives?" His Australian accent lilted at the end, making his every sentence sound like it might've been a question. "Like a manga chick."

It'd been Yasuo who'd told me what those knives of hers were called. She carried two of them, long and thin, each blade framed by two sharp prongs, making them look almost like tridents. They did seem like something a manga badass would wield.

She reached the edge and smoothly pulled herself up and out of the pool. We weren't friends, but we were friendly enough, and she spared me a curt nod as she walked by, headed for her towel. I noted how she didn't spare a glance for Josh, or any of the other guys for that matter.

We were surrounded by half-naked cuties, but Kenzie didn't care. She was in her own world. It made me realize something: I'd never seen her with one vampire in particular, which implied she'd made it to Guidon by consuming only the shooters of blood they served in the dining hall. She probably didn't drink from the source, and yet there she was, power and ease, swimming all over the damned pool. Without breathing.

I'd been nervous about the water, but Kenzie was an inspiration. Not that I'd break my bond with Carden, but if she could accomplish all that, if she could be that strong without a blood bond, then how far could I go? Could I truly break into the keep? Might I uncover their secrets? Discover what'd happened to all those fallen girls?

My journey started now. Here. I'd go to the pool more. Work out more. I'd be a force.

"Earth to Drew." Josh was looking at me funny. I registered how he'd gone for his towel and come back, and I was still in the same spot, staring at that pale blue water. "You'd better shower up. Curfew's soon."

I was the last girl in the showers, hurriedly rinsing the conditioner from my hair as I heard the heavy metal door to the locker room slam shut. I turned off the water, the ancient knobs squealing. There was total silence. I was the last one. I scampered to my locker, careful not to slip. I'd dallied too long.

"Dammit." I struggled to get my clothes on—I hated putting clothes on damp skin—but I needed to hustle. My hair was soaking—the ends of it would surely freeze on my race back to the dorm. "Damndamndammit."

I hobbled out of the dressing room, forcing my heels into my boots. I'd just reached the pool deck when I heard a noise—a loud electronic sound reverberating through the pool area. *Whoomp.*

The lights cut out. I was in pitch-darkness.

CHAPTER FOURTEEN

I froze. I mean, how much would it suck to accidentally fall in the pool fully clothed? "Hello?" I called out. It was probably just some nighttime janitor out there, doing his job. "Is anybody there?"

There was another click, quieter this time, the sound like a flicking switch. The overhead lights were still off, but the pool lights switched on, looking like white orbs glowing underwater. The pale water shimmered eerily, making the black stripes along the bottom waver. I strained my ears for some movement, but there was just a distant *drip-drip*. The natatorium at night— creepiest thing ever.

"Hello?" I called again, but there was still no answer.

A door slammed, and I panicked. I'd seen the chain they used to lock up with—I was not about to spend the night at the nata- torium, thankyouverymuch.

"Hey!" I called again, louder this time. "I'm still here!"

"That's the problem." There was another click, and light

flickered behind me. Not the overhead light, but a small bare bulb in the custodial closet.

"What?" I spun, looking for who'd spoken.

He was illuminated from above. In the darkness, the effect was freaky, like holding a flashlight under your chin only flipped the other way. "You're still here, and that's a problem."

"What?" I squinted to see better. "Is that you, Yasuo? What are you talking about?"

"You're here. She's not. And now it's time to eradicate the problem." He flew at me, grabbing my neck before I had a chance to act. His fingers curled and tightened until I felt the delicate bones of my throat begin to give. He was going to kill me.

I grabbed his wrists and struggled backward. He squeezed tighter, and my body spasmed, fighting for air. I opened my mouth to shout, but couldn't get a breath in or out.

The rubber soles of my boots skittered on the wet tile of the pool deck and my feet slid from under me. I had to hold on to his arms to avoid breaking my own neck. Finally, my boots got purchase. I got my feet back under me and tried to speak. *Stop*, I tried to say, but nothing came out. My mouth just opened and closed like a gasping fish.

I stared into his eyes, trying to communicate that way. His were bloodshot, giving him an insane, unhinged look. I wanted to connect. Tried to telegraph something with my pleading expression. Maybe he'd remember how I wasn't so bad. How we used to be. But he wasn't there. I stared into those eyes, and he wasn't home. His gaze was flat and dead. Cold. He'd become something different. Whoever this creature was, it wasn't my friend Yasuo anymore.

His fingers curled tighter, and I felt my eyes bug. Black spots popped into my vision. I was dead if I didn't act.

Alarm, terror, grief . . . My emotions were so haywire, I expected Carden to appear any minute. But he didn't.

Had Yas chained the door? Either way, it looked like I was on my own. Which meant I needed to stop the magical thinking. *Strength*, I told myself. I'd be strong, not terrified. I was strong.

I uncurled the fingers of my right hand and forced myself to release his arm. Hitching up my leg, I reached down. My fingers splayed, flapped, grasped toward the stars in my boot. But the farther I stretched, the deeper his fingers dug into me.

The black spots in my vision melded together. Became a black veil. My chest was spasming now, my throat making disturbing little croaking noises. But I sensed it as though from the end of a tunnel. I was passing out.

This was it.

I sensed movement. *Carden*. He'd come at last.

There was a slamming door, a rush of fresh air and light. But Yasuo didn't take his eyes from me, so surely it was only my fantasy. This was my brain shutting down, me going into the light.

But suddenly Yasuo's fingers were gone. His spine shot straight and his arms sprang from his sides like he might flap away. His back arched, and he bucked, then bucked again, eyes shut like he was having a seizure.

It was the last thing I saw before my own body took over, and I doubled over, dropping to my knees, coughs racking me. My chest shuddered to pull in oxygen, the moist air burning as it passed my throat.

Finally, my vision cleared and I looked up, expecting to find Carden. But my savior hadn't been a vampire. It took me a moment to make sense of what I was seeing.

Yasuo was on his belly, and Kenzie sat straddled over him. She'd plunged her sai knives hilt-deep in his back.

She calmly met my eyes and said, "I forgot my goggles." She glanced from me to Yas. "Just in time, apparently." She stood and dusted off her knees, giving me a smile. "I hate missing a pool party."

"Oh my God." My voice was ragged, barely a rasp. "You killed him."

She gave me an impatient look. "I'm better than that."

"You did." I pointed at the twin hilts, sticking out of him like an *X*. "His heart. You staked him."

"Anatomy 101, Acari Drew. I'm a Guidon—I know *exactly* where his heart is." Looking almost bored, she drew her finger down to a point just below his left shoulder, between her knives. "His heart is exactly between these two blades. The kid will be fine."

She pulled out those blades, and Yasuo's body shivered. So he was really alive?

Oh crap. He was really alive.

And he'd be really pissed when he came to. I wavered to standing. "We should get out of here."

"He's out for a while." Seeing my questioning look, she grinned. "Not my first rodeo, girlie."

She was cleaning her blades on the hem of his uniform sweater, her posture so cool, it ratcheted her several notches up in my estimation.

"Whose side are you on anyway?" she asked.

My eyes shot to hers. "What?"

The word brought on a fresh bout of coughing, and she waited till I was done to say, "If I'm not mistaken, this Trainee just tried to kill you."

I gazed at Yasuo's face. His features were slack, but his chest rose and fell evenly now. Alive, just as she'd said. He looked so peaceful—more peaceful than I'd seen him since Emma's death. "He's confused."

"Confused?" She nudged his leg with her foot. "These guys aren't worth the trouble, if you ask me."

I thought of Josh, my Australian pal. "Some of them are okay."

She rolled her eyes at me as though I'd lost my mind. "If you're into that sort of thing."

Kenzie had obviously not bonded with a vampire. Lately, I'd thought a lot about strength versus power, but she didn't mess with thoughts of who controlled whom. She fought. She survived. She was pure strength. A warrior.

I vowed to be more like her.

I hopped into step, catching the door before it swung shut. "Right behind you."

CHAPTER FIFTEEN

⸺⸺⸺

This thing with Yasuo had to stop.

Maybe if I could definitively prove that Emma was alive when she left the ring, he'd finally understand that her death wasn't really my fault. In fact, Alcántara had probably targeted her way back in our first semester, when she'd pulled out of the original Directorate Challenge.

I needed to get closer to the truth, which meant getting closer to Alcántara. It all came back to him.

And, I just realized, he was currently eyeing me again. I shifted in my seat, pretending to write something in my notebook. Every time he looked at me, I felt it, like a warm breeze blowing over my skin or a little shiver of relaxation at the base of my spine.

I girded myself. Sat tall. I'd lost my best friend. My other best friend was doing his best to kill me. And it was all the fault of this vampire.

He was lecturing on assassination techniques. Historical examples. Issues of distance. Questions of proximity, of position. And I wasn't hearing a word he was saying. I was plotting.

I dared not confide my plans to Carden . . . and where *was* he, anyway? I hadn't seen him since that intense night we'd spent together.

Had I done something to make him keep his distance? I replayed our final conversation in my mind. I hadn't said anything too strange about Ronan, right? I would've known at the time if he were upset.

He was probably just busy.

So why hadn't he come when I needed him? I'd gotten used to my vampire coming when he sensed me upset, and when your supposedly good friend tries to *kill* you, it definitely falls under the Upset column. Surely Carden had felt my alarm. My anguish.

Maybe since Kenzie had come to my aid so quickly, he'd felt he hadn't been needed. Maybe Carden even purposely stayed away to avoid discovery of our bond. Both were good excuses, but neither completely erased the pang of hurt.

I was telling myself to grow up when I heard Alcántara pause and clear his throat. *Crap.* I looked up, and those fathomless eyes were waiting for me.

A smile curved the corner of his mouth. An *I'm-watching-you* smile.

Pay. Attention.

It was no secret that Alcántara was one of the main baddies in this place, but how could I get more insight than that? I pretended to take notes, writing down random phrases from his lecture—secrecy . . . motives . . . Shakespeare's *Macbeth*?—embellishing the words with squiggles and curlicues, considering Alcántara's secrecy. Alcántara's motives.

Lissa asked a question, and as I turned to look at her, only then it struck me. There were empty seats—like, a *bunch* of empty seats. The realization shot me back into the present. If Emma were alive, she'd want me focusing on guarding my own hide and less on what'd happened to hers.

I wish I'd done a head count that first day. Just how many girls were missing from class? Did those empty seats represent girls who'd tried—and failed—to execute Alcántara's assignment? (Pun intended.)

Rather than listen to Lissa's question, I was mesmerized by the look of her. She was pale and drawn. I realized her pert-nosed friend was conspicuously absent. When Alcántara had given our assignment, he'd told us the cost of failure would be our life. So I guess Lissa's friend was a fail.

My roommate, Frost, rose from her seat.

What the—?

My attention snapped completely back into class. Frost was about to report on her project.

Already. She'd already killed her assigned Trainee.

Jeez . . . these people. I was still trying to wrap my mind around what this whole business entailed, and yet there was my roomie, going to the front of the class so calmly you'd have thought she was about to give an oral report on *Jane Eyre* instead of detailing for us the finer points of her first successful assassination.

Bloodthirsty much?

"Acari Frost." Alcántara purred the name—and how annoying was it that even the vampires no longer called her Audra? "Tell us, did you successfully complete your assignment?"

"Yes, I did," she said proudly.

"Well?" Alcántara looked like his patience was wearing thin already. Apparently, Frost wasn't *every* teacher's pet. My feelings for the Spanish vampire aside, I found his distaste to be just the slightest bit gratifying. "Why don't you begin by outlining the details of your personal assignment? For example, do you know *why* you were assigned the target you were?"

So there *was* a method to Al's madness. What did it mean that my assigned victim was Trainee Farm Boy? He'd asked that our assassinations have some sort of poetic twist. *Horrific.* Alcántara wanted a story, and I was suddenly curious to hear Frost's.

"Yes," Frost said. "Trainee Marlin Grosse was my assignment."

I searched my memory banks . . . Marlin Grosse. I'd never met him—I mostly knew the Trainees in Yasuo's circle—but I pictured a tall, gangly guy with a blond buzz cut. Grosse—I'd assumed it was German, but it could've easily been Norse. Had he been in one of Frost's advanced Norse classes? She was obsessed with it—if he'd been competition for Dagursson's attentions, I'll bet she hadn't liked that one bit.

"Due to our mutual interest in Old Norse literature and my-thology, we've had several classes together," she said, confirming my suspicions. "I believe he was my assigned Trainee because . . ."

She faltered, and I shot up in my seat. Was I about to glimpse into the truth of Frost's tiny heart?

She cleared her throat. "Marlin has troubled me in the past. I believe this is the reason he was my target. To force me to face my . . . problems."

She'd been about to say *face my fears*—I'd have put money on it.

Alcántara steepled his fingers, cocked his head, and furrowed his brow. "What is the nature of the trouble he's given you?" His fake sympathy made me sick.

"He tried things," she said simply. From the steel in her expression, I could guess what those *things* were. Some of the guys on this island were real scumbags. Rob had *tried things* with me. I got where she was coming from.

"This made my strategy easy." The way her eyes pinched at the corners told me not all of it had been that easy. "I got him alone. I told him . . . I'd changed my mind. About him, I mean."

She slowly began to unfold a square of linen, and everyone— even Alcántara—leaned forward to see. "The next question was, which weapon to use?" She revealed the long, thin knife that'd been tucked inside.

I craned my neck to get a better look. I knew for a fact this wasn't her weapon—she carried some obnoxious Viking ax thing (of course)—and at closer inspection, this didn't seem like the typical choice at all. Sure, it was a knife, but the blade looked shoddy, like it was a kitchen implement bought on the cheap rather than a prized weapon.

"Tell us about this crude blade," Alcántara said.

"When considering how to do it," she continued, "how to kill him, I began with his name. *Marlin Grosse.* From there, it was simple."

"Simple . . . how?" Alcántara seemed interested now.

Frost clearly liked the attention. I watched her loosen up. Warm to it. "It's a fishing knife that I . . . *borrowed* from the kitchens." She looked up through her lashes and smiled at Alcántara. She loved the vampires, loved life on this island, and it made me sick to watch her fawn like this.

"Fine, fine," Alcántara said, sounding impatient again. "Perhaps you'll share with the class the significance of this choice."

"I'm from Maine," she continued. The warmth had bled from her voice and she was robotic again. "My father was . . . is . . . a fisherman. I know how to use a boning knife."

There were a couple of chuckles in the room, and her eyes shot up. "Yes, ha-ha, *boning*. A boy like Marlin would've had the same reaction."

"And that is why you chose this particular blade?"

"Well, that and the fact that his name was Marlin. You know"—she paused, waiting for the dimmer kids in the class to get it—"like the fish."

"Lovely," Alcántara cooed. "Tell us how you orchestrated your execution."

She nodded, and though her gaze was aimed straight ahead, I was sure she was focused on nothing but what she saw in her own head. "Marlin was going to, you know, force me."

Jesus. I stared. I might've even stopped breathing. What the hell had Frost gone through? What were we *all* going through? And why were so many of these girls set on going it alone? She hated me, but she could've trusted me. She could have told me all this stuff was going on for her.

"He kissed me," she went on. "He told me if I let him . . . do things . . . he said it would only hurt a little bit. I let him kiss me while I slipped the knife from my coat pocket. And then I told him he was wrong. That it would hurt a lot. For him. And that's when I did it. I stabbed him."

You could've heard a pin drop. Nobody made a sound. Nobody, that is, until Alcántara broke the silence with a majestic slow-clap.

"Brilliant," he said as a blissful smile spread across his face. "That was lovely. Thank you for sharing. Truly, that was a triumphant moment for you." He turned to the rest of us. "Acari Frost has followed my instructions to the letter. Her assassination had meaning. It was clever and brave and, I daresay, poetic."

Elbows on the desk, my chin was resting in my hands, and I curled my fingernails into my cheeks to keep myself from scowling. *Poetic*. Give me a break. Sociopathic, more like.

Alcántara's eyes swept the room till they met mine. My breath caught at the intensity of his gaze, heavy on me. "Class is dismissed," he said. But then he caught me, stopping me with a single finger crooked around my arm as I tried to breeze past. "I look forward to your contribution, Acari Drew. And, *querida*?"

I forced myself to breathe in and out. I didn't know what power he was capable of, and I forced my mind to remain clear. "Yes, Master Alcántara?"

"I expect results." He gave my arm a lingering, creepy squeeze, then let me walk out of the classroom.

I rubbed my arm where he'd touched me. I'd show him results. I'd show him poetic.

I'd need to be very careful as I formulated my plan. Very patient. I couldn't raise suspicion. Which meant, even though I found this whole assassination thing repellent, I had to participate.

I'd have to deal with one Toby Engel.

How, though? How was I supposed to kill someone named *Trainee Toby*? I mean, even his name sounded like he belonged in an animated cartoon. But it was life or death, and I'd always fight for life—my own, at least.

And besides, the Trainees had their own assignments to

perform. Rob *would* attack me again—only this time, he wouldn't just want to bite for class credit. He'd probably attempt to kill me, simple as that. There was also Yasuo to consider. It broke my heart to think my best buddy wanted me dead.

And where was Carden? It was long past time for him to show up. To steal a kiss, snug me close, and make me forget my troubles.

But then someone else appeared, bringing my thoughts to a whole other preoccupied place. "Annelise," Ronan said, his long legs catching up to me easily.

"Uh, hi," I said a bit awkwardly. Last term, I'd barely seen him, and now the guy was all over the place. It was unnerving. It didn't matter, though. Our chat wouldn't last long because now Carden really *would* appear any second—he always did when Ronan was around.

The path forked, and I stopped and pointed in the direction of the dining hall. "Well, I'm this way," I said, kind of wanting to ditch him. Carden was out there somewhere, probably sensing even now how we were chatting, and a testosterone showdown was the last thing I felt like dealing with.

"You're headed for dinner?" He turned down the path. "I'll go with you."

I cut him a look as he fell into step. "You will?"

"I'm a growing boy, aye?" He gave me a smile that cheered me despite myself. "And besides, you seem like you could use the company."

Now I cut him a longer look. This was suspicious behavior.

"Fine," he confessed. "I've spoken with Kenzie."

I braced myself. "You did?"

"You should trust her," he said mysteriously.

"What did she say?"

"She told me about Yasuo's attack. I don't like the danger you keep finding yourself in."

"You don't?" Now this really was weird, especially seeing as I've been facing danger since the first moment *he'd* brought me here. I stopped short when I realized he was making one of his ominous *thoughtful-Ronan* faces. "And?" I asked warily.

"She is disturbed that you might not be able to . . ."

"To fight back?" I shrugged, suddenly very depressed. "What's your point?"

And where was Carden? He *always* came when I talked to Ronan—especially when I felt any sort of strong emotions. *Sort of like right now, Carden.* I concentrated very hard. *Earth to Carden, come in.*

Had I done something to upset my vampire? He'd tucked me in so sweetly the last time I'd seen him. But he had said the word *good-bye.* What did it mean? Had it been *good-bye* good-bye? I tried to recall his exact words in my head, but I'd been so out of it when he left, practically drunk from the excessive feeding.

"You need to be ready to act against Trainee Yasuo with appropriate force," Ronan said, and the preposterous notion drew me back into the conversation.

I huffed a cynical little laugh. "*Appropriate force.* Of course I don't want to use *appropriate force* against Yasuo. Wasn't fighting Emma enough? Just how many friends do I have to kill in this place?"

"Don't be angry," he said, his tone unexpectedly gentle.

"It's not that I'm angry." Between Carden's unexplained absence, Alcántara's unwanted interest, and Yasuo's fury, anger wasn't exactly what I felt. "I'm sad. Lonely, maybe. Confused and scared, definitely, for sure. But it's not quite anger. I don't know . . . I'm worried about Yas. I mean, above and beyond the whole trying-to-kill-me thing. His eyes were all wonky, and he didn't seem like himself . . . like, *at all*."

Ronan's expression shuttered, but he gave a slight nod that told me he knew a little something about loneliness and uncertainty. "It's only out of concern that I . . . that Kenzie and I," he quickly amended, "bring this up."

I thanked him, but my throat grew tight. *Kenzie and I.* Did Ronan ever take any responsibility for his own actions or feelings?

"You must be prepared," he warned. "Yasuo won't be satisfied until he feels he's exacted revenge."

My mood spun on a dime. "Alcántara is the one who killed Emma, not me. Yasuo should get revenge on *him*. How is it I'm the only one who seems to want to know what happened to her? Because if she wasn't dead when she was taken from the ring . . ." Emotion stabbed me like a stiletto in the chest, and I sucked in a breath, needing to gather the guts to finish the thought. "If she wasn't dead," I continued slowly, "he should want to know what happened to her. Hell, as a vampire Trainee, he's the one with the ticket inside the bowels of that castle. He's the one who can find out."

"Maybe he knows already," Ronan said evenly.

"Then maybe he should tell *me*."

"Maybe *you* should forget this foolish idea," he snapped.

"Foolish idea?"

"That there's something in the castle for you to discover. There are all kinds of nightmares in that keep. And no," he said, seeing my look, "I don't know what they are. Certainly, you could break in and satisfy your curiosity, but you'd bring the

knowledge to your grave because we'd never see you again."
Something flickered across his face, something tight, like pain.

Ronan cared, and at the moment, it just made me sad. I sighed.
"Look, I've been getting stronger. But Carden—Master Mc-
Cloud, I mean—he says that the difference between strength and
power is—"

"Don't," Ronan interrupted. "Annelise, you will please re-
frain from quoting vampire politics to me."

"It's not politics," I said, but my protest was weak. His jaw had
tensed at the mention of Carden. For whatever reason, I was
walking a fine line here. "It's survival."

"Survival." He sneered. "I'll see you in class, Annelise." He
stopped and turned to head back the way we came.

"Wait." I stopped, too, staring dumbly. "I thought you were
going to the dining hall."

"I've lost my appetite," Ronan said. And he left me standing
there.

CHAPTER SIXTEEN

As it turned out, an early dinner wasn't a good idea. In fact, it proved to be a very, very bad idea.

I'd shoveled down my food, pocketing a roll to snack on later, and was back out the door before too many other kids even had a chance to show up. Head down, hands jammed in my pockets, I walked as briskly as I could, teetering on the very outer edge of the path headed back to the dorm.

But it wasn't inconspicuous enough. A chorus of guy voices greeted me.

I didn't look up. I just upped my pace. The voices got louder. More specific. "What's her problem?" one shouted, and another followed with, "Bitch is scared."

Then I heard Yasuo. "She's too good for us. Isn't that right, D?"

Crap. It wasn't just any group of guys. It was Yas and his pals.

I walked faster, my eyes glued to the ground, and passed by them. Just as I began to release a pent-up breath, I felt them stop.

Like a herd, they turned as one, dutifully following me back up the path.

What the hell? These were growing boys—shouldn't food be the most important thing on their minds? I laughed nervously, still not daring a glimpse at them. "I'd get my butt to the dining hall, if I were you. Food goes fast on casserole night."

"You're much tastier," the Trainee named Colin said. He was one of those swaggering, quarterback types, which apparently translated in life as on the field. "What do you think, Dan? What would you rather eat? Cafeteria slop or Acari slut?"

Redheaded Danny laughed hard and shouted an answer, but between me huddling extra deep in the hood of my coat and his thick British accent, his words just sounded like *oi oi oi oi.*

I picked up my pace, but felt a hand swipe at the sleeve of my coat. *Dammit.* I could break into a run, but that'd probably only trigger some pack instinct. They'd simply chase me back to the dorm and eat me alive.

I was out of options. I stopped short and spun on them. "What?"

They were a huddle of about a half-dozen boys, staring at me. Some glared (Yasuo), some gaped (Toby-My-Trainee), and others goggled as though mine were the first breasts they'd ever seen (Colin, Dan).

I hardened my stance, not in the mood. "What are *you* looking at?"

"You." Colin curled his lip, taunting. *"Trash."*

Nice. Here we go. I put my hands on my hips and stood as tall as my five-foot-two frame could stretch. "I knew you were a dumb jock, Colin, but do you think you could do us all a favor and maybe dream up a better comeback?"

I scanned the rest of them, doing the mental tally. Fangless Rob was notably absent. I was desperately curious to know where he was and what would come of a one-fanged Trainee, but this was definitely not the crowd to ask.

My gaze came to rest on Yasuo, standing front and center. This was obviously his party. "What's the deal, Yas? You've got yourself a little gang now?"

"Gangster is in my blood." He'd pronounced it *gangsta*.

I fought not to roll my eyes at the posturing. "Seriously? And I suppose these are your homeboys?"

"Dude's from LA," Colin cut in with a tough-boy nod.

"Dude's from *the valley*," I snapped, then turned my full attention to Yasuo. "You hated your father. But now you're . . . what? Supposed to be all Yakuza like him?"

His response was a silent glower.

Now I did roll my eyes, taking in the lot of them. "Okay, gangsters. Riddle me this: I thought vampires were supposed to be solitary creatures."

Yas took an aggressive step toward me. "You don't know shit about me *or* vampires."

I put my hands up. "Easy, cowboy." I knew shit about both, in fact, but now wasn't the time. Instead I asked, "What's the plan here? You're going to . . . what? Jump me? Do you really think you can do that here?" I glanced around to prove my point. "In the middle of the quad?"

Actually, I feared that was exactly what they wanted to do. And what would I do then? I'd felt so strong after my last feeding with Carden, but the effects were wearing off.

Where was he? I couldn't get much more anxious than I was now. If he didn't appear any second, I had a problem . . . actually, *several* problems, on many gut-wrenching levels, none of which I could spare a moment to contemplate just then.

Guidon Kenzie had helped me before, but there'd be no Proctor to save me now—she was in the dining hall, probably fork deep in beige slop. We'd given each other a nod in greeting as I walked out of the building and she'd walked in.

"Jump you. Right here." Yasuo smiled a disturbingly vicious little smile. "Maybe that's exactly what we're going to do."

I held my breath and waited, opening my senses to the universe, but I sensed only my complete solitude. Nope, no Carden. Despair wended its way a little deeper into my heart, and I blew out that breath. No knights in shining armor for me. No *deus ex machina*. It was just me. And I'd need to face this head-on. By myself.

But then a voice of reason spoke up, declaring a definitive "Chill out."

I found the speaker easily enough—giant, blond, freckled farm boys tended to stand out from a crowd. It was Toby Engel. *My* Toby Engel.

"Take a chill," Toby repeated. It wasn't exactly sticking up for me, but it was close. This was his way of trying to get them to leave me alone. "Let's just go, man. I want to eat."

It appeared I wasn't exactly *completely* by myself. I had Trainee Toby on my side. The Trainee Toby I'd been assigned to kill.

Alcántara really was an evil son of a bitch.

Common sense told me I needed to use this situation, to find my opening and finish my "assignment" for Alcántara.

Here was Toby, after all. His guard was down. Maybe I could come up with a way to take him. I could announce I'd go to the dining hall with him, and instead I'd find a way to hit him with one of the stars tucked in my boot and then run like hell out of there, hoping the other guys didn't catch me. I'd be done with my assassination. Forget poetic. I could make something up after the fact. Something about how the stars come out at night, maybe. I could come up with some fancy explanation that'd satisfy Alcántara.

But I couldn't do it. I caught Toby's eye. Dim as a post, this one. Why was he even here? Ronan had said the word *tractable*, and that must've been it—the kid was dumb, easily swayed, and yet unnaturally brawny. But despite all that, Trainee Toby lacked the gleeful taste for violence that Yas and the others had discovered. This could've been my moment to take him unawares, and I couldn't.

Ultimately, it didn't matter. The guys made the decision for me.

"Fuck dinner," Danny said, and they closed in.

They leapt for me, and it was an explosion of chaos, of arms and legs. Of *my* arms and legs, kicking and flailing, trying to wrestle free, all the while trying not to topple. I didn't want to consider what would happen if I fell to the ground.

Where was everyone else? But I knew—Yasuo's gang had chosen their timing perfectly. *Everyone else* was in the dining hall eating cream-of-beige casserole.

I was fast and tough and good at flailing, but I was going to lose this battle. There were too many of them crowding all around me, too big while I was too small. Gradually, hands found purchase on my body and I was less able to wriggle free. Soon fingers clamped around both arms. I felt someone's grip at my waist. I was in a vise of many hands.

So much for me having strength or power. Cunning, smarts,

grit . . . All those things I'd thought I had meant nothing when it was me versus a half-dozen guys. I thought my heart was going to explode out of my chest. Trapped—it was the worst feeling ever.

Danny leaned close, studying my face. "How should we do this, lads?" Then he hauled back and sucker punched me in the gut.

It was a shocker, and I hadn't had a chance to flex my ab muscles to prepare. My body tried to double over in protest, but hands held me tight from behind. My stomach churned and spasmed, and I retched up and convulsively swallowed back down a bit of dinner. I vowed I'd never eat cream-of-mushroom anything again.

"That's no fun." Colin shouldered Danny out of the way. "The fun is in making marks."

Oh shit. I clenched, flexing every muscle, from cheeks to toes.

Toes, I realized. I inched my leg forward along the path, and the feet that'd initially hooked around my ankles were gone.

The guys might've had me in a vise, but that meant they were holding me *up,* too, and I used it, bracing my elbows against them. I swung up my legs, curled my knees to my belly, and then kicked. Both feet shot out like a bucking donkey. Aimed straight for Colin's groin.

He doubled over, arm curled over his boy parts, and then he just hung there, his body gone rigid, looking like a freeze-frame from a movie.

Meanwhile, the other guys exploded all around him, shouting, "Oh!" and, "Right in the nuts!"

Apparently, getting kicked in the testicles was a spectator sport with boys, because they'd let go of me and were springing around like they were on pogo sticks, hopping, clapping their chests, smacking one another's shoulders, shouting their sympathy or amusement, and words of advice, like, "Breathe, dude." Or "Jump up and down!" But Colin ignored them, focused only on gasping for air. It looked like he was trying to speak, but when his mouth moved, nothing came out.

I began to back away, slowly sneaking my way out of the cluster, but a hand wrapped around me, feeling more like talons in my flesh than the other grips had. "We're not nearly done with you," Yasuo snarled. There was something dark in his expression, something that told me he wasn't just toying with me. He was playing for keeps.

I scanned the guys, mentally assessing my options. As Colin was coming to, they gradually brought their attention back to me. I could've handled one Trainee, two even. But a whole gang? Even if I could've taken them down, I had no idea what the repercussions would be. All these cute, floppy-haired boys, and every one of them was a killer.

"Check out her bug eyes," Danny shouted. "You scared, D?"

Yasuo whispered in my ear, "You should be."

My eyes sought Trainee Toby. He was on the outskirts, a witness but not a participant. Not yet, anyway. *Great.* The one guy in this gang I needed to kill happened to be the last one I wanted dead.

Someone called, "Is the little girl scared?"

Well, yeah. I was frightened out of my wits. I thought of my dream, of breaking into the castle and spying on the vampires. This was just a handful of Trainees, and I couldn't stop them. What would happen if I was caught *in the keep*? Who knew how many dozens of vampires awaited me inside? But I knew not to show my fear. I wouldn't be daunted. I wouldn't fail before I even began. I could handle this.

I pinwheeled my arm, breaking Yasuo's grip, then pivoted and jogged a quick few steps back. "Scared? You're a bunch of lame-ass douche bags."

"Language," a voice called in half laughter, half warning.

I spun, momentarily startled and confused, then spotted Priti, jogging toward us on the path, a handful of older Guidons following dutifully behind. I never thought I'd be so thankful to see such a thing.

"Be more creative," one of them said as she passed, and the girls' laughs and the easy *thump-thump* of their pace began to neutralize the tension of my situation. "Yeah," another added, "call them apes instead."

The last girl in the caravan turned and jogged backward to address me. "Boors," she said with a smirk. "Call the boys *boors*. Vampires dig the old language." She spun around again, continuing on the path toward the dorms.

Was *she* scared of the Trainees? She sure didn't seem it. With enough blood, could I be stronger than these guys? I knew I could never beat a vampire, but could I beat a Trainee? Watching Priti and the Guidons head down the path, something told me that, yes, I could.

I'd figure out how to spy on the guys. I wouldn't be afraid— I just needed to get stronger. Be more wily.

I broke into a dash before the Guidons shrank too far in the distance. Who'd have guessed I'd ever race *toward* the older girls? But, I decided, I'd choose whatever evil hazing they could dish out over Yasuo's gang any day.

The guys grumbled something; then I heard Toby say, "Leave it. I want to get dinner."

Good old Trainee Toby. I couldn't kill him in a million years—I was screwed.

Yas shouted at my back, "We're not done."

I raised a hand in a wave but didn't turn around. He was right: We weren't done, not by a long shot.

I dug deep, knowing what I had to do. I'd get back to the dorm, but it wouldn't be to lock myself in and hide for the night.

I needed to hit the gym.

CHAPTER SEVENTEEN

L eaving the dining hall so early meant I had extra time to work out, plus I had the gym almost to myself. Normally, I would've liked that . . . though, *normally*, I wouldn't have just come from being accosted by a boy gang led by my former best buddy.

Before I'd headed back out, I'd given myself a moment to wallow. Frost was at dinner, and having the room to myself was too irresistible. Besides, now that I was alone, I couldn't shake this trembly feeling, like my insides had turned to Jell-O. I told myself it was because I'd changed into thin workout clothes in our chilly room, but after that showdown with the guys, I couldn't help but wonder, *Where's Carden?*

I wasn't sure whether I should worry or be mad. Surely he'd felt me freaking out. So why hadn't he come? Even if he hadn't sensed my alarm, usually he would've found me by now, simply to say hi. To steal a kiss.

Just the thought had me putting a hand to my mouth. The guy

had some kiss—not that I had a lot of experience in the matter. There'd only been Carden, plus the one time with Alcántara, if you counted being touched by his cold, precise lips a kiss, which I hated to.

It wasn't like my vampire not to pursue me. I missed it. Missed him.

My eyes went to the book he'd given me for my birthday, and before I could tell my hands otherwise, I was pulling it from my shelf. All the better to feel sorry for myself, right?

I flipped through, straight to the secret compartment in the back binding, and pulled out the photo of my mother. I'd shown it to Carden—was that why he was upset with me? It was probably lame of me to open up so much. Had it been too much too soon? Maybe he'd panicked.

If vampires were immortal, it sure put a different spin on relationships. Like, forever really was *forever*. Maybe he wasn't ready for the sort of commitment implied by pictures of one's dead mother.

With a sigh, I put away the picture and pulled out the rubbing I'd done of runes found in a cliffside cave. Viking graffiti—how cool was that? It was such a human thing, looking at it often made me feel better. Like, maybe I wasn't alone in this whole humanity thing. A sort of reminder that *this too shall pass*.

I tore out a sheet of notebook paper and hastily copied the runes on a piece of scratch paper before tucking the rubbing back in its hiding place. I had to know what those symbols said, and now, just a few weeks into my Old Norse Dialects class, I finally had the tools to translate. Besides, there was nothing like a project to take my mind off my troubles.

Master Dagursson had taught us the runic letters, and they

actually weren't too hard to get the hang of. It was what Old Norse was written in before it was Latinized, and there weren't that many runes anyhow. As for the Norse itself, though German was my expertise, the two languages shared some links, and my grasp of basic grammar was improving.

It took me just a half hour to get it.

ᚾᚨᛗᚲᛁᚱᚾ · ᛞᚱᚨᛏᛏᛁᚾᚾ · ᛋᚨᛏᛁᚨ

I worked it through, finally, slowly reading, "*Vampíru drottinn Sonja.*" I deflated. "Goddammit." The thing translated to "Sonja, ruled by vampires." Well, of course she was. Because if there was a Sonja, that poor girl was ruled by the vamps, that was for certain.

I kicked back in my chair, for the moment putting aside the annoyance of it all to let it blow my mind. There'd been some girl on this island, as many as a thousand years ago, named Sonja. She'd maybe been like me, tucking her body into that same niche on that same cliffside, probably hiding from vampires just as I had. *She'd* been ruled by vampires. Just like I was. It was nuts.

I felt a connection across the ages. What'd happened to her? Had boys also turned against her? Mocked and tormented her?

Had Sonja been forced to kill her best friend, too?

Enough. My own drama made me sick, and this stupid translation was no longer helping one bit. I slammed the dictionary shut. Enough wallowing.

I had to get out of there. Feeling bummed wouldn't help anything. It was time to hit the gym.

It was an impulse I never usually had. Seriously, *never*. But my interaction with the guys had thrown me. I'd been feeling so strong. But pitted against those big almost-vampires, being physically overwhelmed, trapped and held, it was a rude reminder of how weak I really was. I'd work out till my muscles burned. Till I was too tired to wallow.

But when I entered the gym, I almost spun and walked right back out.

Ronan had beat me there. What was with him lurking every-where all of a sudden? I wanted to leave, but there was no turning back. The place was empty, and he'd spotted me the moment the metal door screeched open. His head swung up, those haunted eyes meeting mine.

I gave him a tight nod.

He gave me a tight nod back. Well, as good as one could nod while on the mat doing—what *was* he doing?—alternating one-armed push-ups?

Wow.

He stood, mopped his face. Approached. His navy blue T-shirt was almost black with sweat—it clung to a particularly muscular bit of his chest, to a muscle in his upper arm.

My eyes shot to his. His gaze didn't budge from mine, and though there wasn't warmth there, it wasn't cold either. It was like he was waiting. Questioning.

Did he think I'd come to the gym looking for him?

Had I come looking for him? He was always here, after all.

No. I hadn't come for Ronan or any guy. I'd come to work out. To get strong.

Though, now that we were both here, I knew what I had to do. When I'd last seen him, I'd casually chatted about Carden-this and Carden-that, when I knew how he felt about vampires. . . . Or were his strong feelings reserved for *my* vampire in particular? Either way, I owed him an apology.

I realized neither of us had spoken and it was about to get weird, so I slung my coat and bag onto the bleachers and said, "Hey."

"Hey," he said back.

Uncomfortable silence.

I looked around the gym, hoping for a distraction. Maybe some jerky Trainee would come and interrupt us. Or another Initiate would come bitch at us about something. But, aside from a Guidon I'd seen go into the locker room, there was nobody.

I girded myself. "Look, I'm sorry about . . . you know . . ."

Wait. *What* was I sorry for? For talking about one of the few residents of this godforsaken island who actually cared about me? Why was I supposed to apologize, *exactly*?

Before I could go too far down that path, he surprised me. "It's I who should be sorry."

I gave him a startled look. "It is?"

"I shouldn't have reacted as I did. You're just trying to survive. In the only way you know how. I understand."

Now he really had thrown me. "You do?"

"This place has a way of stealing a person's humanity. When you—" He stopped abruptly, and his eyes sharpened, narrowing in on my arm. "What happened?"

The bruises hadn't yet formed when I was in my room, but they were there now. The Trainees must've hurt me worse than I'd realized. I flexed my right hand and arm. My wrist was the real problem—it didn't look as bad as the flowery purple marks sprouting on my biceps, but it was way more tender. "Yeah, ow."

"You didn't answer my question."

"Your question," I repeated flatly. What happened . . . ? There was no avoiding it. He'd hear about it eventually. "Yas and his friends decided to have some fun with me." I cringed to avoid the sudden wash of emotion. The topic was too painful—losing Yasuo's friendship hurt more than any sprain.

I brushed it off and abruptly strode to the back of the gym where we kept things like tape and chalk. "Where's the tape?" I asked coolly. "I think I should wrap up this wrist."

"You must keep yourself safe," he snapped, following close on my heels.

"Here it is." I snagged one of the rolls of athletic tape and used my teeth to tear off a strip.

"I warned you against this."

I met his eyes. "Look, it's not like I wanted to get manhandled by a bunch of guys with mini-fangs."

"You must avoid walking alone as much as possible."

I knew he hadn't intended his comment to hurt, but it had nonetheless. "Whom do you recommend I walk with?"

There was a steadiness in his presence that told me he'd registered how my wounds were more than skin deep. "Then you should do all you can to avoid such situations," he amended gently. "How was it they were able to corner you?"

I didn't look at Ronan, but I felt him, his attention heavy and silent at my back. He may have understood my pain, but still, he was waiting for an explanation. I guessed it meant he cared, but it gave me an epiphany: Sometimes it was easier when nobody cared.

"I guess I'm still getting used to the fact that my former best friend wants me dead." I tried to wrap the tape around my wrist, but my trembling fingers managed only to attach the tape to itself. "Dammit."

I ripped off another strip to try again, but Ronan took it from me. "Let me," he said gently. Slowly, he wound strips of white tape around my wrist. Between my fingers. Around my palm. The rhythmic movements—rip, wrap . . . rip, wrap—lulled me. Calmed me. "I didn't realize how deeply this situation with Yasuo had hurt you." His voice was suddenly husky. Hoarse.

The sound of his concern made my throat tight. "I'd say the whole thing bums me out, yeah." I didn't have the guts to meet his eye. Instead, I let his hands mesmerize me. They were guy's hands. Strong, clean, and broad. Not pale and immaculate vampire hands. Just dinged-up, weathered guy's hands.

He adjusted, and I realized he'd stopped working. He needed to rip off more tape, but I'd held on to his fingers for a beat too long. I held my breath as—I couldn't help it—my gaze met his.

Those forest-green eyes burned into me.

I felt slack in my limbs. Warmth tingled up my legs. Did Ronan know what I was feeling? Surely *Carden* was out there somewhere, knowing I felt these sensations.

Wasn't my vampire jealous? Apparently not enough to appear. It made me feel abandoned . . . cut loose and flapping in the breeze.

I let go of Ronan's hand, and he continued with the tape. Had I imagined our connection just then? Carden's absence had cracked something deep inside me, a tiny hairline fissure apparently wide enough to let one or two traitorous thoughts steal past. Because, while Ronan was in his own world, focused on wrapping my injury, I found myself focusing on his long black lashes. His skin was darker on the very bridge of his nose, probably from all that surfing. I drifted back to his hands. His movements were so sure. What else could his hands—

I froze, reminding myself what else those hands were capable of. Their hypnotic touch. How they could convince me to do things I didn't want to do. How they'd convinced me to come to this island.

I pulled away abruptly, smoothing the tape down along my forearm. "I can finish."

Needless to say, my workout was performed in a daze. I think I did circuit training and some kettlebell work, but who knew? My damp shirt could just as easily have been the result of a cold sweat.

Ronan . . . there had been something between us this time. I'd imagined it in the past, but tonight I'd felt it, the brush of his fingers like an electric pulse. Or was it? Maybe it was just him using his powerful touch on me.

But he couldn't fake the expression in his eyes. I'd caught it. Something seeking as he'd looked at me. And wow, how I'd felt something in return. A sensation in my gut, like loosening and tightening all at the same time.

So, now, really, where was Carden? Because he *always* appeared when I got those feelings—though usually it was after midnight and I was dreaming of him. But still, he always showed up when I felt this achy wanting feeling. If he were going to appear, now was the time.

But no vampire. Just me.

Alone again.

CHAPTER EIGHTEEN

I got back to the dorm, my mood even worse than it was before. My roommate hadn't turned to say hello as I'd come in, of course. She just nodded and made a *hmph* sound. "Hello, Frost," I said to her back, enunciating the words.

What was her problem? In class, she practically did backflips to get attention, but when it was just the two of us, she treated me like I was contagious. Why would she want to shut me out so thoroughly? I mean, she clearly had a lot of problems—that stuff she told us in class was seriously messed up.

I decided to take a risk and said, "That was some intense story you told in class. I was sorry to hear you went through all that."

Her shoulders stiffened, but she didn't stop me, which I took as a good sign, so I continued. "I've had some issues, too. With Rob." For an instant, I even considered telling her about the fang incident, but I feared it'd be too much. I was curious to hear her story, but it didn't mean I trusted her yet. "Some of those guys are such jerks," I said, because that was obvious, right? Safe territory. "And I don't get what the rules are," I added. Her silence emboldened me, and I decided to go a little further. "Like, can we fight back? What happens if we do? I think I'm going to try."

She still hadn't turned around, but I could tell she was considering my every word, and just when I thought she was going to confide in me, she said instead, "I'm working on my dialects project. I bet you forgot yours. It's due tomorrow."

Jeez, we couldn't even talk about getting mauled by a couple of asshole boys? Was everyone on this island so completely and irrevocably damaged?

"Right," I said flatly. We were in the same Old Norse Dialects class, which, if you're Frost, is clearly more important than the completely screwed-up gender conflicts happening in this place. "The project." I *had* completely forgotten, but there was no way I was telling her that.

My panicked mind was fumbling for some explanation—and a solution, too, because *crap!* I needed to devise and complete a project by tomorrow—when she announced, "I saw the runes on your desk."

Double crap. I'd returned the rubbing to its hiding spot with my mom's picture, but in my dumb wallowing state, I'd forgotten about my scratch sheet of paper.

I dropped into my desk chair to look at those runes, my mind racing for an explanation. It couldn't be so bad, right? There wasn't anything wrong with having some random runes on my desk. It wasn't illegal, not like having a photo of my mother. And thank God I'd stowed *that* away.

"Is that your assignment?" she asked.

Brilliant. Thank you, Frosty. "Yep. That's my project." We had to do an unusual translation of our choosing. Most girls probably weren't even thinking about runes yet, so ironically, this might even get me some much-needed brownie points with Master Dagursson. "I'm just finishing it up now."

Finally, she turned to face me, presenting me with the snottiest expression. "Well, I'm glad to hear you're still working on it."

"What's that supposed to mean?"

"It means, I should *hope* you're not done yet." She was speaking slowly, like I was hard of hearing or something. "Because you've gotten it all wrong."

"Wrong?" My jaw clenched as I snatched the paper to study it. How had I gotten the runes wrong when I hadn't even been the one to write them in the first place?

"Yes, *wrong.* Those runes you wrote . . . they're ridiculous."

"What do you mean *ridiculous?*" I'd copied them from a fricking cliffside, for chrissake. Not that I could tell her that.

"Well, I've done several of these translations now."

"How awesome for you."

"Thanks," she said with a prim smile. She hadn't caught my sarcasm. Apparently, irony wasn't in Frost's little toolbox. "I hate to tell you, but what you've written there is gibberish."

"Gibberish?" I'd just translated it before the gym. *Vampíru drottinn Sonja.* Seemed simple enough.

"Yes. You know, gibberish. Nonsense." Her eyes lit, like she was about to win some game I hadn't realized we were playing. She adjusted herself in her chair, looking eager to rub my face in something. "What do *you* think you wrote?"

Screw roommate bonding. This girl was a freak, and I didn't like her messing in my private business. All I wanted was to blow her off and get back into my own head. I turned, pretending to busy myself with some papers. "It says 'Sonja, ruled by vampires.'"

"Just like I thought." She scooted from her desk and headed over to mine. "Don't worry. It's to be expected you'd make some mistakes if you're using *this* thing." She ran a finger down the spine of the special book/hiding place Carden had given me. "This edition has been out of print since the forties. Where'd you even get it?"

"It was a gift." I stared at her stubby fingers with their chewed-off nails. "Don't touch it."

She recoiled like I'd accused her of intellectual slumming. "As if."

I sensed her about to return to her desk, but I was too curious now. Tamping down my frustration, I turned my attention back to the runes. Was I going crazy? I translated them again in my head. Doodling a wavy line under them, I muttered, "'*Vampíru drottinn* . . . Sonja, ruled by vampires.' I don't see the problem."

"The problem is, your runes suck. Maybe you'd have seen that if it weren't for the fact that your translation sucks even more."

"Okay," I said slowly. I knew the runes weren't messed up, because Sonja, whoever she was, had written them, not me. And if Sonja was expressing herself *runically*, then it was a safe freaking assumption she knew what she was doing. "Let's start with my translation," I said, my voice flat. "You're saying it's wrong?"

She shrugged, acting coy. A snitty little look like triumph pursed her lips.

"What?" I demanded.

Frost made a giggly sound, and not being a giggly girl, it sounded really messed up. Like, menacing almost.

I stared at them, growing angrier by the second, until the treelike shapes started to blur in my vision.

ᚢᚨᛘᚲᛁᚱᚢ · ᛒᚱᚨᛏᛏᛁᚾᚾ · ᛋᚨᚾᛁᚠ

I sounded out, "*Vampíru . . . drottinn . . . Sonja.* Sonja," I emphasized firmly, "ruled by vampires." I shifted in my seat to glare up at her. "Right?"

"Well, what you have there doesn't say *that*." With a smug look, she leaned over me, resting her hand on my desk, and I fantasized about elbowing her in the gut.

She shifted closer and I got a whiff. *Ick.* The girl smelled dry and papery, just like Dagursson. I cringed away, ever so subtly. "A little space, please?"

Frost ignored me, getting off on full lecture mode. "If 'Sonja, ruled by vampires' is what you want to write, you need to start again from the beginning and rewrite the runes."

"Let's just translate what I have here, shall we?"

She rolled her eyes. "Fine. We can address this gibberish. This doesn't say 'ruled by vampires.' You've confused the verb *'drottnun'* with the noun *'drottning.'* *Drottnun* means 'overlording.' Here, the usage is feminine."

I scooted away, peering up at her. "No, it's masculine. In Old Norse society, kings were *'Drottinn.'*"

"Just because the noun is masculine, doesn't mean it can't refer to a female." She sneered at me like I was the most moronic person on earth. "Duh."

"But there are no female vampires," I snapped. "DUH."

She stood—finally, a little space!—and put her hands on her hips. "No need to be rude. You wanted to know what this nonsense is that you've written, and I'm just telling you. If you wanted to write 'Vampires ruled Sonja' then it would be *'Vampírur drottnuðu yfir Sonja.'* You see," she said with exaggerated patience, "it's easy to play with the similarity of the word *'drottnun,'* which means 'to rule over.' And although this passage is confusing, contextually speaking—"

"Jesus." I grabbed my hair, ready to pull it out strand by strand. "In English, Frost, please, just tell me whatthehellthissays."

She gave me a blank look.

I sucked in a breath. "Please, Frost," I said more evenly. "Would you please tell me what *you* think I wrote. These runes." I stabbed a finger at the page. "What do they say?"

"This gibberish?" Looking like she had a bad taste in her mouth, she gave a funny little perplexed shrug. "It says, 'Sonja, ruler of vampires.'"

And, like that, my world imploded.

CHAPTER NINETEEN

O hmyGodOhmyGodOhmyGod.

    Frost had been right about one thing—I *had* made a mistake. But not like she thought. My error hadn't been in writing the runes; it'd been transposing active for passive verbs: *Sonja ruled by* versus *Sonja ruler of.*

Sonja. Ruler of vampires.

As in:

A woman.

In charge.

Because there was no other way to read that. *Sonja.* That was a woman's name. It wasn't the sort of name that could go either way—not Pat, or Taylor, or Carter. It was so surreal, I'd repeated it in my head over and over, considering it from all angles and all nationalities, until it seemed like an unreal mashup of vowels and consonants. But it *was* real. Sonja was a name, and it was undeniably feminine.

Did that mean there'd been a ruler of vampires who was a woman?

I blew off Frost as best I could after that, head reeling and hands trembling from the revelation. And, by the way, thank *God* she didn't see the original rubbing. As it was, she just thought I was crappy at Old Norse, and that was fine by me. Those original runes were burning a hole in my bookshelf, but I dared not take them back out now. Who could I even show them to?

Carden. I could show them to Carden. I *wanted* to share them with him.

Yeah, right.

Screw him. He'd apparently ridden off into the sunset, leaving me to deal with this by myself.

All right. Not *screw him*. Not really. I was hurt, not angry. Heartbroken. Aching to see him. Missing him physically. Longing for his touch. For the feel of our bond igniting whenever I fed from him.

How had I ever let myself get so vulnerable? I replayed our last night. *As you grow stronger, as our bond grows deeper, you will be able to part from me. . . .* Like he was setting it up so he could leave me. And though he'd said we could part for longer periods, I was beginning to feel that familiar unpleasant ache in my belly—the ache of the blood fever.

Why would he put me through this? What had I done wrong? Should I have gone further with him? Was that what he'd wanted?

And then there was all that stuff he'd said. Had it meant anything to him? Or had he just been trying to get in my pants? *You are an innocent. You help me to remember. Blah blah blah . . .* Helped him to remember what? That I was an inexperienced virgin who wasn't ready for more, while he was?

Of course, his disappearance had another explanation, one that I dared not consider. He might've disappeared because he'd . . . disappeared. Something bad might've happened to him.

But wouldn't I have felt it? I was certain I'd know if Carden were ripped from this earth. The thought was too painful—I couldn't even touch it. Much easier to think I'd been blown off. And how pathetic was that?

Which put me back at squares one and two: hurt and pissed. If and when I saw Carden again, I'd be too angry to tell him anything but off.

There was Ronan—I could've confided the whole Sonja thing to him. Yeah, except for the fact that I couldn't even think about that interlude in the gym without feeling heat creep into my cheeks.

Besides, getting Ronan involved in something this big could only put him in danger. First off, Carden might not want me, but he surely wouldn't want any other guy to have me either. Confiding too much in Ronan would only set him up for some major conflict. Ronan might've been a Tracer with some crazy powers, but he'd never survive a fight with a vampire. Secondly, even if Carden weren't an issue, asking Ronan to help investigate the monsters that *employed* him? Talk about putting the guy in harm's way.

No, I was on my own with this.

Sonja, ruler of vampires. I might've been curious about the keep before, but now I was on fire with it. I needed to act, once and for all.

And Alcántara was the key. So many secrets began and ended with him.

Keep your enemies close. . . . Wasn't that how the saying went? Getting closer to Alcántara could prove illuminating, and with Carden missing in action, this was my moment. At least that was what I told myself as I approached his office. Because doing what I was about to do, I needed every mantra, motto, and saying I could muster.

"*Mi querida,*" he purred. "What a surprise."

I closed the door behind me. "Good evening," I said, using my most polite-young-lady voice.

Master Dagursson might've smelled like musty old papers, but the office of Master Hugo de Rosas Alcántara wrapped me in scents of aged leather, antique mahogany furniture oiled to a fine sheen, and crystal snifters of brandy. It smelled dangerous.

I pasted a smile on my face. I'd purposely come at the end of his office hours so we wouldn't be interrupted. I reminded myself this was *a good thing.* For my plan to work, we needed to be alone. So why was my heart knocking in my chest, feeling as fragile and fluttering as a bird's?

The wingback chair creaked as I sat down, the leather a deep— and deeply disturbing—oxblood red. "Thank you for making time for me." It was a halting beginning, but I had to start some- where. I was in it now. And besides, I was convinced this was the best first step in my plan to uncover every secret in this place, because who was closer to the heart of the mystery than Alcántara?

The Spanish vampire sat utterly still, fingers steepled, watching me like some magnificent predatory bird. One false move, and I had no doubt he'd swoop across the room and devour me.

I had to admit, the guy sure was pretty. Long and lean, in black jeans and black sweater to match his artfully tousled black hair. He looked like a bored rock star.

Bored and silent.

I waited, because wasn't this place all about *speak when spoken to*?

It didn't take too long before I began to squirm. He was using the silence. It was his tool, his weapon.

Because I could no longer bear not saying *something*, I said, "I appreciate you seeing me."

Silence.

"I know it's the end of your office hours."

I could practically hear the crickets chirping.

"I had an idea I wanted to discuss with you."

Immortal black eyes, watching. Calmly. Waiting.

I couldn't help it—that stare was too disarming. Apparently, his silence was, in fact, an awesome tool, because here came my babbling questions. Anything to make him speak. "I mean, you do have a minute, right? Is this an okay time? Do you need me to come back tomorrow? Because I can, if that's better."

The inelegant outburst made me cringe.

Finally, a small smile curled his mouth. "I always have time for you, *cariño*." The words rippled over me, a rich and sensual hum, warming me. Teasing me.

Check that. *Toying* with me.

But this wasn't my first tango with Master Alcántara. He'd tried this crap before, using eyes and voice and touch, trying to mess with my mind. I inhaled deeply, until my lungs burned, and held it. As my head cleared, I gave him an artfully naive smile.

He laughed then, a bright, crisp bark of a laugh that seemed to surprise him as much as it did me. "Truly, it is lovely to spend time with you again," he said. "Just when I'd begun to fear you were avoiding me." He kicked out his feet, no longer looking like he was plotting either how to bewitch me or bite me, and I relaxed a little. "I confess," he said, "your roommate surprised me. I hadn't thought she had such depths."

"Frost?" I smiled, going with it, because my roommate was an infinitely better topic of conversation than me. "Yeah, who knew? I thought her inner world began and ended with irregular Norse declensions."

"Funny, is it not? How two talented minds can be so very different. But I'd guessed you wouldn't be friends. Not your type."

He'd guessed? "So then why'd you assign me as her roommate?" I had no doubt the vampires micromanaged every decision on this island. Who roomed with whom, who got which weapons, hell, what food they served on any given day—it would've all gotten equal attention.

"Not I, *querida*. Acari Frost"—he shrugged like he found the name as silly as I did—"she is Alrik's project, not mine." Alrik, meaning none other than Master Dagursson, our resident Viking vampire.

"Master Dagursson can rest assured," I said blithely, "that girl is just as fascinated by him as he is by her."

His eyes shuttered. Note to self: Vamps don't like gossiping about other vamps. Unless that vamp was Carden, who did enjoy a nice rousing round of gossip . . . And you can bet I shoved *that* thought away as quickly as it'd appeared. God only knew what mind-reading talents Master Al was privy to.

"Why have you come?" he asked frankly, those coal-black eyes suddenly laser focused. "Certainly it is not merely to tell tales about your peers. Is it that you have . . . extra time at your disposal?"

Crap. He was slipping back into our old rapport, a rapport that involved his creepy flirting and my panicked evasions. Clearly this was a reference to Carden and how he'd disappeared—a fact that surely hadn't escaped Alcántara's notice. Carden was gone, and *boom*, Drew had free time.

I must've looked freaked out, because he added an amused, "Am I mistaken?"

"I do find I have some extra time on my hands," I said, too smart to lie. There was no pretending with Alcántara, just avoidance and redirection. "That's why I came. I have a proposition." I blushed furiously. "Not that kind of proposition. I mean—" Oh God . . . where was I going with this? Well, if he thought I was flirting, so be it. Whatever I had to do to get closer to that castle. "I was wondering if you needed an assistant for this term."

His eyes widened. I could tell he hadn't been expecting *that*. "An assistant?"

"Yes," I replied, feeling a tiny rush of triumph. Anytime I could keep a vampire on his toes was a good time. "You know, a research assistant, like they have in college."

"What would you do as my assistant?" That last bit came out in a low, suggestive drawl.

Oh. God. Yuck. Not like that.

I needed to become intimate with the secrets of the keep without, you know, getting intimate with *Alcántara*. Some things I just would *not* do.

"I could help with papers," I said, keeping a breezy smile pasted on my face—that good old avoidance and redirection strategy. "Sometimes you come to class with lots of materials. I could help you carry and keep track of things. I can do additional research projects for you, too. Just like at a real college."

He tilted his head back to study the ceiling. Apparently, our vampire instructors weren't accustomed to assistants. While he studied the dark, gabled ceiling, I stole a furtive glance around the room. There were all manner of mysterious cabinets and books and boxes . . . a gold mine for a girl in search of answers.

I sensed him shifting and zipped my attention back to him. My innocent smile was beginning to hurt my cheeks.

He sighed thoughtfully, studying me. If he suspected my motives, he didn't show it. Which wasn't to say he didn't suspect me, because I was certain he suspected me of all kinds of things. No doubt—the sky was gray, the sea was cold, and Alcántara was suspicious.

Worse, he'd probably end up making my life miserable. But if I kept on my toes and stayed sharp, I hoped I could avoid the sort of creepy overtures he'd tried in the past.

He appeared to be seriously considering it. I thought of all those locked cabinets and mysterious tomes. Could it be this easy? Aching cheeks or not, I kept my face frozen in a pleasant, girlishly expectant expression. He might've been skilled at the use of silence as a weapon, but I had a few tricks up my sleeve, too.

"*Cariño*, I admire your ambition. But I must reflect on such an arrangement before I agree."

"Of course." I tried to look innocently hopeful. If I could eventually get him to trust me enough to access his office when he wasn't there . . . It was almost too exciting to consider. "Please do think about it and let me know. I would relish the opportunity."

"I'm certain you would," he said, and his tone had an edge that gave me the chills.

It struck me just how dangerous this was. Forget his creepy attempts at flirtation. He could very well use this as a way to spy on *me*. I'd need to be careful—if he ever gave me access to his office, I wouldn't be surprised if it were to secretly watch my every move.

The clock on his wall chimed, a low *bong-bonging* announcing the dinner hour. "Uh-oh," I chirped. "It's six o'clock already. Sorry I took so much of your time."

It'd been perfect timing, actually, and I made a mental note— meeting at the end of office hours gave us alone time, but not so much alone time that I couldn't find an excuse to escape.

Maybe I was overconfident from the successes of the last hour, but when he began to gather an unwieldy stack of books, without thinking, I stupidly asked, "Do you need me to help you carry those back to the castle?"

I instantly regretted it. I mean, duh. *Subtle, Drew.* What was I thinking? That now he'd just let me stroll wherever he went?

He peered at me, managing to look both suspicious and amused. "You know you're not allowed in the keep."

"Yes." I laughed. "Kidding, kidding."

But as he locked up, his expression wasn't humorous at all. He just gave a grim nod and left me standing alone in the hallway.

It was okay, though, because my mind was racing already. Eventually, I would find a way into that castle.

Surely there were deliveries. Laundry. Housekeepers. Something. I'd once spotted a janitor in the science building—surely there was a team of custodians in the castle, too. I was certain the vampires wouldn't sully their pristine hands with such banal concerns as toilet scrubbing. I mean, not even we girls had to scrub our own toilets . . . aside from the odd bathroom hazing, of course. No, the cockiness of the Trainees suggested somebody else handled their domestic concerns. I vowed to find out.

Meantime, I'd just need to watch, and wait, and learn. If I kept a close enough eye, I'd spot my chance. Too bad someone was also keeping a close eye on me, which I realized the moment I stepped outside.

I zipped my coat. Tightened my messenger bag against my side. My eyes adjusted to the darkness.

And then he pounced.

CHAPTER TWENTY

Y asuo. I recognized him instantly, even in the darkness. I'd
know that telltale silhouette anywhere—tall and lean,
with wiry muscles and black hair that still managed to have a hip
LA vibe despite the fact that we were on an island in the middle
of the North Sea.

He tackled me, and I shoved him off easily. "What the hell?"
I rolled to my feet, dusting off my arms. The attack had felt halfhearted, so maybe he didn't really want to hurt me. Maybe he just
didn't know how to broach talking with me. I jogged back a step.
"If you want to talk, just say so."

His only answer was the rasp of his heavy breaths.

"Earth to Yasuo," I said uneasily. "Please, can we just stop for
a second?"

But he still didn't answer. He just stood there, trembling.

It was full dark now—most of January was—and I angled my
body to let the moonlight hit his face. Something was wrong
with him, and it wasn't that he had that detached, vampiric thing

going on, either. He appeared stricken, with glazed eyes that stared out to some distant place.

I stepped closer. "Are you okay?"

His attention snapped to me—it was like he'd forgotten I was there—and he leapt again. His fangs were bared this time, and I narrowly ducked out of the way of his gaping mouth.

I shrieked and stumbled back. "What the hell?"

He came again and kept coming, slashing his hands, pawing at me, diving for me, but I skittered backward, using quick left and right hooks to deflect his advances. I shouted, "What is your problem?"

There was clearly something very, very wrong with him, and I needed to do something before he sank his teeth into me. I couldn't turn and run—no matter how trembly he was, with those long legs, he'd beat me in a foot race. My only hope was to fight him off. Maybe talk him down enough to get some answers.

First step was getting away from his crazily windmilling limbs. I lunged and ducked under an arm, grabbing his coat and shoving him in front of me. He doubled over easily, and I hopped onto his back, snatching him into a basic choke hold, using both arms to trap his neck from behind.

He wriggled madly, clawing at my forearms, but my wool coat was too thick for him to get purchase. His moves were spazzy and weak. Had something happened to him? Was he sick? "Did someone attack you?"

He laughed, a disturbing cackle, and dropped to his knees. The hideous noise he was making faded, but not completely, and I realized he was muttering to himself, nonsensical sounds, with no real words coming out.

"You're freaking me out." I released his neck and shoved him to the ground, quickly readjusting my pose, straddling him as he lay on his belly, and wrenching his arms up behind his back. I curled my full body weight over him and snarled in his ear, "Tell me. Just . . . dammit"—I struggled to keep hold, riding him like a bucking bronco—"tell me, Yas. What's going on?"

He was shaking like mad now. I could feel the tremors reverberate up my body. "Do you think I'll see her?" he said, and his cracking voice made him sound like a boy.

What the—?

I froze. "Emma? But she's not alive." I told myself hope was dead, that he was just hallucinating.

"Stop," he shrieked, turning his head, resting it on the ground. "Stop saying her name. Emma's gone. So just . . . fucking . . . stop."

He snapped then, just lost it completely. His body gave up, and he became boneless beneath me. A horrible keening sound cut between us—and oh God, *Yas* was making that sound—as he began to cry great heaving sobs where he lay in the icy dirt.

It was like his mind snapped, too, and he began to babble again, but loudly this time, manic, scattered gibberish. About Emma. About the castle and vampires.

About her heart.

For the first time, I wondered if there'd been a bond between him and Emma. Could Trainees even bond? Surely they'd had some sort of connection. Would her sudden death cause a pain even deeper than grief? Would it be a pain great enough to drive a person to madness?

I shook him, pleading, "Why are you acting like this?"

I knew if a vampire left, it could be devastating to his bonded partner, but how did it feel for the vampire?

How had I never broached this with Carden?

Carden. Damn him. This latest attack only served to remind me of his absence. I blamed *him* for my vulnerability.

A long breath shuddered from Yasuo, and I actually had to pause and tune in to see if he was still even breathing. A thin rope of foamy spit dribbled from his mouth onto the dirt.

He was making some sort of transition, and it wasn't a good one. Was he injured? Was this a broken bond? Merely grief? Something haunted Yasuo deeply, and it gave me a chill.

I slid from him and rubbed between his shoulder blades. He was limp as a rag, and I was confident—kind of—that his attack had paused for the moment. "Are you okay?" I asked quietly.

He hitched up to his elbows and stared at me.

It was then I noticed his eyes.

"Oh, Jesus, Yasuo." I sprang backward in the dirt, snatching my hands to my chest as though burned.

He dragged himself to his hands and knees and began to skitter away. Finally, finally, he uncurled his body and stood, loping into the night.

His eyes, they'd glowed red. Gone was the stillness and blankness of Vampire. When he'd looked at me, he'd looked like a rabid animal, lacking reason or focus.

He'd looked like a Draug.

CHAPTER TWENTY-ONE

I t took me several minutes to calm down. My heart pounded, my hands shook, but still I managed to do a body check. Adrenaline could mask pain. I'd seen girls so involved in a fight, they were unaware they had a weapon sticking from them. But as I tugged my clothes back into place, I saw I was relatively unscathed—physically, at least. Emotionally, I was a wreck.

I was shocked. Shattered. Grieving. I was steeped in my grief—choked by it.

Yasuo was Draug.

Draug meant dead.

Yas was dead.

Or he might as well be, if what I'd seen was really true. I still couldn't wrap my brain around it. I couldn't believe it. But I'd seen his eyes, those red, soulless eyes that I'd seen before. I thought of the Draug in Tom's pens, remembered those hands reaching through bars, clawing the air, mindlessly swiping for food. Anxious to taste blood. To taste fear.

Was that why Yas had been so unhinged lately? I'd imagined that when a Trainee turned Draug, it would be an immediate thing. An instant change. But if Yas was any indication, it was a slow, laborious process. Like devolving into madness.

It was a madness that had its roots in the castle, in what they did inside the castle. What they did to the guys. To the girls. To all of us.

"Annelise?" The familiar voice pulled me from my morbid thoughts.

"Ronan?" I gaped at him, completely thrown now. I was reeling, unable to make sense of anything, and it was surreal to see *Ronan*. In my moment of need, it wasn't Carden who'd appeared, but him.

"Are you going to dinner?"

"Huh?" I looked from him to the dining hall and back again, realizing I'd just been standing there, staring at the students spilling from its doors. For an instant, each was illuminated by a pool of light before walking into the night. Their bellies were full; they were sad or happy or anxious, each immersed in his or her own world, completely unaware of me in my hell.

A hell where Yas was gone from me. From everyone. Forever.

"Annelise?" He peered at me, equal parts concern and puzzlement. "I said, are you going to dinner?"

"Dinner." I shook my head, shaking my mind back into reality. "No. Not happening." I doubted I'd ever eat again, my stomach was in such knots.

"Are you all right?"

I couldn't deal with this right now, this concern from Ronan. Was he here to protect me or simply because he'd wanted to seek me out? It made me feel confused and exposed. "Yeah," I answered tightly. "I'm fine."

"I say you're not." He stepped closer and took my arm, and I flinched away, but he took it again, at the elbow, with a grip both firm and gentle. "Come."

I looked over my shoulder at the dining hall and asked, "Don't you need to eat?" But deep down I hadn't really meant that. If I'd wanted to voice what I really thought, I'd have said something like, *I want out. . . . I need help. . . . I want someone to take me away.*

But those were dangerous thoughts, each one a brutal reminder of why I was here in the first place. "You." I tugged at my arm. My life in Florida had sucked, sure, but it hadn't been like *this*. This unending parade of terror and heartbreak. "This is your fault."

His face fell, hearing my words. He knew what I meant, and still, he didn't let go. He only pulled me closer. "Come with me," he said, and this time his words were a soft lull.

Even through my thick coat, I felt the warmth begin to buzz from his fingertips. I stared at his hand nestled in the crook of my arm. "You're doing your trick," I said, though at that point, I didn't even care. If it could put me out of my misery, I welcomed it.

He shrugged and gave me a sad, halfhearted smile. "It seems an emergency, aye?"

"Fine," I said numbly, falling in to step beside him. "I'll go with you. You don't even need to do your special voodoo grip."

We walked for a while, headed toward the cove where we'd had so many of our swim lessons. Finally, my curiosity got the better of me. "Where are you taking me?"

"It's where I go when I'm low."

I sighed. Whatever. I'd lost Amanda and Judge. Emma was dead in a way I presumed so horrific it'd been enough to make her boyfriend snap. Carden had disappeared off the face of the earth. And now Yasuo was transforming into a monster before my eyes. Maybe this little jaunt would make Ronan feel better, but I doubted I'd ever feel better again.

I assumed we'd head down to the water's edge and was surprised when he led me off the trail. "Off the path? Hasn't there been enough trouble?"

"And can't you be quiet for two minutes?" he snapped back, but even in the dark, I saw in his eyes how he wasn't truly angry. He led us to a spot looking down at the shore. It was nestled in the hills, perfectly situated so that neither people on the path nor those on the beach would've been able to see us.

"You're full of secrets," I said.

"I'm not the only one." The way he sat next to me—sat *close* next to me—swept the thoughts from my head like a bracing breeze might clear smoke from a room.

As he watched the waves, I stole glances at him. Because, *why?* Why was he doing this now? Why couldn't he have taken me on moonlit walks to secret spots *before* I'd bonded with a vampire? What was he up to?

For once, he was the one to break the silence. With a heavy glance, he asked, "Are you going to tell me what's on your mind, or are you going to just sit there and brood?"

I whipped my eyes away from him, looking down at the water instead. Bright shards of white moonlight danced on the inky black waves. "I'm not brooding."

He laughed. A Ronan laugh was a rare thing, and it unsettled me.

I changed the subject. "So your family lives here somewhere?" My gaze swept south, imagining the distant fishing village I'd once spotted from the water.

"I have people here, yes. In a manner of speaking. They're like . . . my foster family, I guess you'd say."

Foster family? This was news. "What happened to your—?" I trailed off, uncertain what the protocol was for conversations like this. Already we were navigating depths that Ronan and I had never plumbed before.

"To my blood kin?" he finished for me. "They're . . . elsewhere. But aye, they live." He phrased it awkwardly, his words bearing a strange echo, like awe, or fear.

"Why aren't you with them?"

"It's not my time," he said. "I grew up here. I am required here."

His time? How weird was that?

But I quickly forgot about weirdness as something he'd said clicked. "So the sister you told me about . . ." My heart soared. "She was just a *foster* sister?" He'd once said I reminded him of his sister, but really, who wants to be sisterly?

"No, Annelise. Charlotte was my real sister." Damn him, he'd sounded amused. Or patronizing. Something I couldn't quite put my finger on.

I cringed. Again I wondered, why was he doing this? It made me feel embarrassed, or like a kid. I didn't even understand why we were having this conversation. Why had he brought me here? It gave me a stab in my chest that sharpened words I might have softened otherwise. "Where exactly *is* your blood family? Are they on another island?"

I thought of Mei-Ling, who'd escaped. Tom the Draug keeper

had put her on a boat, headed toward what he'd called "friends." Might Ronan's family be with "friends," too?

"Aye," he said, his words clipped and tight with emotion. "My mother . . . she's on a different island. With others."

The honesty surprised me. There were so many stupid, frustrating secrets all around me. A million more questions sprang to mind, but I knew not to push it. This was already way more than I'd ever thought he'd tell me, more than I'd ever expected.

Again, why? *Why* was he confiding in me like this? Why this casual little glimpse into his life?

Aside from my Scottish vampire, Ronan knew me better than anyone on this island—now that Emma was gone, at least. I was certain he'd guessed at the connection between me and Carden, and yet, thus far, he'd kept his judgments to himself, and for that I was hugely grateful.

He got it. Got how complicated and lonely life on this dark isle could be. But he'd always maintained a veil of formality between us.

What had changed?

Did he just feel sorry for me? He'd seen how distraught I was, how much I needed it. Was this pity bonding?

The optimist in me said it was because he finally trusted me, but my inner pessimist countered that it was because I served some mysterious interest known only to him.

Who knew? Maybe the explanation was as simple as him assuming Carden had already confided everything.

Or . . . maybe he just felt safe telling me these things precisely because Carden *was* out there, somewhere, with a claim to me, and therefore Ronan couldn't make one himself.

That last one gave me a shiver.

Regardless, he'd confided and now it was my turn.

"At least your mom is alive," I said. "All I've got for family is a no-good dad and my"—I made air quotes with my fingers—"stepmom." I couldn't even say *her* name without irony, she'd been that crappy to me. "I had what felt like a family here for, like, half a second. Emma and Yas. Amanda and Judge. Mei-Ling. But they're all gone." I stole a look at him, a quick millisecond under my lashes, before looking away. I spoke the words before I chickened out. "Everyone's gone except for you."

I could hear in the cadence of his breath that he'd heard what I was really saying—the implication that he was also like family. He didn't press it, though. He didn't make some elaborate show of thanking me or act like he had to return the sentiment, and I was grateful.

Instead he said, "Yasuo. You've seen him?" Something in his tone told me that he already knew what I'd suspected.

"I did see him. He's been on me like white on rice, actually." I let out a humorless laugh. "He blames me for Emma."

Ronan slid a hand onto my arm. Not the special hypnotic touch . . . just *his* touch. "Emma wasn't your fault."

"I know." I shifted away, quickly changing back to a subject that was no less heartbreaking. "Yasuo, when I saw him, he was acting funny. Not like funny ha-ha," I clarified. "He was off."

"Yes," Ronan said, and there was a heaviness in his voice, a heaviness that told me he knew exactly what I was talking about. "I'd hoped to find you myself, to warn you. I've been growing concerned. But I suppose you've seen for yourself—?"

I did see, but it didn't mean I understood. "Will he be okay?"

"No, he'll never be okay again. Yasuo is becoming Draug."

Draug. Even though I'd guessed, hearing the word made it real. My stomach dropped. "Why? How?"

"I don't know," he said, sounding suddenly angry. "There is much I don't know about the vampiric transition. I know what I'm told, and I'm not told much. Something happened to derail the transformation. I've seen it before. Many times." His anger collapsed into sadness. "He's gone, Annelise. You must give up on him."

"On Yasuo? No way. I can't."

"You can," he said sternly, "and you will."

How could I mourn Yas when he was still here physically? And more than that, there'd been something left of him, something more than just that shell of bones and fangs and wild red eyes. He'd had some memory—he'd spoken of Emma. The last remnants of him were in there somewhere.

Did that mean he still had a soul? Was it leaving his body? Would it eventually leave him completely? I hoped so. I hoped there was a heaven for kids like us. Who knew, maybe there was a big juvie in the sky.

Or was that what ghosts were? These Draug, bearing wisps of memory of a life lived, but cursed to walk the earth. Would Yasuo haunt me?

Tears burned my eyes.

"I'm sorry, Annelise. Truly I am."

It was an easy, standard sentiment to say, but from Ronan, I appreciated it. I'd lost roommates, friends, and was now watching Yasuo devolve into some mindless monster, and yet I got the sense Ronan understood the desolation I felt.

Could it have been mere pity that drove his words? Did he

simply feel bad for me because I was ditched by my vampire boy-friend?

I'd had a million questions about why Ronan was all of a sudden around at just the right times, but oddly, just then, the reason didn't matter. Whatever his motives for seeking me out, there was one thing I knew: Ronan had lost people, too. He understood my grief.

Which meant he'd understand my need for vengeance.

I decided to take a risk. "Ronan, I found something. Some-thing crazy."

CHAPTER TWENTY-TWO

"Crazy?" Ronan looked thrown by the strange direction the conversation had taken. "What have you been up to, Annelise?"

"Nothing," I protested instantly. Must he always think the worst of me? "I was on the cliffs, near where Trinity—"

"*What* were you doing on the cliffs?" he interrupted angrily.

"I wasn't doing anything bad." I rolled my eyes, but he'd narrowed his. "Okay, fine, nothing *that* bad. Anyway, I found some runes, like old Viking graffiti. I took a rubbing and translated them."

I paused, waiting for him to look impressed, but apparently it took a lot more than that to impress Ronan, so I went straight for the punch line. "The runes read: *Sonja, ruler of vampires.*" I gave a weighty pause. "Like there'd once been a woman." Another weighty pause, this time with brows raised. "*In charge.*"

He only nodded quietly.

Nodded.

"What do you mean?" I mimicked his nod. "Did you already know that?"

"No . . . not that specifically. Not *Sonja*. But I've had . . . suspicions."

"Suspicions? What on earth would make you suspect *that*? I mean, this is huge, Ronan, and you *suspected*, and you didn't tell me? Or anyone," I quickly amended, because really, why would he have told me anything?

"I said I suspected. I didn't say that I knew."

"What made you suspect?" I demanded.

"I can't say." He shrugged, looking uncomfortable. "It's merely that the . . . nature of things strikes me as suspect. I told you before, I don't *know* anything."

"Can't say, or won't?" I was too frustrated to give him a chance to answer and waved it away. "Whatever with your *nature of things*."

"The keep is the realm of vampires and Trainees only," he protested. "The knowledge, theirs only."

Carden could've found out. There'd been a day when Carden *would've* found out for me. Now more than ever I needed my vampire here. The thought made me cold. I realized the freezing ground was leaching my heat, sending aching tendrils up my spine. I tried not to care—I could no longer afford it.

I scowled, plucking at the grass around me. "I bet the vamps don't even tell the Trainees everything. I mean, I sure wouldn't. So many of those guys are such knuckleheads." I couldn't imagine kids like Danny or Rob being entrusted with all the Ancient Secrets of Vampire. The Robbies of the world would never flourish into Alcántaras, no matter how much blood they consumed.

If his response to my Sonja translation surprised me, then this next bit floored me. Because instead of scolding me as usual and treating me like a child, he said, "If I tell you something, the one thing that is known outside the castle, do you promise to give up this quest of yours?"

My heart skipped a beat. "I promise to consider it. Now, what *thing*?" I edged closer, lowering my voice. "You have to tell me. What goes on in there?"

He angled his head to meet my eyes, and crap, I'd scooted a little *too* close. But he didn't seem to notice. He simply continued quietly. "I don't know much, but I've heard the villagers speak of a ritual." He hesitated, and for once I didn't press him. It took everything I had to keep quiet and let him come to the conclusion that I was mature enough, trustworthy enough, to share things with. He seemed to make some decision and finally—*finally*—he spoke again, and when he did, it was as though something shifted between us. Maybe it was because of Carden's departure, or my ascension to Initiate, or maybe it was simply the waves of raw misery wafting off me—but all of a sudden he was treating me more like a peer than a student. "There's a holiday. In the old religion, it marked midwinter, a celebration of the end of the yule season. On the Anglo-Saxon calendar, it was called Antonsmas."

"You're trying to tell me the vampires still celebrate it?"

"Those who hail from these parts would've celebrated it as men. Whether as Antonsmas, or the more modern festival we call Up Helly Aa."

I'd heard of such things before, how Pagan holidays became modernized into Christian ones, but I'd never heard of this one. "What the heck is heely-yah?"

"Up Helly Aa," he corrected. "The folk of the Northern Isles see it as an ode to their Viking ancestors. Traditionally, it's a night of fire and boisterousness."

"You mean they like to get drunk and burn things," I clarified.

He gave me one of those Ronan smiles, one of the rare ones where the corners of his eyes crinkled in a way that said he'd thought he might never smile again yet here he was, surprised by one. "Something like that."

I glanced out to sea, marveling. "And you think the vampires like to party, too?"

"I think they like to party, too, yes."

I dusted off my hands, suddenly feeling very chipper. "Well, I can't miss that."

The magic broke the moment I said it. "You most certainly can miss that," he snapped. "You promised you'd give up this silliness if I told you."

So much for the shift between us—we were back to grumpy Ronan scolding the misbehaving Annelise. "I promised to *consider* it." Before he could dive into the rant I read on his face, I quickly added, "There must be some way to spy on them. Think about it. You said you'd heard about this in the village, but how do *they* know about it? I'll tell you how. The vampires can't hold a whole celebration by themselves. They need cooks and cleaners and launderers and . . . I don't know. . . . What else do you need for a party? Whatever it is, they need them. I mean, they won't even stoop to driving their own cars—you can't tell me they'll be the ones tapping the kegs."

He'd gone ice cold. "You will not be finding out who is *tapping their kegs*," he said, enunciating each word.

I watched his face for a moment, trying to figure out my

strategy. I couldn't do this alone—or at least I didn't want to. But how to get Ronan on my team? He'd already said enough to prove to me he was more on my side than on theirs. He might not be willing to help me—yet—but I sensed somewhere deep down, he probably wanted to take the vampires down as much as I did.

"Listen," I said. "I think there's a way."

"There's no way."

"Would you please *listen*?" I leaned over, shoving him with my shoulder, and just that brief brush of my arm against his made my skin buzz. I edged away the tiniest bit in an effort to focus. "I've gotten one step closer to the inner circle," I said, using my best serious professional voice.

"Inner circle? What are you talking about?" His expression went slack. "You best not be telling me you're getting involved with the Directorate."

I waved that thought away. "Oh God, nothing like that. I met with Alcántara, and he's thinking about taking me on as his TA."

Ronan's features contracted to life, and he looked *angry*. "His *TA*?"

"You know, like a teacher's assistant."

"What are you doing?"

With an innocent smile, I joked, "Don't you mean, *what am I thinking*?"

But this time, he didn't so much as crack a smile.

"Fine," I said. "I know I'm treading on dangerous ground—"

"Deadly ground."

"Okay, I'm treading on some *badass* ground. But I need to do this, Ronan. I've got nothing to lose."

"I do," he said, his voice tight.

He shifted, angling his body toward me, and I automatically shifted to face him. I was ready for battle, expecting to face off with Ronan's anger, but what I saw instead floored me. His face was mere inches from mine, wrenched with worry and something else . . . something that looked like longing.

"Don't do this," he said. "I cannot lose you. I've lost too much already."

I tried to swallow, but it was like I'd forgotten how to operate my throat. He was saying that he didn't want to lose another friend—right? Because it wasn't like we had a thing. He knew about Carden. Ronan and I were just buddies. And even if there were no Carden, why would a guy like him ever be interested in me? No, surely I wasn't sensing what I thought I was sensing. He'd told me once how I reminded him of his dead sister, and there was nothing less romantic than *that*. He had brotherly feelings for me; that was all.

Right?

I had to look away and glanced down instead, which unfortunately had me staring at his hands, fisted on his crossed legs, clenched tightly enough that I could make out the ropes of tendons and veins in the moonlight. I looked at those hands and remembered his touch as he'd so gently wrapped my injured wrist.

Gently and without his powers.

He could've used his powers now. I was sure I had no idea at the extent of them—he probably would've been able to grab me and just hypnotize me into doing his will. But he wasn't. His hands were clenched on his lap, so close, and yet a million miles from me.

My eyes shot back up. I was suddenly desperate to understand him . . . understand *this.* "Why do you care? And don't say you don't," I quickly added. "You once told me I reminded you of your sister, so I know you have some feelings."

"I have an interest in your well-being . . ."

"But?" There was always a *but.*

He had brotherly feelings for me, but . . . *it became more?* Or *But now I've decided I hate you? But now you've got your own vampire?* But *what?*

He looked to the water, shutting me out. "Feelings are a luxury I cannot afford."

I wished I'd learned that lesson before I let myself be gutted by Carden.

And yet this confession was hard to believe. I took in the sight of him. The scruffy black hair—I could tell he'd surfed that morning from the way it was pointing every which way—and the shadow of razor stubble on his jaw. All that darkness and shadow and it only made his green eyes more haunted.

"Never? You've never allowed yourself feelings?"

His head swung back to me. "Of course I have feelings. And I must guard them."

I let the truth of his words sink in. Ronan tried not to let himself have feelings. Did that mean he'd never been with a girl? "Do you mean you're afraid of being with someone?"

His expression hardened. "I'm afraid of what being with someone would do to her. The risks it would expose her to. You should know this lesson better than anyone." The words struck me like an accusation, a reminder of how Emma's death had been orchestrated as a punishment for me.

Such a serious statement, and yet I couldn't get clear of the speculation currently clouding my brain, because really, was he saying he'd *never* been with *anyone*? How could that be possible? Ronan, never touching a girl? Surely in all his time roaming the world, he'd hooked up with someone.

In a normal world, he'd have been knee-deep in girlfriends . . . but this wasn't a normal world. It was one where *hooking up* could—and often did—mean death. I thought of Amanda and Judge and how they'd died trying to be together. Ronan would never choose to be responsible for that.

I let myself look, really look, in his eyes. At the moment, he seemed so . . . tormented. Like, he had so many wants and no way to let any of them out. "Ronan, what kind of life is it where you're afraid to touch another person?"

"I'm not afraid to touch another person," he snapped.

He was getting frustrated, but I was frustrated, too, with the sense that there was some truth just out of my reach. "But you're obviously not happy. So why not leave? What keeps you here?" My roommate Mei-Ling was a diminutive ninth grader and *she'd* managed to escape. "Your blood kin aren't even on the island with you. I don't get it. Why do you even stay?"

"A man must do as a man must do," he said mysteriously.

"That didn't stop Carden." I'd said it dismissively, intending the words only as a sting to myself, but I saw instantly how they stung Ronan instead.

"You are in over your head with that . . . *him*. I'd think that you, Annelise, more than anyone would strive for better than what he offers you. I tell you, a man does as he must, but Carden McCloud is no man."

His anger, so quick and sharp, startled me. "And you are?"

He reached out, resting his hand in the dirt at my hip, leaning closer. "I am."

My breath hitched. I stilled, waiting to see what would happen next.

He raised his other hand, slid it around my neck.

What was happening? Was this a lesson? Had I offended him—did he think I was accusing him of being afraid to touch a girl, and now he had something to prove?

His hand was warm and gentle gliding over my skin, and my scalp tingled as his fingers laced through the hair at the back of my neck. He leaned closer still, until I could no longer see his features clearly. Only impressions of Ronan filled my view. The dark stubble. His full mouth. A fringe of black lashes on lids half-closed. Those features had once rocked my world. Once, in a Florida parking lot, they'd been enough to convince me to get into a car with a stranger.

And now? Now Ronan was no longer a stranger. He'd become so familiar to me. Somehow, Ronan had become all I had.

How I missed Carden and the comfort he'd given me. I longed for connection. I missed my friends. All of them, they'd been so dear to me, and yet here I was, alone, aching, steeped in desolation and uncertainty. Carden had vanished. My friends were lost to me.

Everyone was gone, but Ronan was here. Right here.

Would it be so bad, so wrong, to seek just a little bit of comfort with him?

I leaned in to him, testing. He didn't move. Was this solace that he was offering? Was it more? I leaned closer, and he still didn't move away. My heart began to pound. All my fear and desolation and abandonment . . . it all catalyzed, becoming this need I felt now. Ronan was going to kiss me, and even if he was using his hypnotic touch, I'd take it. I'd take him. I just wanted to feel him, because somehow I knew. He wasn't using his powers. This was just a touch—the touch of a guy on my skin.

Then suddenly . . . cold air.

I opened my eyes—when had I closed them?—and saw he was staring at me, his gaze so heavy and dark.

"I can't," he said. His jaw was tight, and it was like he had to grit out the words.

And then he was gone.

I stared after him, even though I couldn't see anything in the darkness. Breathily, I asked the universe, "What the hell was that?"

I collapsed onto my back, grinding my fingers into my hair as I stared up at the sky. My heart was still skittering in my chest, my pulse as shallow as the air in my lungs.

Holy crap.

I guess I no longer reminded him of his sister.

CHAPTER TWENTY-THREE

I plopped onto the sand, panting for breath, clutching a hand at my side. I hoped the pain was just a stitch from my run and not the beginnings of the blood fever.

Okay, fine . . . so maybe it wasn't as dire as all that.

Check that—emotionally, it was pretty freaking dire, but physically? I was feeling some discomfort, but nothing crippling, not yet. Just . . . a needful sort of thirst. I thought back to last term. I couldn't go through *that* ordeal again, through the pain of separation and the early stages of breaking a bond.

Carden. He was the opposite of stupid Ronan. I didn't get stupid Ronan at all—lurking, popping up at unusual times, *almost kissing me.* When Carden had wanted to kiss me, he'd kissed me. He was so easy, so predictable . . .

Until he was no longer easy and predictable.

Was it me? Was I just lame with guys? My vampire had been gone for too long now. Either something had happened to him—which I honestly thought I'd have felt—or he'd simply . . . bailed.

But he couldn't just dump me, right? Logically, I knew: We had a bond. So whether he really wanted to be with me or not, physically he *had* to come back at some point.

And there was the crux of it. I wanted someone who *wanted* to be with me.

Someone who liked me. Maybe loved me.

I thought of the difference between my parents. When my mom had been alive, presumably she'd wanted to be with me because it gave her joy. My memories of her were vague, but they were happy—we'd both been happy—and it wasn't such a leap to deduce that she'd *wanted* to spend time with me. As opposed to my father, who'd kept me around merely because he was obligated.

Was that what I'd become to Carden? An obligation? All those words he'd said. *Dove shmove.* All of it meaningless crap.

"Stupid," I muttered, stretching into the ache. My train of thought was stupid. This situation was stupid.

I felt stupid. I'd been too smitten to sense what'd been going on in Carden's head our last night together. While I was experiencing the most amazingly special night of my life, he'd already checked out. He fed me over and over that night because he'd known all along that he'd be leaving.

Sure, eventually he'd come back. He'd saunter back one of these days, grinning all Carden-like, feeding me again, just enough to sustain our bond. And then he'd probably turn around and saunter right back out.

All that intimacy I thought we'd shared for all those weeks . . . did none of it count? Had it been my imagination?

Hey, at least the guy had done me a solid and overfed me. Because of his foresight, I'd had minimal physical symptoms since he left. Though this pang in my side made me wonder just how long I had until the blood fever set in. One month? One year? A decade?

How long would he be gone anyway? I couldn't last forever—minimal physical symptoms wasn't the same as *no* physical symptoms.

I shaded my eyes, staring out to sea. We didn't get much sunlight on this rock, but what we did get irritated vampire eyes, and I'd purposely taken my run smack-dab in the middle of a Saturday afternoon. Lately, 12:01 had become a favorite sight on my digital watch.

Though why I'd chosen to run in the shadow of the damned Needle, the chimney rock formation that Carden could scale and leap from like he was some kind of superhero, was beyond my understanding. Or maybe it wasn't—maybe this particular workout spot had been an entirely intentional choice. Because, let's be honest: I *wanted* to think about Carden. Duh. I wanted him to appear, as he had so many times, coming from out of the blue to nestle next to me in the sand.

The thing with Ronan had upset me, and I just wanted everything back the way it'd been before. But if Ronan was going to be all weird and Carden all gone, then that left me with nobody.

Waves slapped and churned against the base of the Needle. Had I really thought Carden's head might bob into view, that he might spring from the water, clambering up the side as I'd seen him do before? I decided I was like that rock—alone in the middle of a bleak sea, pummeled by waves . . . until stupid Carden had climbed me and then leapt free.

"Jeez." I had to laugh at myself—I really hated my own drama sometimes. "Pathetic."

I stretched on an exhale, grabbing my toes, pulling hard, folding myself over my aching belly. I inched my fingertips lower on the soles of my feet, wrenching my torso lower, daring my hamstrings to quiver and burn. Daring the pain to wipe out everything else.

"You'll snap in half," a male voice said from behind me.

I sprang up on a startled yelp. Josh. "I'll snap *you* in half if you scare me like that again." I glanced around, looking behind him, but he was alone. "Where'd you come from anyway?"

He cupped his hand over his eyes. "I had a Trainee thing. At the keep."

Sure you did.

"I was looking for you earlier," he added. The sun wasn't that bright, but he kept his hand shielded over his eyes, like he was in pain.

"You all right?" I remembered the rogue vampire I'd fought—that *Carden* had fought for me—and the eerie pale eyes, hidden behind sunglasses, that'd betrayed his ancient years. The older the vamps got, the more sensitive to light they became. It made sense that Trainees would be no different. "Shouldn't you wear, like, a hat or something?"

"Nah, I'm good." He plopped next to me on the sand. "It's just your radiant beauty, it blinds me, yeah?"

I laughed and picked at my sweaty shirt. "The only thing I'm radiating is sweat." I was lonely and uncertain, but Josh and his easy, Aussie good humor always made me smile. It didn't hurt that he was pretty cute, too, in a scruffy sun-kissed beach-boy way.

He clutched a hand to his heart. "She denies my compliment."

Wait . . . was this real flirting or playful friend flirting? If my tense interactions with Ronan were any indication, I had no clue how to tell the difference between the two.

"Easy, sailor." I really looked then, reconsidering him. Not as a friend, or as someone I'd gotten to know, but as a *guy*. Honestly, by that point, I was just that angry at both Carden and Ronan. If they were going to blow me off, then I'd feel free to look at other guys, dammit.

I looked at him, and though I saw the appeal, I didn't *feel* the appeal. No butterflies or any of that other good stuff. *Sorry, mate*, I thought. Maybe in another life.

"Hey, a boy can try," he said, still doing the flirty thing.

"And a girl could get the wrong idea." Feeling a mite uncomfortable, I erected the barest of shields between us. Carden had warned me not to trust Josh—not to trust any of them. Though, clearly, I should've taken the advice and not trusted *Carden*.

But when Josh and his flirty eyes still didn't stand down, Carden's advice nagged at the edge of my mind. "Hey," I said, in a bright tone that indicated Major Topic Shift, "why were you looking for me anyway?" Sitting tall, I crossed my legs and began to stretch my arms in front of me, loosening my triceps. That was me, all chillaxed, just doing my workout.

"Looking for you," he repeated with a smirk. "Looking out for you is more like it."

The comment had a weird edge that cut me the wrong way. "Oh, so I need a big guy like you to look out for me, is that it?"

"Hey, nerd bird, is that what I said?" He nudged me with his shoulder, his good humor back with such gusto I had to wonder if I'd imagined the dig in his earlier statement. "I've just been worried is all. I've heard some of the guys talking. I don't know what you did but, dude, some of them have a real hard-on for you"—he squirmed at his own crude phrasing—"I mean, you know, not in the good way."

He looked abashed, and it endeared him to me.

"Oh. That." I dug out a clump of wet sand and crushed it between my fingers. Deciding these weren't exactly secrets, I explained. "Yasuo blames me for Emma." I paused, studying his face—did he know about Yas? His expression didn't betray a thing. Deciding there might've been a little truth in Carden's warning after all, I used care as I continued. "And Rob, well, he was assigned to . . . I don't know . . . bite me, or whatever you guys have to do for schoolwork—" I glanced up, hoping he'd fill in the blanks.

But he raised his hand, stopping me altogether. "Hey, we're not the ones who are supposed to go around *assassinating* people."

"You heard that, huh?" Wary, I caught his eye, but all that met me was his broad grin, and I couldn't help but smile back. "By the way," I added with pretend solemnity, " 'assassination' is so *gauche*. We prefer the term 'elimination.' "

As our smiles faded, he grew serious, quietly mimicking what I was doing, picking up and breaking apart wet clumps of sand. "Just look out for yourself," he said finally. "This island would be pretty boring without you."

The sentiment was unexpected. He might not have been my type, but I took companionship where I could get it, and I was happy to be getting it, period. I flicked sand at him. "You're just nervous because I still owe you a favor."

The comment puzzled him for a moment, and when it registered, his eyes widened. "You still remember *that*?"

"How could I forget it?" He'd once saved me from some

pretty gnarly hazing—involving *urine*—and I felt I still owed him, even if he didn't. "It was my first big run-in with Rob."

"Kind of like your anniversary," he teased.

I shuddered. "Puhleez."

We were laughing, which meant I was sideswiped when, totally seriously, out of the blue, he said, "So tell me for real, Drew. What are you plotting?"

In a matter of seconds, my heartbeat went from calm to chaotic.

Panic must've shown on my face because he burst into laughter. "Chill." He patted my shoulder. "Kidding, D. *Kidding.* But look at you. All alone here." His sweeping arm took in the empty beach and the gray, roiling sea. "You look depressed and you're way too much of a little hellcat for that, which means you must be plotting. So tell me."

"Hellcat?" I exclaimed, but he just sat there, waiting for an answer, so finally I just said, "Fine. I'm not plotting. I was just . . . thinking."

"Uh-oh. Sounds painful."

He looked like he might've bought the lie—because I sure as hell *was* plotting—but then I thought, maybe I could trust him. Maybe I should, just a little. After all, as a Trainee, he got to go inside that castle every day of the week. I'd need to trust *someone* if I were to get anywhere with my plan.

Baby steps, I warned myself. Asking about the keep could make him suspicious.

So what *were* my next steps? I'd been working on a strategy, trying to figure out how to convince Ronan to help me, when he'd almost kissed me. Was that why he'd done it? I had to hand it to the guy; it sure had been a clever way to put a stop to my scheming. Before the weird tension, though, he'd mentioned villagers.

There were villagers on this rock who knew about the vampires' midwinter ritual. I needed to know what they knew. Any insight I could get into the vampires' world was information that could help me take them down.

"Did you ever wonder where the people live?" I asked suddenly.

"Huh?" Josh looked flummoxed. "The people?"

Cool, a train of thought he hadn't expected. That was a good thing, because if he'd expected me to ask about the villagers, then it'd mean he was suspicious of me. Gawd, all these paranoid mental acrobatics. It was proof that sides had already been taken— with me on one end and Trainees on the other.

"You know, the *people*." I consciously maintained my pleasant expression, feeling my shields reinforce just a bit more, because what was that thing I just saw flicker in his eyes? "The people who drive the trucks and operate the boats, that sort of thing. I heard someone talking about a village. And where there's a village, there are villagers."

Josh's pause wasn't long, but it was enough for me to glimpse the machinations going on in that mind of his—a mind that was, I guessed, not nearly as laid-back as he pretended it to be. I couldn't let myself forget how, in his life before, he'd been Harvard premed. Not quite the sandy surfer dude he liked to portray.

No, there were definite machinations. He was weighing what he was and wasn't allowed to tell me, all the while wearing a pleasant expression that mirrored my own. Eventually, he said, "I guess they have to live somewhere."

I not only guessed. I knew. They lived north of here. I'd seen the settlement from the water, tiny white dots that had to be homes. But I didn't share that much with Josh—it was too fun testing the boundaries of what he was willing to tell me. I decided to move down the map. "Have you ever been to the southern end of the island?" I asked innocently.

Finally something clicked in his expression, and I knew I was seeing the real Josh. "South?" He shivered. "There are all those Draug out that way."

His reaction made sense. The Draug would probably freak out any Trainee—the monsters would serve as a reminder of how it could all go very wrong on their own road to Vampire.

I knew *I'd* never be able to look at a Draug again without thinking of Yasuo.

Wait a minute.

I bit my lips, trying not to lose that pleasant face I'd been working hard to maintain. But my mind was whirring a mile a minute.

The Draug. There was my strategy. Or rather, the Draug keeper.

I let my chat with Josh peter out. He cracked some jokes about growing up in a village on this rock. I cracked some jokes about men with thick accents unburdened by a surplus of teeth.

I stood, brushing off. I needed to get rid of Josh, which meant it was time to bring this meeting in for a landing. There was another man I needed to be talking to right now: Tom, the guy who acted as a sort of shepherd of the Draug, keeping them in pens like livestock. He was older, quirky, and plainspoken—and not surprisingly, not a big fan of the Directorate. He'd helped me before, in a big way, and I was hoping he'd be inclined to help me again.

Tom would know secrets of village life. And I knew just where to find him.

Josh might've been scared of the southern end of the island, but I knew better. South didn't scare me.

Well, not too, too much.

We said our good-byes, and I jogged inland, taking a short-cut—a dangerous shortcut—through Draug country. To say I needed to be careful would've been an understatement. They were terrifying, mindless creatures who rotted like corpses, but were cursed with the thirst, strength, and immortality of vampires. In ideal circumstances, the Draug might've behaved like livestock, but like livestock, one or two sometimes slipped through for a little rampage, which was where the careful part came in.

I stayed on the path as long as I could, then swerved off in a dash, picking my way along the desolate landscape, going fast enough to make good time and avoid company, but not so fast that I broke an ankle. Random snippets of an old Beastie Boys song ran through my head, the same lyrics running on a loop . . . *Listen all y'all it's a sabotage.* God, how I used to love music. What new songs were out there now? Which new bands? It'd once all been so important, and now it was so unreal. A universe away. I'd have given a week's ration of blood to recall the full song, but I was left with the same few lines, and I chanted them over and over—*I can't stand it . . . I know you planned it*—anything to push other thoughts from my head.

To push away the fear.

I couldn't let myself be afraid. I couldn't afford it. On this part of the island, fear smelled like dinner.

Tom had been the one who'd told me that, though the Draug

fed on blood, it was fear that sustained them . . . the taste of it, the whiff of others' terror, that was what they really craved.

I upped my pace, mouthing lyrics. Good thing it was Saturday—no classes. The island was small, but still, it'd take me a good forty-five minutes to find his cottage. If I hustled, I'd have time to find Tom and double back to the dining hall before it closed.

I stopped to check my watch—early afternoon yet. But this time of year, I was looking at three thirty twilight. Full dark by five o'clock. I grabbed my right foot and pulled it to my butt, stretching my quad. I looked to the horizon, scanned the terrain around me, gauging my location.

It meant I was distracted. Checking the time, the sky, the landscape, my leg muscles . . . I was minding everything else but what I should've been minding.

My back.

CHAPTER TWENTY-FOUR

"Bitch." A pair of hands shoved me, hard.

No time to brace, I lost my footing and slammed face-first into the gravel, my right ribs and elbow taking the brunt.

"God*dammit*." I instantly curled my legs, reaching for the stars in my boots, but before I could grab them and roll to standing, a large male body flung itself onto me. My lungs expelled a disturbing *whump* sound, and black spots swam before my eyes, resolving into snapshot images of lanky hands and dishwater brown hair.

Rob. Scrambling to pin me in a standard-issue wrestling hold.

I burst to action, squirming beneath him. "You gonna bite me?" I managed, wriggling into an angle that bought me more air. I coughed, gasped for breath, coughed again. "Oh, right. You can't."

He sawed his arm, aimed at my neck. I tensed and tucked my chin down, but he managed to pry past my hunched shoulders, crushing my throat. "Go ahead and joke. Like a prisoner's last meal."

I twisted from my side onto my back, and in the half second it took for him to readjust, I snapped my hands up, guarding my neck with my forearms and bucking my hips, trying to fling him off.

He lost his balance and fell forward. He was still on top of me, his chest crushing my face, but with a quick scramble and scoot, I turned my head, clutched him close, and wrapped my legs around him, pinning him to me. Not a great position, but at least it gave me some control of his movements. "You're lisping, Rob."

"I don't need fangs to draw blood." He relaxed into me, crushing his body to mine as he grabbed for whatever he could get hold of. He grabbed, and I squirmed, and we grappled, him trying to use his weight to immobilize me, while I wiggled like a wind-up toy, bucking my hips, fighting to free my arms.

"What are you going to do?" I said, pausing and panting. "Hug me to death?"

"Nope." He reached down, his hand clawing for my neck. "Strangle."

I bit his wrist. As he flinched away, he dug his fingers into my forearms and slammed his elbows onto my biceps, bending my arms and pinning me. Grinding me into the dirt. "You're going to suffer for what you did."

"Oh, Robbie, did the other boys make fun of you?" I couldn't budge, and I couldn't budge him, either. My arms began to burn, my muscles quivering—he was just too heavy. I could drink all the blood in the world and I'd never be able to fight a big Trainee boy, especially one who'd also been getting doses of the blood.

My words were one of the last weapons left to me, and I let them rip. "Just think how special you are. There can't be many other vampires who have just one fang. It's actually quite piratical."

"Shut up."

"Do you even want to grow it back? You might want to consider—"

"I'll shut you up." He let go with one arm and clawed for my neck. I hunched my chin into my chest, but he just snatched at the collar of my coat instead.

"That all you got?" With my free hand, I punched at him, but I couldn't hold him back for much longer. "It's not over yet."

His fingertips grasped the fabric, then began inching lower, twisting and tightening it around my throat until it became hard to breathe. "Isn't it?"

As I struggled to loosen my collar, his other hand wrenched between my forearms. I tried to block, but I must've slipped, because suddenly I felt his thumb on my skin. His palm on my throat. He laughed.

Then he squeezed.

Instantly, I flashed back. Instantly, I was in the ring with Emma, her hands on my throat, choking me just enough to make me black out, our plan to fake my death.

It'd worked.

And then she'd been the one who'd died.

Despair swamped me. My legs thrashed and my feet kicked the dirt, just as they had with Emma. My lips opened, mouth gasping for air that wouldn't come. Just like that day.

And, like that day, the world went dark.

SOMETHING COLD SLAPPED MY FACE, and I gasped. Deep in my muzzy brain, I rejoiced at the rush of sweet air. Greedily, I sucked it in, but was slapped again.

Cold water. I accidentally inhaled it. Choked and coughed. Panicked.

My eyes shot open.

The sky was dark gray. Late afternoon. I could breathe. But I was . . . tied.

I shifted, assessing. My arms were numb, bound behind and under me. Something sharp dug into my spine. A rock. I was lying down, tied on top of a rock.

I wrenched my arms, adjusting my hands, nestling them into the small of my back. Rope cut into my wrists with every movement. Two lengths of it were stretched over me—one slashed across my hips and the other across my collarbone. I wriggled, but that only cinched the bonds tighter. "What the hell?"

There was rustling and I craned my neck, peering up over my head. Rob had knocked back the last of his water and was zipping his canteen into his pack.

"Hey," I shouted. "Hey, moron. Is this how you fight? You tie me up so you can—what?—gnaw me to death?"

He approached, his face peering over me like a great moon dawning in my line of sight. "I'm not going to fight you. *They're* going to fight you."

My heart burst into a gallop. Frantically, I scanned the perimeter. "They who?"

"You'll see." He hitched his backpack onto his shoulders with a cocky little laugh. "Not me, though. I'm leaving. But don't worry. . . . I doubt you'll be alone for long."

"Wait." I tried to scoot down. Ignoring the rock cutting into my hands, I kicked lamely at him. "Are you serious? You tied me to a rock?" I kicked and flailed, but he only dodged out of the way. "Is this some kind of Greek mythology thing? What kind of poetic crap did Master Al order you to do, anyway?"

Alcántara wanted us to attack one another in moving and poetic ways, and I wouldn't have put it past him to insist Rob reenact a great moment from literature.

"No way, dude. This is all me. Wait"—he stopped and stepped close—"just one last thing." He eased into a squat, running his hands down my legs as he went.

"Get the hell off." Ignoring the rope, I kicked like a maniac now, but he was too close for me to do any damage.

Crap. I hadn't thought he'd try to get physical. I shuddered at the creepy feel of his fingers running along my calves. But then I felt him fumbling at my boots . . . and, *double crap* . . . he was reaching for my stars.

"Get off," I screamed, bucking and jerking wildly now. Warmth bloomed along my wrists and knuckles as the rock scored my skin.

I rammed my heels into his stomach, but he'd tied me up too well. He was able to dodge me, making my attempts laughable. And laugh he did.

Laughing, he stole a star from my boot. Standing, he tilted the star, studying it in the deepening twilight.

Even though I hadn't budged, I was panting, glaring. It was the star Carden had given me.

Pain and regret stabbed me. I missed my vampire with such fresh longing. Like thinking a wound healed, only to remove the bandage and tear the scab away with it, I was left feeling as raw, my heart as battered as on the day I first realized he was gone.

"Isn't this pretty?" Rob tested a point of the star with his thumb. "It's etched. Like feathers."

The wings of a bird, you asshole. But I'd never tell Rob that. Carden was the only one who knew the significance. I was his dove with wings of fire. *Was.*

I hitched my hips and pistoned my feet toward his groin, but he hopped back, laughing harder. I tried again, and as I did, the rope across my chest shot up an inch, slipping close—too close—to my neck. I froze.

"Careful, little D." He smiled and tapped my star on the rock. With a little toss, he adjusted it in his fingertips.

My eyes went wide. "What are you doing?"

He opened my coat.

"Don't touch me," I shrieked.

Rob slashed a giant hole in the belly of my pretty new catsuit.

"Stop!" The rope near my neck forgotten, I thrashed like a wild animal. "What are you doing?"

He placed a cool hand on my stomach. "Easy now. You might hurt yourself." Slowly, he brought the star down. Traced it around my navel. "Alcántara will enjoy this bit of poetry, don't you think? Slashed by one of your own stars."

I grew still and stared, proud of the smile I managed to muster. "But will it be moving enough for him to forget you're a fangless freak?"

He slashed then, quick and deep, a diagonal slice across the soft flesh of my belly. "Do you know where we are right now?" he asked as he used the hem of my coat to wipe my blood from the blade.

I gritted my teeth, refusing to give him the satisfaction of seeing my pain. "Yeah, Rob. *I'm* with the asshole who's going to die when I get out of here."

"Wrong answer." He struck then, a sucker punch in my gut, tearing the wound deeper, dizzying me, releasing a fresh wave of blood, drizzling down the sides of my torso. "You're in Draug country," he said. "They'll scent your blood and come running. Which means I'm going to leave you now. Dark will come soon. They'll be hungry."

"They feed on fear," I said, as much to convince myself as him.

He shrugged. "That's cool. You go ahead and try not to freak out when they swarm you." And then he simply turned and left.

"Coward," I shouted after him. "Fangless freak can't fight a girl."

But my taunts were met with silence. I tried to tug my hands free, but it was hopeless. My movements only cut the rope deeper into my wrists.

I lay there for a minute, heart pounding.

Blood had pooled in my belly button. In the crease of my waist. It was oozing down my sides. I was dripping with it. If it didn't call the Draug, it'd be sure to call *something*.

"Shit," I said, looking left and right. Nothing. No one. I was stuck. "Shit."

The blood cooled instantly. The evening was getting colder. The sun had already dipped below the hills. It was twilight. Soon full dark.

Draug craved the fear of others. They looked like demons, but they'd once been scared boys who'd not survived the transition to Vampire. Despite what Rob thought, I believed I'd have the mental strength to be brave. To stave off that fear.

Draug might've craved fear, but they survived on blood. And although I was able to moderate my fear, the pumping of my own blood was something I had no control over.

Draug were thirstiest as the sun set. They'd be too thirsty *not* to attack me.

It wasn't yet full dark when they came.

CHAPTER TWENTY-FIVE

———

I smelled him before I saw him. A Draug, coming.

    I tugged my arms, testing my bonds, but that only brought a fresh gush of blood from my belly wound. "Oh shit," I whispered, holding myself very, very still. "Here we go."

The stench grew. I heard shuffles and snarls now. More than one Draug—a lot more. Craning my neck, I saw them, cresting the hill, ambling toward me, senseless and hungry, looking like something from a zombie movie.

My mind skittered to manic places. Wishful thoughts—how I might be saved, how I might have some undiscovered power to heal my wound—plummeted to grim musings. How best to get myself killed quickly, put out of my misery.

I heard rustling, apart from the Draug. It was the sound of someone elbowing their way through the mob.

Would it be Carden? For an instant, I half dreamed it might be.

But then an artificial sound cut to me. A *bzzt*, followed by a pungent smell like ozone. Like electricity.

Electricity. I'd heard that sound before. Relief washed through me, listening as the Draug keeper zapped his way through. A mass of them had already gathered around me, staring and drooling like I was the turkey on their Thanksgiving table.

Tom's wizened face popped into my line of sight. Our eyes met, and he didn't smile, not precisely. But there was a tiny quirk at the corner of his mouth that said he wasn't entirely unhappy to see me.

"Excellent timing," I said, sounding more blasé than I felt.

"What trouble you in now, girl?"

"No trouble"—I shrugged, and the gesture sent a fresh trickle of blood down my side—"just hanging out. Thought I'd pay you a visit."

Finally, he smiled, baring teeth badly in need of a dentist. He shook his head, *tsk*ing. "You're aye reddin the fire, aren't ye?"

"Huh?"

"Stirring trouble." He tugged the rope at my shoulders, and I bit my lips against the flash of pain. Fresh blood oozed from my belly, and one of the Draug snarled. Tom took the cattle prod from the belt at his waist and zapped it. "Back," he shouted, then muttered, "Damn beasts." He met my eye. "Shall I help you, then?"

"Um . . . yes please?"

Sucking at his teeth, he studied the ropes. A few of the Draug jostled him from behind, but Tom cursed under his breath, quickly zapping them back. "I thought they was acting funny. They got all riled, of a sudden. I thought I'd take a look. See what's what. Didn't expect to see you again—though don't know why I should be surprised." He considered me for a minute, looking very perplexed. "Wee troublemaker, you are."

I gave him a toothy, pleading smile. "Do you think you could cut me loose now? Please?"

"Aye, I'm at it. I'm at it." He pulled a knife from his sock and began to saw the rope at my shoulder. "What are you doing out this way anyhow? Girl like you? I told you to stay away from these creatures. You're a braw thing, and they won't bother you, one-on-one like. But you're a wee thing, too. And I don't care how brave you are; you're nothing to a pack of thirsty Draug."

As though on cue, one peered over his shoulder. It was clear he was newly transitioned, his skin less rotted, the hair on his head still full. His eyes flicked to and fro, as though he might remember something if he only tried hard enough.

Oh God. I gasped as a nightmarish thought struck me. Soon that'd be Yasuo.

Moving faster than his age would suggest, Tom reached for his prod and zapped the thing under its chin. He shot me a look. "Keep still."

"It's just . . . I have a friend," I said. "He's becoming . . ." I couldn't drag my eyes from the new Draug at his back.

"Your friend?" He slashed the first rope free. "Ah, you mean the Chinaman."

"He's Japanese," I snapped. "Japanese American."

"Whatever you say." He began to saw the rope at my hip. "Don't matter what he is. He'll be Draug by month's end." At my shocked look, he clarified. "Yeah, I seen him. He's mighty close now. They don't usually turn so soon. Musta had a hard time of it. He'll be coming to my side any day. You'll be keeping your distance, if you know what's right."

"Don't worry." I couldn't bear to get close to Yasuo. I'd had my suspicions about his fate, but hearing it from Tom's lips made it real.

Despite what I'd said to Rob, I *did* blame myself. If I'd figured out a way to save Emma, she'd be here now, and I had no doubt that Yasuo would be right there with her, his arm slung across her shoulders. Tears stung at the thought. "So there's no way to help him?"

Tom glared. "Don't go weak on me now." He worked the other ropes free. "You know as good as I, there's naught to be done for that boy but mourn."

As I eased to sitting, he pulled a handkerchief from his inside coat pocket. He shoved it toward me, looking more unsettled than I'd have thought him able. "Take it." I gave both him and the rag a skeptical look, and he simply foisted the thing into my hands. "It's clean," he scolded. He nodded to my belly. "You stop up that cut now, and I'll walk you back to the path. Them Draug aren't the only ones who'll catch this scent. Vamps'll come soon, sure enough. Best get yourself back in your world now and out of mine."

I was feeling uncharacteristically fragile. I didn't know whether it was due to my near death, the run-in with Rob, Yasuo's fate, or the simple fact that I needed to feed, and I shoved every bit of it back into an increasingly precarious compartment in my mind. Time was short. I had questions, and I suspected Tom had answers.

As we walked back, I glanced uneasily at the Draug. They shuffled behind us, reminding me of confused sheep. "They won't bother me?"

"Not when there's this." He held up his prod. "They're beasts of habit, anyhow. This ain't their normal feeding spot."

I didn't want to ask what was. Instead, I peppered Tom with questions, a steady stream of things like, "Do you know the villagers? Do they have a celebration? Is it soon? Some fire thing, right?"

He'd given vague nods to each, but at that last, he gave me a sidelong look. "You always talk this much, girl?"

"I thought you knew that already."

He chuckled to himself. "So I do. But you have a care." He glanced around. "This island has ears."

"So will you answer the question?"

He waited but eventually gave a curt nod. "Aye. But that's the last one."

I asked it again, more specifically this time, just in case he really would answer only one more question. "Do the vampires celebrate *Up Helly Aa*?"

He gave me a baffled look. "That there's a strange choice of question."

I was silent, waiting—hoping—he'd continue. Or at least finish before I bled out . . . The slash in my belly throbbed with each step. The lack of Carden's blood was taking its toll, and I was afraid what I might find when I went back to the dorm to survey my injuries. "Please?" I whispered, hunching in to my pain, hoping a bit of pathos might help my cause.

"Fine," he finally growled. "The vamps, they celebrate something that night. I don't know what, but there's always lots of comings and goings. Sometimes there's boats—maybe day before, maybe day after—but boats come."

"Boats?" I pictured the keep in my mind. It was close to the coast, but it was just land on one side and a sharp drop into the sea on the other. Even if the surf wasn't a roiling, rocky mess, there wasn't a single dock in sight. "What do boats have to do with it? I wanted to know what they do in the castle."

He shot me a glare. "Is that a question? Because I told you. You get just the one."

"Please?"

He mimicked, "*Please, please,* she says." He shook his head, looking very put-upon. "All right, girl. But you keep this to yourself." He shot me a pointed look. "And I didn't tell you nohow."

We stopped walking as we reached the path. "Tell me what?" I asked impatiently.

"The boats—"

"Not the boats," I interrupted. We were running out of time. I was bleeding. It was getting dark. The Draug were groaning now, their thirst palpable. Other beasties were out there, too, and they'd be just as eager to snack on a morsel like me. "You were going to tell me about the castle."

He stared at me like I was an imbecile. "I *am* telling about the castle. Get that? The boats come . . . to the castle."

"But it's at the edge of a cliff."

"So it is. But there's more than one way into that keep." He let the notion hang for a moment. "Them boats pull right up, girl. Right up along that cliff. Up to the sea door."

CHAPTER TWENTY-SIX

———✦———

I headed out first thing Sunday morning, climbing along the coast to check it out. Eyeballing a straight line from the water inland to the castle, I had to guesstimate where this mysterious entrance might've been. I refused to think about the series of tunnels I'd need to traverse to get from the sea gate to the bowels of the castle—the prospect of navigating in pitch-darkness gave me the heebie-jeebies.

Also shoved from my mind was the glaring fact that lately it seemed every time I stepped out alone, I was jumped by some murderous creature or other. But seriously, a secret entrance into vampire central? I was too impatient. In fact, I'd impressed myself by waiting *this* long.

A sea door . . . I'd always assumed such things were the stuff of fiction. It sounded too much like something from an old pirate story—tall ships, their sails snapping, timber creaking, and cannons booming as they sneaked into coves, smuggled booty, that sort of thing.

"Shhhhoot," I hissed under my breath, swallowing my curse, as I grabbed at the underbrush to stop myself from slipping and sliding along the gravel into the roiling water below. I had to pause, clutching my stomach, waiting for the throbbing to subside. The gash in my belly felt like it might rip back open at any moment.

The heavy kit bag I'd slung across my back was throwing me off balance. But I had no choice—it was my fail-safe. I'd packed my wetsuit and towel inside, knowing if I was caught, I could always say I was out for a swim, and "swim" was exactly what was going to happen if I wasn't more careful.

I got my feet back under me and continued to pick my way down, but the hill was rapidly steepening into a cliff. I managed another few steps before I slipped again, my foot shooting out from under me, and landed hard on my knee. Gravel bit into my kneecap—I'd be lucky if my uniform hadn't torn—and I had to bite my lips against the pain. A warm tickle along my stomach told me the impact had finally reopened my wound.

"Shhhootshhhhhootshooot." It wasn't exactly the curse I'd wanted, but even this distance from the castle, I dared not mutter so much as a *damn*. The vamps demanded propriety at all times, and despite this little off-road hike, the impulse was ingrained in me.

There were nooks and crannies up and down these cliffs, and edging along on my butt, I aimed for one. My muscles were trembling, and I needed a spot where I could relax for a minute without worrying that I might tumble to my death. And who knew? Maybe I'd find more crazy Viking graffiti.

The morning sun hit the water at just the right angle, and I had to squint to see. It was a happy development, though. I'd thought noon was the best time to go out, but morning sunlight beaming directly at the cliff was even better than the midday sun overhead would've been.

I couldn't shade my eyes, needing both of my hands simply to hang on, so I peered hard against the white glare, trying to make sense of the rugged cliffside. I'd been looking for a nook to scoot into, but a shadow below and to the right told me I was coming up on a cave—even better.

It took mental effort to ignore my panic and pain as I inched down feet-first, all the way on my belly now. I had to put my complete focus on this little trek, which had surpassed *hike* and was well on its way to *free-climb*. It was pretty much as steep as I could go without the use of ropes and carabiners. One false move and I had visions of plummeting to the rocks below, B-movie style.

Finally, I was on level with the cave. Could *this* be the sea door? It seemed like it might be large enough. Did the tide even get this high? I peered over my shoulder at the water, hoping I wouldn't find out.

Using both hands to hold on to a snarl of roots overhead, I stretched out my foot, blindly fumbling for footing. My toes met hard ground, and I crab-walked along the wall, inching over until my whole foot was inside, then my leg, then my other foot. It was dark and dank in there, and I collapsed to my knees in relief.

But then, an explosion of motion. A shrieking wind came whipping toward me from deep in the cave.

Bats.

Hundreds of them shot out, screeching, flapping, careening toward me, close enough to tangle in my hair. I bit my lips to silence a scream and dropped to the ground, curling into a ball and covering my head. Like the fluttering of a single black veil, they swooped out, then whipped right back at me. *Scree-scree-scree-scree.*

"Holy shit holy shit holy shit." I crushed my face to the ground, my body rolled up tight. So much for not cursing.

I waited. Gradually, the flapping and screeching subsided until all I heard was my own panting breaths echoing off the walls and the heavy *thump-thump* of my heart.

I risked a peek. The bats had gone back to wherever they'd come from, and this part of the cave was empty once more. Shuffling forward on my hands and knees, I peered hard into its depths, but there was just blackness. Deep blackness and a sharp tang, the odor of innumerable nesting creatures.

Gathering my courage, I got to my feet. I had to hunch to stand and tiptoed as deep as I could. I didn't get far. The cave soon narrowed to a point tight enough that it wouldn't allow passage to anything much larger than those flying rodents.

So much for finding the sea gate on my first try.

I returned to the ledge and peered over, gulping in the fresh air, ignoring the bloody implications of my now completely soaked belly. I scanned the cliffside, but it was too jagged. The mysterious sea door might've been right below me, but I'd never know it. It was just too impossible to make sense of all those chinks and cracks.

I'd need to find it from the water.

The decision was easy. But explaining myself to Ronan later that afternoon? Not so much.

"Deep-water techniques?" He narrowed those forest-green eyes at me, not believing me for a minute.

I'd wondered how it'd be to run into him—after all, the last time we were together, we'd almost kissed. Seeing him now, although he was distant, he wasn't cold, but it was hard to say for sure. He was always so impossible to read. Was he angry? Resentful? Regretful, even?

I'd have put off this meeting—and those questions—altogether, but I didn't see any other choice. Who else had access to a boat? Who else could take me out into the water without raising suspicion? When I'd tracked him down, he was even at the car already.

"Yes," I insisted. "I've been practicing my breath-holding techniques. I want to work up to more difficult conditions." I hoisted my kit bag higher on my shoulder and flinched against the searing pain along my stomach. I needed Ronan to make up his mind ASAP, but he still looked far from convinced. I brightened my smile, adding, "I'd eventually like to try, you know, maybe like a free dive."

The corners of his eyes crinkled in a skeptical look. "'Maybe like a free dive'?"

Uh-oh. Too far. "I've been thinking about what you've said, about preparing myself. Making myself more competitive. Watchers need to have experience with deep, breath-hold dives, right?"

He ran a hand through his damp hair, and I refused to contemplate how that dark mop poking every which way was like girl kryptonite. "But I already went out for a swim, just now."

"That's right," I said brightly. "Which means it'll be easy to hop back in the car and go again." Pasting a bland, expectant smile on my face, I waited, and it was like a game of chicken, seeing who'd cave first. When he didn't say anything, I busted out the big guns and sighed heavily. "I guess, if you don't want to, I could probably handle the boat by myself. . . ."

"Truly, Ann? You're truly going *that* route?"

The nickname stopped me cold. He'd called me Ann just a couple times before, and it never failed to punch through my armor. It was what my mother had called me.

He dug his keys out of his pocket and went around to the driver's-side door. Placing a hand on the hood, he leaned over to look at me. "Are you coming or not?"

I got in before either of us had a chance to change our minds, holding my body carefully against my pain.

"By the way," he said as he pulled onto the main road, "manipulative isn't a good look for you."

"It worked, didn't it?" I settled in, careful of my injury, and buckled up. I had to hide my grin—no need to rub this in.

We bounced along in the SUV, and for a while, neither of us spoke. But, oddly, it wasn't an uncomfortable silence. Sure there was some tension—romantic and otherwise—but where my relationship with Ronan was concerned, friction and awareness had come to feel like normal states, so this was like slipping into something comfortably familiar.

After a while, I caught him peering at me from the corner of his eye. He looked away quickly, eyes glued back on the road.

"What?" I asked, instantly on the defensive. Was he going to find a way to blame our almost-kiss on me?

"Nothing."

I shifted in my seat to get a better look at him, but his profile gave away nothing. "You were thinking something just then."

"It's just . . ." He considered for a moment.

"Jeez, Ronan. Just what? What'd I do now?"

"What did you do?" He gave me a startled look. "Och, silly girl," he muttered, then simply reached over me to pop open the glove box.

It took a conscious effort not to flinch away. The closeness of his hand to my knees made something pulse low in my belly, so completely was I aware of him.

But then I registered what he'd pulled out. An old cassette tape. "Where'd you get that?" I asked incredulously.

The slightest of smiles quirked the side of his mouth. "As you said, I have my secrets."

"Don't I know it?" I snatched it from him. It was a plain black tape with *#14* written on the white label in black marker. "What's this?"

He snatched it back. "Something I think you'll like."

He slid it in the tape deck. The hiss of static filled the car, followed by a clicking, and then . . . music.

It stole my breath—literally. My entire body seized stiff as I held my breath, not daring to move. Music. It'd been so long since I'd experienced it privately like this. Not Baroque classics played by a vampire string quartet. Not Dagursson's waltzes. Just sitting in a car, riding and listening. Letting the notes wash over me.

It was a piano solo, and I heard it with such texture, it was as though I'd never truly *listened* to music before. Higher notes unraveled their tune on the treble clef, while the low bass keys were played so tentatively, I felt the emotion behind each stroke of the pianist's fingers. The ponderous pauses, the mini silences between notes—every second was a revelation.

Was it the blood that'd attuned me like this? Or was it merely my own deprivation? Had my raw emotional state made me vulnerable? Sitting in this confined space, with Ronan, the guy who'd tricked me here, then had the gall to turn around and care.

Like the notes, I let these thoughts wash over me, letting myself be brave enough to truly face and contemplate each one.

"Evgeny Kissin." Ronan's subdued voice broke into my thoughts. "That's the name of the pianist. It's my favorite recording."

"Number fourteen," I said. "That's the Moonlight Sonata." Some fundamental tension, a knot that'd been clenched deep in my chest, unspooled. Even the throbbing along my belly subsided. I let my head sink back and sighed a blissful sigh. I loved lots of bands and musicians—Foo Fighters, Cat Power, Nick Cave—but before them all there'd been Beethoven, and I loved him maybe most of all. "How'd you know?"

"How'd I know what?" Ronan asked. I opened my eyes to peer at him, and his questioning gaze was waiting for me. "How did I know that the girl who'd risked her life just so she could smuggle her iPod onto this island might like to listen to a spot of music?"

His humor lightened the mood, yet somehow that only made the moment more serious. More meaningful.

I didn't take my eyes from him as I asked, "Does this mean I'm to add intuition to the list of your many gifts and abilities?" I quirked an affectionate smile, feeling it in that newly unwound place in my chest.

He laughed then, and the free sound of it was a warm rush along my skin. "Aye, I'm a regular superhero."

The tape quality was miserable, all raspy and fuzzy, but even so, I leaned back again, letting the music wash over me. "I love Beethoven." I'd shut my eyes to savor it, but then shot them open again. "Wait. Isn't this illegal?"

His probing look added some other layer of meaning to my question.

I felt myself blush as I added, "The tape, I mean. Is it allowed?"

"Are you going to tell on me?" He took his eyes from the road to give me a slow smile.

Another smile? Another light comment? The guy was slaying me. We'd never had this. Never done this before. What did it mean, this easy banter with Ronan? Was he *flirting*?

"We'll see," I replied, attempting to sound just as flirtatious. "Maybe if you're good, I won't tell." I blushed furiously—that hadn't come out right. "I mean, if you're good with me in the water. For our class," I quickly added. "As a teacher." My cheeks were really flaming now, and I turned to watch out the window, letting the leather headrest cool my skin.

Crap . . . I couldn't flirt if I tried.

But the little exchange had clearly made him uncomfortable, too, because when he spoke again, it was stilted. "Recordings like this aren't illegal," he informed me, answering my question with a formality that, at that moment, I appreciated. "For instructors, at least. We're allowed to listen to music. As long as it's classical."

"No Led Zeppelin?"

"I said classical, not classic." The look he shot me—once more relaxed around the eyes—said he was beginning to loosen up again. "Definitely no Led Zeppelin. I imagine even Debussy is too gauche for the undead."

It was my turn to laugh. "Ronan," I exclaimed. "Was that *another* joke?"

"Mm." He nodded, looking pleased with himself. "Terribly clever of me."

I laughed again, and like that, the tension was gone. It was a place I never thought we'd go—one of easy comfort, where we joked like friends. It made me feel safe enough to ask something that'd been nagging me.

"So . . . can I ask you a question?"

He smirked. "I'd be shocked if you didn't."

"The vampires on this island . . ." I took a steadying breath. Formulating the words in my mind, I realized how ridiculous it was.

"The vampires?" he prompted.

"They don't, you know"—another breath, slower this time, exhaled through the teeth—"they're not the kind who turn into bats, are they?"

A raucous laugh exploded from him, reverberating through the car. "Bats? Now you're the one to joke."

I crossed my arms at my chest. "You don't have to laugh at me."

"Aye." He dabbed tears from his eyes. "I really do." One last *hee* escaped him—was that a guy giggle?—and he asked, "What on earth made you ask that?"

"I saw a bat is all," I mumbled.

"You what?"

"Bat," I snapped. "I saw a bat."

"You keep company with ancient vampires, and yet you're afraid of a wee winged rat?" He chuckled one last time.

"I didn't say I was afraid." I squirmed low in my seat, embarrassed.

We were quiet after that, and I suspected it was the one brief mention of ancient vampires that'd made him serious again.

Was he thinking about Carden? And what did it mean that, for a moment, I'd forgotten about him?

The cove where he stored the boat came into view, and Ronan swerved off the road, bumping along the rocks and pulling the truck to a stop.

He didn't open the door, though. Instead, Ronan turned in

his seat to face me, and dread shot through me to see how his expression had gone from serious to totally grim. "Why are we here?" he asked skeptically. "And don't lie to me, Annelise. I know you'd rather set your hair on fire again than—what was it?—do deep-water breath-holding free-dive prep exercises?"

I gave him an overly innocent grin. "I've been practicing."

He stared at me, silently challenging me to speak the truth.

It was a look I was powerless against. "Fine," I said. "I'm looking for something."

He raised his brows, waiting.

"Fine," I repeated, emphasizing the word. "I'm looking for a sea gate. I heard there was some sort of door carved into the cliffs." The coastline was jagged, an uneven ribbon of small coves and inlets, and I pointed north, back toward campus, to the cliffside jutting between Crispin's Cove and the sandier beaches. "Back that way."

He gave me a startled look. "By the keep?"

"Is that where the keep is?" I asked innocently.

"Annelise," he said in a tone stern with warning.

"C'mon, Ronan. I just want to see it. I heard the vampires have things delivered to them during that celebration you were talking about, that *Up Helly Aa* thing."

"I made a mistake telling you about that." He pinned me with his eyes. "So what does that have to do with this gate?"

"Apparently, boats pull up at high tide to deliver things."

"You've been busy." He leaned back, looking tired all of a sudden.

"Am I right?"

"You must forget about this whole business."

"So I *am* right."

"Aye," he admitted. "You're right. I've seen it with my own eyes. Boats come delivering things. Or people." He'd leaned against the headrest, but he slowly turned his head back to me. "Please have a care."

"I will. I just want to see the door. That's all. I promise." I crossed my heart. "Seriously, I'll be safer if you show it to me. I almost broke my neck this morning trying to hike down to it."

His knuckles went white, gripping the steering wheel. "You climbed the cliffs beneath the vampires' castle?"

"I said *hike*. It was more of a hike."

"I see." His eyes narrowed. "Fine," he said, mimicking our earlier exchange. "I'll show you the sea gate. But in return, you're going to have your swim lesson, too."

"What? No way."

"Yes way." He got out, and I followed him to the back of the truck.

"It's going to be dark soon," I protested.

"All the better for this extensive training you've been telling me about." He opened the back hatch and pulled out my bag. "If you're thinking what I think you're thinking, then I'll give swim lessons till you believe you'll die from them if that's what I feel will keep you safe."

I peered closely at him, wondering if I'd misunderstood. "Does that mean you're not going to stop me from investigating the whole sea gate thing?"

"If I asked you to stop, would you?"

I shrugged. "Guess not."

He tossed me my gear. "Then get in your wetsuit."

CHAPTER TWENTY-SEVEN

W̲e walked up the beach to the boat. It was an old wooden dory, stored upside down, its oars nestled in its belly. Like the Range Rover, all Tracers had access to it, but as the resident surfer and sea fanatic, Ronan was the only one I'd ever seen use it.

He'd grabbed rags from the back of the truck, and once we cast off from the shore, I watched, somewhat baffled, as he wrapped them around the paddles. "What's that for?" I smirked. "To keep them from getting chilly?"

The look he shot me told me this was no joking matter. "It muffles the sound of the oars. Sound carries on the wind. You want a closer look at the vampires, but we don't want them to get a closer look at us."

It struck me then, how great the risk was that he was taking for me.

We both had much to think on in silence. It took an eternity to row out, his expression growing more tense with every pull.

"Do you want me to take a turn?" I whispered, showing off my flexed arm, trying for a little good humor. "I've been working out." Though, secretly, I was pleased he was doing all the work—I doubted rowing was good for abdominal injuries.

He glared silently as he skimmed the scarred wood in the water, pulling the boat to a stop.

"I guess that means no," I muttered. Surreptitiously cradling my belly in my arms, I turned to look back to shore. Ever careful, Ronan had made certain to row out farther than we usually did. Like, really far. How would I ever detect the gate from here? Unease made my voice sharp. "We're pretty far away."

"I dare not go closer," he said grimly, and I didn't have to look at him to detect the clench of his jaw. "You endanger us both with this foolish endeavor."

What to say to that? He was right, of course. Responses like *Thanks* or *I know* didn't quite cover it, so I only nodded. I knew exactly how much he was risking for me.

I tried not to wonder why.

The keep loomed far in the distance, and yet I shivered as though its shadow fell directly over me, its evil and darkness hungry to subsume me. A chill crept along my flesh, and I chafed my arms, telling myself I was being silly. That the black maws in its facade were merely castle windows and not watchful eyes peering at me, detecting my treacherous heart.

My hands ached—I'd been gripping the boat's edge harder than I realized—and I gave them a sharp shake. "Where are you, little gate?" I'd said it lightly, just enough to prove to myself that I wasn't afraid. That I didn't secretly fear I was making a terrible, terrible mistake. I shaded my eyes, peering hard. "Now if only I could figure out where the cliff ends and the castle begins."

Something hard nudged my back. "Calm yourself," Ronan said, and the gentleness in his voice surprised me. My tone hadn't provoked him. Rather, he'd discerned my anxiety, knowing the more snarky my commentary, the more stressed I really was. He was one of the few who understood that about me.

Him . . . and Carden.

I bit my cheek till I tasted blood. *Forget Carden.*

The only vampires in my life were the ones I would take down. And it began here and now.

A nudge again, harder this time. I turned, a sassy remark on the tip of my tongue, when I saw he was just handing me a pair of binoculars. Our eyes met and held. His were a studied blank, but the shrug he gave me said all I needed to know. He was looking out for me.

I quirked a half smile, but it made me feel too vulnerable, so I quickly averted my gaze to the binoculars instead. They were compact enough to fit in his pocket. "Cool," I said tightly. "Thanks."

It took me a moment to sight through the tiny lenses. Blurs of gray jostled in narrow frames of black; then, in a sudden explosion of clarity, breaking waves and weed-tangled rocks zoomed into view. It took me a moment to make sense of what I was seeing. I tracked upward, finding the keep as a reference point, and then slowly brought the binoculars back down, systematically tracing the cliffside.

Just as I began to doubt I'd even know a sea gate if I saw one, it came into view—a large hole covered by what looked like a thick iron grate. I squinted. A gate—*the* gate. And it wasn't nearly as poetic as it sounded, either. If anything, it put me in mind of sewage, of rank tunnels hiding beneath highway overpasses, spilling into concrete runnels like urban riverbeds.

Deep black, this wasn't just a flaw in the rock face; it had to be an entryway. A tunnel. And it was much lower down the cliff than I'd guessed—the tide wouldn't need to rise so very high in order to access it by boat. Concealed beneath a wall of shrubbery, it would've taken me ages to find by climbing alone. So close to sea level, waves licked mere feet below. Did the tunnel ever fill with water? It was something to consider.

"I assume you've found what you're looking for?" Ronan sounded tense—more tense than usual. Did he not like being this close to vampire central, or was it my desire to get so close that worried him?

I offered him the binoculars, trying to bring the mood back to normal. "Do you want to look?"

But he'd begun rowing away already. "We're done here."

Vampires forgotten for the moment, I plucked at the neck of my wetsuit. "I don't have to swim?" I practically shivered with relief.

"Oh, you'll swim," he said with a wicked glint that told me he'd make me pay for this little errand.

Damn. He couldn't mean I was going to swim . . . from *here.* Right?

A small swell smacked the rear of the boat, tossing us forward. I gripped the hard bench to hold on, and . . . *ow.* I felt the tiniest tear in my tenuously healing wound. If Ronan were bent on punishing me, he was doing a fine job.

"Don't get mad at *me,*" I told him. "If you didn't want to row me out here, you didn't have to."

He raised his brows. "Is that so?"

"Yeah. It's so."

He was grimly quiet as he rowed on, giving me ample time to consider his reaction. I'd threatened to take the boat out myself, and he believed he had no other choice but to help me. The bigness and trueness of that impulse sank in. Blew me away.

I'd need to be more careful—I didn't have enough friends left to be risking them so.

Back in sight of Crispin's Cove, Ronan once again dragged the oars along the water's surface, pulling us to a stop. The boat bobbed, and he waited, but I didn't budge. Our eyes met in a moment's standoff. He really was going to make me do deep-water exercises.

I huffed. "Fine."

I reached for a mask, but he stayed my hand. "No," he said.

"No?" I curled my fingers more tightly around the plastic.

"You were studying the sea gate."

"The what?" I asked in my best innocent voice.

He only shook his head and snatched the mask from my hand. "No mask." He met my eyes again, only this time he was the one with the feigned innocence. "You're the one who wants difficult conditions, Annelise. I'm simply preparing you for 'difficult conditions.'"

I had to laugh despite myself. "Touché."

But my agreement didn't mean acquiescence. In a moment of defiance, I heaved my weight as I stood, making the boat lurch, and bit back a grin to see Ronan startle and grab the side against the sudden rocking. But I was enjoying it a bit too much and, stupidly disregarding the wound in my belly, I flung myself over the side in a way that'd create maximum splash. As I hit the water, I knew instantly I'd done wrong. The fragile seam in my skin tore open further, and salt water slashed like a blade, searing into my tender flesh like I was being stabbed all over again.

I could barely get my head above the surface before I hissed and curled into the pain. Salt in my wound was like a hot brand, and I had to grit my teeth and pant away the pain. "Whoa," I said as I finally caught my breath. I shook my head, releasing a weird adrenaline-charged sound that was half sob, half laugh. "Holy crap." I opened my eyes, but Ronan wavered in my vision, so I wiped away tears and then laughed for real, seeing the expression on his face. "What are you looking at?"

"Get out," he said.

"What?" Mindlessly, I massaged my side, feeling my smile fade.

"Get out of the water." He reached a demanding hand down to me.

"I just got in." I shoved away. I'd have loved to get back in the boat, but I needed to buy time—I didn't think I'd be able to exert myself again without bringing on a fresh wave of agony. My wound was pounding. I was certain I was bleeding into my suit. Were there sharks here? Could they sense blood through my thick neoprene armor?

Normally, I would've healed by now. But *normally*, I'd have been taking Carden's blood. I'd been sneaking extra shots of the drink when I could, but if I were to survive at this pace, it was clear I'd need to up my dosage even more.

Ronan stretched his hand farther. "Annelise," he said sternly.

"What if I don't want to?"

"Then that's your prerogative." He scanned the horizon with

a nonchalant shrug. "How many sharks do you reckon are in the North Sea this time of year? As I understand it, they prefer the colder waters."

Two quick scissors kicks, and I whooshed back to the side of the boat, my extended hand begging for a pull up. "You win."

The look on his face was pretend bafflement. "What's that you say?"

"Ronan. Help me up." I began to haul myself over and grimaced at a fresh stab of pain. "Please."

His hands were under my arms in an instant, lifting me back into the boat. "Jesus, Ann."

My wound had really torn back open now, and I crumpled onto the bench, doubled over. "Stop calling me that."

"All right, then," he said stiffly. "Just tell me, what did you do this time?"

"*I* didn't do anything."

"Take off your suit." He placed a gentle hand on my shoulder.

I flinched away. "*Ronan.* I'm not that kind of girl." I chuffed a little laugh, trying to rid myself of the feeling that I might vomit at any moment.

"This is no laughing matter, Annelise."

I glanced up. He wasn't smiling. "How did you know I was bleeding?"

"I've seen you burnt, broken, and near death. You're as stoic as they come." He helped me sit up. "Your eyes, they went distant. . . . I've seen it happen but once before."

He was referring to my fight with Lilac—that had to be it. Then, I'd longed to get as far from my charred body as I could. "It's not nearly that bad." I blew out a breath, regaining my composure.

"I can tell you're injured."

I sighed. "It's not that big a deal." And it was true—now that I was out of the water, the pain was not as bad, though the wet, salt-soaked suit chafed something terrible.

"Then it won't be a big deal for you to show me."

He was right: It wasn't a big deal. I wore a swimsuit, the two-piece I always wore under my wetsuit. The top covered me more than a jog bra would. So then why did it feel like a big deal?

"Can't we just head back?" I hedged.

"Annelise." His tone told me that, no, we couldn't.

"Fine." I stretched up to unzip the back, and hissed as the movement tore some other part of my flesh open.

"Stop." He snatched my elbow, halting me in midair. "What are you hiding?"

"I'm not hiding anything."

"Then show me." He waved his hand, ordering me to turn, so he could do my zipper.

I presented him my back, and the next sounds came loudly to me. There was the rip of Velcro, the crisp snick of the chunky, plastic zipper. The thud of my heart in my ears.

I turned back around and pulled my arms free of the suit. It was a single, fluid movement, torquing my body, but I welcomed the pain now. Anything to stop this feeling of hyper-self-awareness.

Before, Ronan had been my teacher and *only* my teacher. By the time our friendship had deepened, Carden was in the picture.

Carden, who loomed so large in my heart. Hell, he loomed in my *bloodstream*.

Carden and any breathless thoughts of Ronan were completely mutually exclusive.

But where was Carden now?

I knew where Ronan was. He was right here, helping me. Making my pulse hop in a way that had me woozy. A little woozy and a lot confused.

I still didn't get *why* Ronan was here. Or where Carden had gone. Or why he'd gone.

I couldn't wrap my mind around any of it. So I didn't. Instead, I went through the motions, watching Ronan—and me with Ronan—as though from afar. Trying to figure out what on earth was going on. He was looking at my belly, *hmm*ing and poking. A fresh zing of pain brought me back quick enough.

I flinched away. "Easy."

He ignored me . . . of course. "The salt water would be painful—"

I shifted away to give him a good glare. "You think?"

"Aye." As he knelt closer, he tried to hide his smirk, but I spotted it. "The salt burns, but it has antibacterial properties." He poked and prodded a bit more, testing the edges of the gash, pushing together, pressing down.

"Ow." I hated the tone of my voice, but something about this blatant attention made me peevish. I didn't care about my injury. I didn't want to hear about it. I wanted him to explain what he was doing, like, in a fundamental way. "Do you have to do that?"

"It needs to close back up. How well did you clean this?"

"I cleaned it." As best I could, stealing solitary moments in the girls' room without anyone seeing. People seeing me with bruises was one thing, but I'd become very secretive about anything that might betray a weakness. I could've gone to the infirmary—there was such a thing—but seeking help was yet another way to mark yourself as vulnerable. We studied combat medicine for this very reason. We were trained to be tough. To endure extreme conditions. Extreme pain. We should be tending our wounds ourselves.

I wouldn't need to be tending my wounds if *Carden* were around. I felt a flicker of resentment and snatched on to it. Anger was so much easier than loneliness or sadness. I pushed Ronan's hand aside and felt around the wound. It was cool. Not swollen. "It's not infected."

"Keep direct pressure on it." He put my hands over my belly, then took my shoulders and guided me off my seat. "Move." He opened the bench storage and began digging through. "You need to keep it dressed." He pulled out a first-aid kit—it looked ancient, the red plastic box faded almost pink—and fished through it till he found a yellowed roll of gauze and a sterile cotton pad. "Hands up." His voice was devoid of emotion as he staunched the wound with the cotton and began to wind the ribbon of gauze around and around my belly.

A silence followed, and it became unbearable. With nothing more clever to say, I finally told him, "Thanks."

Weak. Lame.

"You should've just told me," he said flatly. "You didn't have to do this today. Why do you continually insist on putting yourself in harm's way?" His hands stilled on my belly. "Have you ever once considered telling me the truth without hesitation?"

"I tell you the truth all the time," I protested.

He looked up and pierced me with those green eyes.

"*Most* of the time," I amended. "Think about it, Ronan. If I told you I wanted to get a look at that gate, you would've hidden the oars and made me swim out here myself."

He'd been fighting it, but a reluctant smile finally quirked one corner of his mouth. "Probably true."

"And, anyway, you were right to challenge me."

The other corner of his mouth curled until it became an actual symmetrical smile. He tied off the gauze. "Indeed?"

My eyes swept past him as I considered, taking in the vast sea. It was the color of a spilled inkpot. Or a bruise.

But not the sky. The sky was so bled of color, the white band of the horizon seemed barely able to touch down.

My gaze returned to Ronan. Drawn to him, as I'd been drawn on that first day we met. He'd been an anchor for me since I'd arrived. "I needed this now more than ever," I told him.

Little did he know, my words referred to so much more than swimming.

CHAPTER TWENTY-EIGHT

I needed to get into that sea gate. Tom had said boats pull up to unload. Surely it wasn't just vampires and Trainees who used it. I doubted those vampires did anything so banal as unload cargo. I had a great big picture in my head of Master Dagursson hauling crates like a dockworker.

Not.

Surely they had cooks and maids and scullions and whomever else people employed in castles. I thought of the vampires I'd seen on the other island. They had an army of servants. I didn't believe these vamps mopped their own floors. Someone did it for us girls; someone had to be doing it for them, too. And that vampires' keep was way bigger than any Acari dorm—they had to employ dozens of someones.

Villagers. It had to be villagers.

I thought of the few I'd met. It was village men who managed the airstrip. Villagers who'd ferried us to the other island. They had to have villagers who helped in the castle, too. How did they enter? I doubted they sashayed through the front door.

Good old Tom. He'd know. Which is how I ended up poking around the Draug pens, but he was nowhere to be seen. The Draug were there, though, snarling and moaning in their cages as I neared. It must've been the scent of my healing wound. I pulled off my gloves, and something about winter's bite helped me clear my head. Staved off the fear. It must've worked, because the Draug made no more than those basic complaints.

My feet crunched through day-old snow as I searched all over, but there was no sign of Tom. Could he be out feeding the animals? He had goats—apparently, their blood was enough to keep the Draug sated—and he kept a paddock of them behind his cottage. I didn't know what was involved in keeping livestock. Did he have to exercise them? Take them someplace for milking? I'd grown up in suburban Florida—how should I know?

I wandered to the paddock, climbing onto the fence for a bird's-eye view, but there was no sign of anyone.

No sign, that is, until Toby appeared. I hopped down and instinctively grabbed a long-handled tool that'd been leaning against the fence. "Hey."

My farm boy. Toby-the-Trainee. My assignment. He looked as perplexed as I felt. "What are you doing here?" he asked.

"I could ask the same of you." I tightened my grip on the wooden handle, grateful I'd already removed my gloves. My hands were growing numb, but if it came to a fight, numbed fingers were a lot more nimble than gloved ones.

He didn't attack, though. He just gave me a dopey smile. "You look like a witch."

"Huh?" I glanced at my impromptu weapon. It was an old pitchfork, with three long, thin, rusted prongs.

"Holding that dung fork," he said. "You look like a witch." His tone was easy, not aggressive at all. Was this a trick? Was my dim farmhand actually a conniving supergenius who was fooling me into dropping my guard?

"Actually, I feel more Amish," I said, playing along. I hefted the fork high, trying to read his expression. We were alone. How was this going to play out? But then his words registered and I gave an involuntary smile. "Wait. What did you call this? I thought it was a pitchfork."

"Nah, that there's a dung fork." Then he nodded to the paddock, which upon closer inspection, did appear rather dung-y. "You know, scoop it up, spread it out. Makes good fertilizer."

"Oh. Ew."

This was the guy I was supposed to kill? Mr. Dung Fork? I probably could take him down pretty easily. He had a good hundred pounds on me, but in this case, all that mattered was who had more IQ points.

"You never seen a dung fork?"

I shook my head. *No, but I've met a boy dim as one.*

My thoughts were churning. I had to "assassinate" him. "I still say it's a pitchfork."

Toby laughed and kicked a muddy patch into the slushy ground. The guy wasn't acting like he was about to attack. In fact, he wasn't acting combative in the slightest bit.

But Alcántara's words rang in my head. In our last class, he'd been furious with me. *How serious are you, querida?* And, *I'm beginning to think you've lost heart.* He'd never take me on as his assistant if I couldn't complete the semester's only assignment.

A snow flurry hit my cheek. One landed in my eye. I wiped my face, clearing my head. I couldn't think of him as Toby. He was *homework*.

He gazed past me. "Looks like weather is coming."

Weather is coming. It was exactly what a farm boy would say. Like something *Emma* would've said. Suddenly, this felt too normal. I couldn't do it. I couldn't deal with this chitchat.

"Where are you from, anyway? Because where I'm from in Nebras—"

"Guess what?" I snapped. "I don't care where you're from. I don't care where you were born. Because guess what? This is where we'll all die."

"Jeez," he said, looking like I'd actually hurt him. "Take it easy."

But it wasn't easy. This wasn't normal. It was survival of the fittest.

My voice took on an edge. "What are you even doing here? I thought being on this side of the island freaked Trainees out." That was what Josh had told me anyway. "Aren't you worried *you* might turn into one these zombified bloodthirsty monsters someday?"

He looked like he didn't want to answer. Finally, he admitted, "Yeah, sure, it's freaky. But we had to follow Yas."

My eyes widened. "Yasuo?"

He gave a baffled shrug. "He's been acting weird."

"Understatement of the year." It hurt that Yasuo was no longer my friend—he'd once been mine to know about, chat with, look for. "He used to be one of my best friends."

"Yeah," he said, with surprising sincerity, "sorry about that. The guys are still pretty sore about the whole Rob thing. You know, the"—he pointed to his teeth—"the fang thing?"

"Yeah. I know."

"You should watch your back. They're pretty balls-out for you."

Classy. But I appreciated the sentiment, if not the choice of words. And wasn't that just grand, because now I could *never* kill this kid. How much easier it'd be if he were as much of a jerk as the rest of them.

Could I put it off just a bit longer? But that was why Alcántara had assigned me this boy, wasn't it? He'd know I'd have trouble "assassinating" someone like this. The Spanish vampire was testing me.

Could I avoid killing him? Evade my assignment altogether? I ran possible excuses through my head. Possible scenarios. Surely there'd be a way to pass my class without killing Toby-the-Trainee.

I heard someone approaching and spotted Rob and Danny, dragging a limp and pale Yasuo between them. "Found him," Rob called. Then he spotted me and his eyes went wide.

Ha. The moron thought he'd killed me.

He shot Toby a glare. "What the fuck is she doing here?"

I gave him my brightest smile. "Happy to see me?"

"This time it'll be the last time." Rob flung Yasuo's arm down, making him stumble, then strode toward me.

Standing tall, Toby put up his hands. "Rob, dude. Take it down a notch."

Yasuo's head lolled up, and spotting me, life snapped into his eyes. Like a flicked switch, he was instantly animated, his body shooting upright. It was like a rabid animal woken from sleep. One minute Yas was absent, the next he was there. Like, *really there.* He shouldered past the others to get in my face. "Nobody trusts you."

Danny chimed in. "I agree with Yas. You're toxic."

I angled away from them. "Hey, didn't you hear Toby? Let's all chill out."

Yasuo's attention turned to farm boy. "Ignore her. She gets people to trust her. To tell her their secrets."

"I'm here, you know," I said. "You can address me directly."

I regretted my words when he turned his full attention back to me. I had to look away from that creepy cold stare.

"Emma trusted you and now she's dead. Amanda trusted you—did you know her secrets, too? How about Ronan?" Then he added slowly, deliberately, "I'll just bet he tells you all sorts of things."

Adrenaline dumped through me, acid blazing through my veins. What was he referring to? Ronan had shared the secret of Lilac's strength with me just before I met her in the ring for the Directorate Challenge. Stupidly, I'd later confided it to Yas and Emma. Was Yasuo threatening me with this? Threatening Ronan? Were my friends his enemies now?

It'd been a secret big enough to save my life.

Big enough to get Ronan killed.

"What are you saying?" I asked carefully.

"I'm saying you'll suffer." His voice was a deep and other-worldly growl. The rationality that'd been in his eyes a moment ago clouded. "There has been a wrong, and I will right it to my death."

Okeydokey. I took a subtle step backward. *Righting wrongs till death* was always my cue to exit.

Draug in the surrounding pens began to come to life, their moans turning to snarls. Someone among us was afraid and it smelled tasty. Toby shot a panicked glance their way. "Let's get out of here, guys."

"Not leaving till it's finished," Yas said in that creepy voice. "Till she's finished."

"Yeah." Rob stepped forward. "Can't leave this mess behind."

Danny snickered. "Hot mess."

Toby put a hand on Rob's arm. "Let it go, man. What if those things smell her blood and bust out of there? I'm not getting eaten."

Rob snatched his arm back. "They won't eat you."

Danny taunted him. "Don't be such a nancy boy, Tobe."

"There has been a wrong," Yas intoned again. Suddenly he was pure rage, unhinged, his madness glimmering until his eyes glowed red with it. This was Draug Yasuo.

The whole scene was disintegrating rapidly. My gaze skittered right and left, searching for a plan.

"Looking for someone?" Danny's voice was cool and amused in a way that scared me more than any Draug.

Crap. The attention was back on me.

"Because there's nobody here but us," Rob said with a smile.

"No vamp to come and save you," Danny said.

Rob stepped closer. "Good times."

"Get her," Yas growled.

Danny loomed over me. "You think you're better than us."

"You're even too good for the island vamps," Rob said, in an obvious reference to Carden. "Where'd you find that skirt-wearing bastard anyway?"

I stood tall, deflecting the pain, dredging some dignity from down deep. "That *bastard* is a Vampire, hundreds of years old."

Toby had wandered closer to the Draug pen, looking uneasy. "Hey, guys, these things are really freaking out."

Rob ignored him and held my gaze. "Then where's the *old* bastard now?"

"Where are any of her little friends?" Danny asked. "Oh, right. She has none."

"None are left," Yasuo declared in that eerie atonal voice. His eyes were really glowing now.

Ignoring Yasuo, I tried to sound braver than I felt and said determinedly, "Carden will be back." Because he would, right? Carden would need to return sometime.

Danny glanced right and left, then gave me a stupid grin and a shrug. "I don't see him."

"Guys, seriously. These Draug things are starting to lose it." That was Toby. At least one of these morons had a lick of sense. I imagined once the beasts were riled up, smell of fear or not, there'd be no stopping them.

"Yeah, guys," I interjected, "aren't you scared of the Draug?"

Danny took a step closer. "We're not scared of shit. Especially not you."

"Let's just get out of here," Toby said.

"You can. I'm staying." Rob leapt at me, with Danny right behind. The pitchfork flew from my hands. Rob snagged my arm and curled his fingers into me, hard enough that I felt it through my coat.

Rather than pulling away, I hurled myself toward him, the surprise earning me a moment's advantage. My hand found his collar, and I slammed my other onto his shoulder, grabbing as much fabric as I could. "Is this still part of your homework assignment? Because I think you failed." I pulled and twisted, trying to choke him with the collar of his own shirt.

Unfortunately, the move gave him some ideas, because he went for my throat, too. "Not yet, I haven't."

We grappled, me squirming to stop him from getting a firm

grip. The collar of my catsuit was snug against my neck, but not so snug he couldn't easily wriggle a few fingers down there if I gave him the chance.

Danny stood close, cheering him on, chanting for blood. Toby mumbled some protest or other, but how successful could he be, really, when he wasn't exactly doing anything to stop this? And through it all was Yasuo, snarling and muttering. Had he completely lost it already? I couldn't tell if this was madness or pure, cold-blooded fury.

Rob had me restrained in a bear hug now. This close, his hot breath stank like stale onions. He tipped his head to scan my neck and shoulders in a lingering perusal that made my skin crawl. "I live for girls like you."

In that moment, I wasn't just fighting Rob. I was fighting everything he represented. Everything he stood for. My body exploded into action, renewed kicking, bucking, scratching. "How can you feed with no fangs?"

"I'll feed." Rob gave me a gloating smile. "That's why you're here. It's the blood in you girls that makes us strong."

The moment the words were out of Rob's mouth, Yasuo went ballistic.

CHAPTER TWENTY-NINE

———⊗———

Yasuo went nuts.
NUTS.

He flew at Rob, ripped him off me and flung him against the fence, repeatedly slamming his face against the post like a person might beat the dust from a rug. There was a hideous sound, a splat and crack like a hammer on meat, and Yas tossed him away, a bloody heap in the muddy snow.

"What the hell?" Toby shouted, backing away.

Danny dove to kneel beside Rob in the slush, watching helplessly as his friend writhed and spasmed, then glared over his shoulder at Yasuo. "Have you totally lost it?" Rob's jaw hung loose, no longer resembling a jaw.

The Draug began howling like crazy, rattling their cages, because now they scented fear *and* blood.

But Yasuo just stood there, panting, his mouth agape, fangs longer than I'd ever seen them. Sharp and gleaming.

"What the hell . . . ? What the hell?" Toby was paralyzed, rocking in place, looking like he was going to tear his hair out.

"You should get out of here," I whispered to him.

"Screw this. I'm gone." Danny hopped to his feet and burst into a jog. He called out a final, "Enjoy, mates," before running off.

At least I heard him run off. I didn't take my eyes from Yasuo, who was now staring like a statue. It was a terrible sight, that stillness. It was menace and hatred, frozen as marble. And it was all aimed at me.

Toby—good old Toby—must've sensed it, because he said, "Dude, let's just talk about this." He sounded as uneasy as I felt.

I sidled closer, telling him in a low voice, "You should follow Danny." Yasuo was spiraling, and it was obvious he was all too happy to take Trainees down with him. Besides, the farm boy was a distraction. I desperately hoped the old Yas was still there, buried deep in that glaring creature, and this might've been my last chance to summon him. "Really, I've got this."

"All you've got is the kiss of death," Yasuo hissed.

"There's death all around this island. Don't pin it on me." I edged sideways, but there was no escaping that stare. He was laser focused on me and yet completely oblivious to my words, my emotions. "Come on, Yas. Try to remember how we used to be."

"Kiss of death. The sure thing."

I put my hands up, taking a few steps back, thinking maybe I preferred crazy-unhinged Yasuo to this cold, calculated-fury Yasuo. "I heard you the first time."

"People around you don't die in normal ways. They meet grisly, fucked-up ends."

"Take it easy."

"It will be easy." He lunged at me, and I darted aside.

"Don't do this." I'd been avoiding another confrontation with my old friend, but I was in survival mode. If he attacked, I'd fight. And I didn't want to fight.

He flung himself at me again, but again I managed to duck and spin out of the way.

"Get a grip, man." Toby was bobbing on his toes, unsure how or if to get involved. Why didn't he just leave? Was he looking out for me or for Yasuo?

"It doesn't have to be this way," I pleaded.

"It does." Yasuo was panting again, that madness once more descending like a film over his eyes. "Does."

He attacked again, a broad swat at my head, then another. But his movements were erratic, and I evaded them easily. This wasn't the old Yasuo—the old Yas had been eclipsed by a monster. This was a creature driven by fury but unable to strategize. Incapable of tactics. His weren't maneuvers; they were motions, crude and predictable.

Maybe if I could stun him, make him stop for long enough, I could get away. The last thing I wanted was to fight him. When Yas leapt again, I deflected him, dropping and rolling to the ground, snatching the pitchfork from the dirt. "Please don't make me do this."

"You guys." Toby tried to insert himself between us. "What the hell?"

Yas elbowed him with enough force to send the big, corn-fed boy reeling. "Don't. Help. Her." His voice had become an animal growl.

I tightened my grip on the tool. Even in my numbed hands, the wood was reassuring.

I thought of Sonja. Ruler of vampires. Had there truly been such a woman? Even if she hadn't been strong enough to rule vampires in truth, then at least she'd had the guts to carve it into rock. Thinking of her words, imagining her, gave me courage. Sonja—if there was a woman who'd been that powerful, then I could be powerful, too.

I tossed the fork up and held it in my two hands like a fighting stick. No longer a farm tool, it was a javelin. A lance. A sword. A *weapon*.

Yas aimed a roundhouse kick at my head, and the stick deflected him easily. I jabbed his belly. I could've hurt him, but didn't. Hurting my old friend was harder than I'd ever have believed. "I don't want to hurt you," I said.

The Draug were really losing it now. Could that be *my* fear they smelled? And was it fear for myself or fear of what had become of my friend?

Rob took that opportunity to moan. He was fading in and out, his breathing a bloody gurgle. The Draug shrieked in response, rattling their iron bars in their hinges.

"Oh fuck, oh fuck." Toby was really flipping out now.

"Just get out of here," I shot at him.

But instead of fleeing, he squatted and scooped up a rock. A coldly self-preservational part of my brain noted how Trainees didn't carry weapons. Did vampires not carry weapons, either? Were they that proud? That arrogant? Something to consider . . . if I survived this.

Toby hefted that rock, and for a chilling moment it was unclear who it was for. Because, for a moment, his eyes were cold on me. Had he not wanted Yasuo to fight me because *he* didn't want to fight me? Would one Trainee side with another, no matter what?

My musings were cut short when Yasuo swept a foot toward my ankle, but I managed to react in time, clocking his knee with my stick.

"Right wrongs," he intoned.

I knew better than anyone how wronged we'd all been. But what if I were the one to set it all to right? This Sonja had become my heroine. My Wonder Woman. If Yasuo wanted wrongs righted, I'd be the one to do it. I parried him again. "Not if I right them first."

He peeled his lips into a snarl. "Go to hell."

"Oh, I'm there." I jabbed him with the fork, but I hadn't used enough force to budge through the thick wool of his coat. "Careful, or I might bring you with me."

"There's been a wrong," Yasuo said.

"Not that again." I jabbed again, and this time he took a step backward. I had the brief and disturbing thought that I might be able to herd him as the most mindless of Draug were herded.

"There has been a wrong, and I will right it."

"You do that, Yas."

He froze, staring at me as though trying to remember why he was there.

"What's he doing?" Toby asked.

"Losing it." I shot farm boy a look. What was he going to do with that rock?

"It's your fault." Yasuo addressed me, speaking in a wondering sort of voice.

"It's nobody's fault." Toby inserted himself between us, his tone aggressively soothing, like he was trying to calm a crazy street person. "Let it go, man." But he still gripped that stone, his eyes flicking back and forth, returning to me over and over like I was a bomb he might have to detonate. "We don't have to fight her."

My heartbeat amped up a notch, my body preparing for something my mind hadn't yet grasped. "What do you mean, *We*?"

"Ignore her," Yasuo shouted, ignited once more. He shouldered Toby aside, pinning me with a murderous glare. "She's selfish. She's a killer."

"Fuck it," Toby said. "It's just a girl."

Just a girl.

It's just a girl.

Yasuo lunged at me. Did Toby lunge, too? Later I told myself he did. Later, I told myself he hadn't been flinging himself between us.

Because when I speared the pitchfork, I speared Toby.

There was a horrific moment. A sharp inhale. A gurgled exhale. His eyes met mine, confused. Bewildered. It was a weird look, like he'd asked me to prom and I'd surprised him by turning him down. It wasn't the look you'd expect from a guy impaled on the business end of a dung fork.

He fell.

Yasuo laughed, a cackling, gleeful sound. "Told you. Killer." He repeated it over and over, manic and high-pitched. "Killer. Killer."

It hit close to home. Too close. I was a killer.

But I wouldn't kill Yasuo. He might've been turning Draug, but he'd once been my friend. I wouldn't attack him. Not like this. Not today.

I dug into my coat pocket. My fingers found my prized possession. Emma's handkerchief.

I rubbed it between my fingers. It was a sacrifice. But a fitting one.

I pulled it out, holding it like a white flag in front of me. Yasuo recognized it at once, his eyes growing wide.

"That's right," I said. I waved it. I hadn't washed it and wondered if it still bore some scent of hers. "You know this."

He took a step forward.

"You want it?" I tied a couple of loose knots in the fabric. Just enough to give it some heft. I threw. "Then take it."

Yasuo went for it.

I ran off. I ran like a crazy person. Leaving Rob and the body of Toby-the-Trainee dead and cooling by the paddock gate. Leaving my friend Yasuo behind, maybe forever. I ran until I realized my feet had carried me all the way to the water.

Screw it.

I'd end this now.

I loped up the beach, running until there was just a thin sliver of rocky sand, and when there was no beach left to run on, I sloshed through the breakers, lifting my knees high, trying to stay upright. Waves slapped at me, the freezing water sloshing over my boots, biting through the thick fabric of my catsuit, each swell rising in a moment of peace and then whooshing, back, trying to suck me out to sea. The waves came over and over, relentless, violent smacks against my thighs, trying to topple me.

But I refused to topple. I was seeing red. I'd lost everything and everyone. Would it kill me? Probably. But I'd see the secrets of this castle once and for all.

Finally, when the water was deep enough to buoy me, lifting

me with each swell of the tide to my tiptoes, I stopped. Looked up. The sea gate was overhead. Not as far a climb as I'd have guessed, concealed from above by a coarse shelf of brush.

I let the breakers sweep me closer and higher, grabbing ahold of the rocky cliff side, using hands and feet and knees to scramble up until I found a shelf wide enough to perch on. The tunnel's stench reached me first, wet and sulfurous, like hot springs and rotting things. I looked back down from where I came, scanning the lay of the land, seeing just how well situated this spot was.

The wind was picking up, and I wasn't in the mood to be blown off the cliff, so to be safe, I shuffled on hands and knees to get closer and assess the gate itself. Almost immediately, I cracked my kneecap hard against something. An explosion of pain like my bone had split in two felled me. Tears sprang to my eyes, and I curled onto my side, swallowing a cry of pain.

When I was able to breathe again, I saw what I'd run in to. Two large, rusted rings had been secured into the granite. Mooring for supply boats? Or did the boats come bearing victims? Who knew what evil visited these shores . . . ? Either way, it was a good sign. *Somebody* used this entrance, which meant it led somewhere.

Resting against the bars with one arm, cradling my nose in the crook of my other, I peered inside. Up close like this, the thing looked more like a sewage runoff than ever. I whispered, "Here I come, boys," and gave the gate a jiggle, but it was much more solid than the rusted iron would suggest. "No problem." I turned my attention to the handle and froze, taken aback. "What the—?"

I'd expected a simple lock, maybe a sliding bolt or a padlock hanging from a latch, but not this. Rather than a single gate, there were two, like French doors opening up the middle. I ran my fingers along the outer edges of the portal, feeling for hinges, but they weren't visible from this side.

A lack of hinges wasn't the strange part, though. Instead of a traditional lock, a circular medallion roughly the size of my palm connected the two doors in the very center. Tracing my finger, I could feel a seam between the doors, above and below the medallion, but the disc itself was a solid whole, not atop the metal, but a part of the iron itself.

How would I ever break into this? There was no keyhole. No lever or latch.

"Weird." I sat back on my heels to regroup. Surely this was pickable. Every lock was pickable, right? Generally, I was a whiz with good old breaking and entering. I always kept random useful bits in my pockets—paper clips, safety pins, pop tops— enough to pick any lock . . . except this one.

I studied the medallion, utterly perplexed. A sideways figure eight, the symbol for infinity, was carved in the center. There were two triangles etched within that, one triangle in each half of the eight, so that they touched, their silhouette like a sideways letter X. The triangle on the right was indented, a little niche in the metal.

Was this the keyhole? I'd never seen such a thing.

My hand hovered over the medallion, and I realized I hadn't yet touched it. Something about it radiated with power. Creeped me out. It was such a peculiar symbol, such a magical symbol. I had the eerie feeling that handling it might have horrific consequences. My hand hovered until my biceps began to tremble, and then I just felt stupid.

I was being weak. It was time to be brave. To be rational. Not to be freaked out by some stupid old lock. I had nothing to lose. I touched it to prove to myself I could.

Exploring it with my hands, I was no less perplexed. I tilted my head this way and that, wishing the ambient light might suddenly catch something I'd missed. But as far as I could tell, this was unpickable—not just hard to pick, but *unpickable*. Impossible. Cryptic. In all the books I'd read, I'd never encountered such a thing.

The metal was cool and damp with sea mist. A thin layer of corrosion felt like dirt under my fingertip. I wriggled my finger, using my nail to feel for some seam or edge, but there was *nothing*. Nothing to pry open, nothing to unfasten, unlock, or unlatch. There'd be no picking this thing. The triangle was hollow.

Not unlike my heart.

CHAPTER THIRTY

I lingered in the dining hall, unable to make myself care enough to move. I'd failed. The more time that passed, the more deeply I doubted myself. The more profoundly I believed there might've been something I could've done differently. Better.

If I hadn't been able to prevent Emma's death, then at least I could've avenged it. But now I couldn't even do that. My sole and final goal had been to break into that keep. There was an entire goddamned hole in the cliff leading inside the castle, but I couldn't even find my way through *that*.

I sucked.

And then there was Alcántara. My defeat was his triumph. I couldn't bear facing him, but I had no choice. Assassination class was next period. He'd know by now how I'd completed his assignment. I'd killed Toby, innocent farm boy. I'd gutted him on the end of a damned dung fork. I dreaded giving Alcántara the pleasure.

The worst part, though? It was the fear that I hadn't needed to kill him. Not really. And yet, not only had I done it, but for an instant, I'd relished it. That was the part that really sickened me.

So I'd gotten Toby after all, and what did that make me? Maybe Yasuo had spoken truly. Maybe I *was* a killer.

Yasuo. He was out there somewhere. How much longer did he have walking among us before he appeared on the other side of those bars? He felt called to the Draug already—the other Trainees had had to go out there to retrieve him.

And what of Rob? Was he even still alive? His last words had been about the girls, how we fed the vampires. Was that why Yas attacked him? Had his comment evoked memories of Emma somehow? I didn't want to contemplate what it said about me that I wished I could've been the one who'd gotten him in the end.

What did any of it matter, anyhow? I couldn't get into the castle. I was a failure all around.

Rob would probably heal. Then he'd seek me out. And I had no doubt he'd eventually find me. He'd catch me off guard, eventually. Eventually, he'd kill me.

I sloshed my spoon in my cold chicken soup, mashing soft carroty bits along the edge of the bowl. Lunch was winding down. I heard the clack of dishes and cutlery. Chairs scraping. Chatter grew louder as kids drifted by, then faded as they bused their dishes and headed out the door. The noises grew fewer and farther between.

I felt a body sit next to me at the table. *Ronan.* Surprise, surprise. I felt his lecture mode vibrate along my side.

"You are too reckless."

I met his eyes. "This is news?"

An instant's vulnerability put me on my guard, and I carefully schooled all emotion from my face. I feared if I let the tiniest bit show, the dam would break and I'd snap completely.

"Going out with me in the dory is one thing, but roving the countryside"—he paused to temper his voice, pitching it calmer, quieter . . . steelier—"that is another matter entirely. I've begged you to have a care. There has been too much sneaking around. You're in danger of . . ."

"Of getting killed? Duh."

He was silent for a moment, and I glanced up expecting to see his Ronan-look, but the tenderness that waited for me instead caught me off guard. "In danger of losing it. Of losing yourself. Losing heart. Forgetting who you are, truly." He touched the backs of his fingers to my cheek. It was the lightest of touches, but I felt it sear through me. Was he using his powers, or was it simply the heat of his touch? "You must protect yourself. And I don't simply mean your body." His fingers traced down my neck to my chest. "You must guard your heart. Who you are."

I could protect myself. The first step would be to put a stop to this confusing interaction. I edged away from him. "Don't you get it?"

That snapped him out of it. "What I get is that you need to stop wandering off campus," he said sternly.

"They have to be stopped, Ronan. *I'm* going to stop them."

He glanced around quickly, ensuring no one was within earshot. It looked like steam might shoot from his ears. "I caution you, Annelise. Do not underestimate the power of those in charge. These little excursions of yours—don't be fooled. The vampires may not catch everything, but they see more than you think. You've been given much latitude, but it's because you're one of Alcántara's greatest amusements. Do not miscalculate the situation. To him, you are merely a toy. A plaything. The days of his patience, tolerance, and I daresay, curiosity will one day come to a close, and the moment Hugo tires of you, the moment he feels you've crossed him, he will dispose of you without so much as blinking."

He paused to let it sink in, then added more quietly, "Do not forget these things. Keep your vision clear, unclouded by passion. You want revenge, yes. But you must not let rage blind you. Blind rage kills."

"Like I killed Toby, you mean?"

He deflated, seeing my pain. "Aye," he said gently. "Like Toby."

The sympathy in his voice was dangerously close to breaking something inside me. To guard against it, I forced some cynical cheer. "They're all just monsters anyway, right?"

But Ronan didn't smile at my joke. Rather, he remained serious as ever. "And you must mind that you don't become like them. You have been reckless"—he put up a hand to stop me before I could grumble, *this again?*—"reckless with your person, with who you are, and if you don't stop, then you have become the monster."

Me. A monster.

My father's daughter. Someone who preyed on those weaker than me.

It cut too deeply to contemplate. Too close to my greatest fear. I lashed out. "Is that all you came to tell me?"

There was a beat of tense silence. A shift in mood. The unspoken mutual agreement that we were changing topic.

"I must go away for a while," he said.

Of course. I was getting all too used to guys going away for a while. I wanted to say, "Not you, too," but dared not draw a parallel between Ronan and any vampires. I'd learned my lesson by now.

Instead, I forced my voice to sound casual as I asked, "Off island?"

"I have business in the village. For the upcoming festival. Preparations must be overseen."

"You'll come back." I didn't know if it was a question or a statement.

"I will." He paused, shifted. I noted a tensing in his jaw. What emotion was he concealing? "You must promise you'll keep yourself safe in the meantime."

I chuffed a little laugh. "Don't you get tired of looking out for me?" I knew what the answer would be, but still, I needed to hear it. Just then, I longed for support. A friend. It struck me how much I'd come to count on him for that since Carden's disappearance.

Lately, my vampire hadn't been here when I needed it, but Ronan had. Ronan spent so much energy concerning himself with what he *should* do, what was right, while Carden was all about what he *wanted* to do. And apparently, what he wanted to do didn't involve me.

"Annelise, I don't trust that look. You must promise you will avoid trouble."

"Check. No recklessness." I gave Ronan a smile. Unfortunately, it felt as weak as my promise.

Assassination class was as hideous as I'd feared.

After Alcántara had complimented me on my kill for the

umpteenth time, I finally snapped. "I beg your pardon, Master Alcántara," I said when I sensed my moment to get a word in edgewise. "The thing is, I didn't *mean* to kill Toby." It felt good to be honest. Ronan's words had resonated with me—I'd keep hold of who I was, of my humanity. I was the master of my soul.

"Ah, *querida*, but kill him you did. And in a most magnificent way."

I squirmed in my seat. "But killing him wasn't my intent." Not truly. Maybe if I repeated it enough, it'd become truth.

"A boy of the land," he continued grandly, clearly ignoring me, "a young farmer, killed by an agricultural implement." He chuckled, looking tickled.

It infuriated me. Because of me, there'd been more death. And I was being praised for it. He was crediting me with the kill. More, he respected me for it.

"Yeah, the ho used a hoe," someone said from behind me. Giggles erupted throughout the room.

I whirled around in my seat to glare and couldn't help noting how the class had thinned even more in the past weeks. Apparently, not everyone was as "successful" at their assignment as I'd been.

Like roots forcing their way into cold earth, my anger—at Alcántara, at this hideous island—twined deeper into my soul. I would not become a monster. The monster Alcántara wanted me to be.

Rather than discipline the girls, Alcántara actually grew serious over the asinine insight. "It is my understanding that Acari Drew used a pitchfork. Although a hoe would indeed have added a compelling layer of meaning."

I sank low in my chair. Because . . . What. The. Hell. We were so not having this discussion, were we?

He strolled to the back of the class, and I fantasized I might trip him as he glided by. But instead he paused at my desk, telling me in a confiding tone, "This was my dream for you."

I remained silent. What could I say to that without digging an even deeper hole for myself? Alcántara would know how much I was hating this. He held my gaze, trapping me further. When he spoke again, it was slowly and with intent. "I knew you'd not disappoint me."

It was my own fault. I'd lost control. My actions had painted me into a corner. I was becoming the island, and Alcántara would know I'd hate that most of all.

Yasuo's fate held a lesson for me. His transition would be my cautionary tale about what happened when you lost sight of the important things—things like mercy, or compassion. My friend might've been gone to me, but *I* had a chance to come back from the edge.

The first step would be to get myself under control. Ronan had said it best: Blind rage killed. All my anger, my self-righteousness . . . all this emotion roiling inside me. I needed to tame it. To be calmer. Clearer about my goal. Because that goal had crystallized, growing beyond a simple desire to break into the keep and un- cover its mysteries. I vowed to myself, I wouldn't become the environment around me. I would triumph over the monsters.

I would triumph over Alcántara.

"As Acari Drew has demonstrated, violence is a craft," Al- cántara said, resuming his lecture. "Today we begin our unit on the *Arthashastra*, an ancient Indian text and one of the first to address the art in such courageous detail." He'd wandered back to the front of the class, looked at his desk, and frowned. "Ah, but I have forgotten the book in my office."

I went on instant alert. There was no "forgetting" with Alcántara. Every single thing was considered and remembered.

"Acari Drew," he said, and I thought, *Here it comes.* "Perhaps you can help."

I stood, bracing. What did he have up his sleeve? "Yes, Master Alcántara?"

He grabbed his black leather man-purse from where he'd hung it on his chair and pulled out a key chain. "Please go to my office and retrieve the book for me."

My breath caught. *This* was not what I'd been expecting. Some bizarre, previously unimagined cruelty unleashed on me in front of my fellow classmates—now, that I'd have guessed. But his keys? I definitely hadn't anticipated *keys*.

Did this mean he'd considered my offer and that I was to be his teacher's assistant? Had he given *Masha* access to his office? I pushed away the thought—I couldn't afford to consider the implications of his trust, only the potential benefits. Because keys made me think of that locked gate.

Surely Alcántara had in his possession the means to unlock his own tunnel.

"Come, come." He jingled the keys. "We've not all day. And this is a task to which you must accustom yourself . . . if you are to be my research assistant."

"Your . . . Pardon me?" Would my plan go this smoothly? Had I heard him right? The gasps behind me suggested I had.

"Children," he said in answer, "congratulate your peer. Her most successful completion of this assignment has merited her the role of class helper."

His little helper. It was just as Ronan had warned. Alcántara and I were playing a game of chess, and with each move, I came one step closer to becoming his pawn. His monster.

By killing an innocent Trainee, I'd crossed a line I'd never crossed before. Alcántara thought this transgression declared me as his. I couldn't change the past, but I could take control of my future. The Spanish vampire wanted to claim me as *his* creature . . . and I wouldn't let him.

I would stop him.

"We've not got all day, *cariño.*"

"Of course." I kept my voice even, while inside my heart was hammering. I accepted the keys. There were only a few on the ring, all of them resembling the ones we girls had been issued— old and tarnished, looking like things that might unlock pirates' chests. "It will be a supreme honor," I lied with a smile.

Ronan's warning echoed in my head. I needed to temper myself. Alcántara's office was just upstairs. What was I going to do? Toss his desk, looking for something—a medallion, a plaque, what?—that had an infinity symbol on it, all in the ninety seconds it'd take for me to go up there and get his stupid book and come back down? Not hardly.

This was a long game. I'd be patient. Work it through. I'd be as canny a strategist as he was.

I allowed myself a moment to scan his office. He certainly had ulterior motives for appointing me his assistant. Did he want to make me feel trapped in a corner? Merely keep an eye on me? Whatever his reason, it didn't matter. I'd make it benefit me as much as it did him and memorized as many details as I could, no matter how ordinary.

I snagged the book from atop his desk and headed back to

class, walking slowly, my mind racing. My hand began to ache, and I realized that, in my nerves, I'd been clutching the key ring so hard it was cutting into me. I looped it on the fingers of my other hand and wiped my palm on the leg of my catsuit. The keys had left a faint impression in my skin, the ghost of them highlighted by rusty smudges.

An impression.

That was it. I'd make an impression of that infinity symbol. Maybe if I made a cast of it, I'd be able to puzzle out the key.

I was just a few yards from the classroom when I realized Alcántara had stopped speaking. He was waiting for me, and I was dawdling. Good way to lose my new job before I even began.

I jogged the last few steps, but my foot hit a wet spot on the tile, and I slipped, needing to catch myself on the doorjamb not to fall. A bunch of girls laughed, and I stamped my boot, glaring at the melting slush we'd tromped in from outside. It was January—it was impossible not to track in the stuff. Gritty puddles were everywhere.

And that was when it hit me. I knew who had materials good for casting. Things like putty and caulk and chemicals that would be easy to steal.

The janitor.

In my whole time on the island, I'd spotted the maintenance man just once—slipping like a ghost into the boiler room—and that was only because I had a penchant for visiting the science library at odd hours.

I placed Master Al's book on the lectern and gave him a great big sunny smile.

Ronan was right: I didn't want to be this person I was becoming. This monster, respected by monsters. I knew now what I wanted, and it wasn't the vampires' praise.

Carden had once told me how I was his light. I'd tasted darkness, and one day I would come away from it. But first I'd need to linger just a little while longer.

I'd think this through and do it right. I'd be like Sonja, the Sonja from the runes, a woman who'd ruled. I'd draw my power from within. I'd be strength and grit and calm vision.

I'd see inside that castle if it killed me. Because now I had an additional plan.

First I'd sit through class. Later I'd go back to the dorm. I'd wait till Frost was at dinner. I'd hone my stakes.

Soon I'd track the Spanish vampire in his lair. I'd track him and then I'd stake him.

I'd stake Alcántara.

My thoughts were that simple.

I'd get Alcántara before he changed who I was.

CHAPTER THIRTY-ONE

I couldn't exactly wander the halls, hoping I'd run into the custodian. And even if I did run in to him, then . . . what? Just walk up to him and ask if I could borrow any materials he might have that were capable of casting a shape at an awkward angle and then hardening despite the cold and damp? Or I could simply sock him on the head and take what I needed.

Not.

Recalling Alcántara's almost comically revolted expression at the sight of that puddle was ultimately what gave me the solution to my problem. I didn't know if it was the result of being hundreds of years old, or if it was the thing that made a creature survive for that long in the first place, but these old dudes, they put a high price on neatness and order. And there was someone on the island who particularly despised untidiness. Someone who had a fetish for all things custodial.

The headmaster.

He gave janitorial punishments all the time. The day Emma

and I had stood together against the Guidons, to chastise her, Headmaster Fournier had forced Emma to clean toilets as her punishment.

I pushed away the memory. I couldn't let emotion cripple me. I needed clear focus. I told myself it was this sort of cool logic that would ultimately help me get my head above the deluge of loss drowning me. But would it be enough to erase the confusion, chagrin, and heartbreak that was Carden? Would anything ever be enough for that?

I stiffened my upper lip. I was roots in the earth. I was cold stone. I was grit and vision. I was Watcher. Or I would be if I lived that long.

I knocked on Headmaster Fournier's door, a cup of coffee in my hand. It was tepid—it wouldn't do well to burn the guy—but I'd waited for the dregs, and I imagined it was all nice and silty with thick, goopy grounds.

His voice was muffled from behind the door. "Come."

"Good afternoon, Headmaster Fournier." I used my most formal tone—I wanted to earn a simple janitorial punishment, not an evisceration. "I hope I'm not interrupting."

It took a lot of gall, doing the casual drop-by like this, and his expression was a mix of curious and surprised. "This is not the best time. But I confess, I'm intrigued." He glanced over my shoulder, as though an explanation for my appearance might present itself. He didn't look angry, though, and that was something. I guessed it took a lot to rouse a vampire's curiosity, and they probably didn't mind when it happened.

I thanked him with a smile and said, "I'll be quick."

There was no stopping now. I walked in and put my cup right

on his desk. It made a ceramic *clack* sound, and coffee sloshed over the sides.

Horrified astonishment instantly marred his handsome face. "Young lady, this is not a café."

Nerves had me giddy, and I had to bite my cheek not to giggle at his expression. "I'm so sorry," I said with my chirpiest voice and scooped the cup back up. It'd left a gratifyingly dark ring, which I promptly set to dabbing with my sleeve. I was walking a fine line here. I needed to be careful—bad enough to earn a minor disciplinary action, but not so bad I'd lose my life over it. "Oh no. This is terrible. My sincerest apologies."

"What did you want?" He addressed me as though he had something distasteful on his tongue.

Okay. So a coffee ring on his antique desk didn't do it. I'd need to go further. If I spilled on his shirt, I might get laundry duty, but what would I do with a bunch of soap? No, I needed *janitorial* duty—maintenance guys surely had all kinds of chemicals and tools at their disposal.

"I needed to ask you about something," I said, thinking fast. Honestly, I'd expected to be punished the moment I walked in. "It can wait, though. If this is a bad time."

"I told you it was not. Now speak before you try my patience further."

"I had a question about . . . an academic matter." I widened my senses, assessing his office as best I could without actually pausing to look around. Beneath his desk was a gorgeous Aubusson throw rug, with a floral pattern in shades of pale peach, sky blue, and ivory. I prayed it wasn't priceless and irreplaceable, because spilled coffee could really mess it up good.

I needed to get behind his desk. I stepped forward.

"Stop," he said sharply. "You have thirty seconds to tell me why you're here before I pursue disciplinary measures."

"I beg your pardon, Headmaster. It's just your office is so overwhelming. I'll make it quick." Thinking fast, I said, "I wanted to propose we establish a TA program."

"TA?" He articulated each letter as though I were speaking some foreign tongue.

I nodded enthusiastically. "Like teacher's assistants, research assistants, that sort of thing. Like at real colleges."

"This is not a real college." He scooted back like he was about usher me out himself.

It was now or never.

I made like I tripped.

My cup spilled, the dregs of my nasty coffee unfurling like a black spiderweb across that pretty carpet.

Fournier made a horrified gasp. He pointed to the door. "Acari Drew. You will report to the janitor, with whom you will spend the rest of your day."

Score.

Custodial storage was in an outbuilding around the back of— go figure—the old chapel. With just a single hanging bulb, the place was dark, cold, and dank, and considering the small garden plot languishing behind the chapel, I guessed that it'd begun its life as a potting shed. I peeked inside, and where most would see basic cleaning supplies, I saw a gold mine. Just a quick scan, and I was able to identify enough materials to assemble several Molotov cocktails, a thrilling number of stakes, and the makings of enough toxic gases to choke an entire building. Surely among all this crap, I could find something to make a simple cast of that medallion.

When my eyes came to the workbench, I gaped. Dozens of keys hung above—there was hook after hook of them, bearing keys old and new, in all sizes, on all manner of rings, chains, and retractable loops. Once I figured out the casting thing, I could turn my attention here. Every locked door on campus would be mine. "Damn," I whispered.

"Mind your tongue or you'll be cleaning toilets with it."

I startled, cursing myself that I'd let the janitor—the *janitor*, for pity's sake—surprise me from behind. What was wrong with me? Letting Trainees catch me unawares was bad enough, but this was just plain sloppy. Was it the absence of Carden's blood that was making me so distracted? I needed to stop tempting fate and *focus*.

I quickly assessed the man, and just one look was enough to tell me what a charmer he was. I hadn't known what to expect, maybe a slice of affable village quirkiness, à la Tom the Draug keeper, but this guy was about as pleasant as dental work. Which he clearly needed, BTW.

"Sorry," I said, on instant alert. I estimated he was in his fifties, with the heavily ridged brow generally associated with Neanderthals, lifelong mental asylum inmates, and the sort of creepy loners who lurked after teenaged girls like me. I decided to play it polite, wanting to make as few ripples in his little pond as possible. "Just tell me what I need to do."

"Swab." He thrust a mop into my hands.

Swab? What was he, a pirate? I scrunched my nose as a rank smell made me consider the thing in my hands. I held the mop as far away from my body as possible, certain I was tempting all manner of fungal infections simply by holding it. It'd been cleaning floors for decades, and if I'd assumed that'd make it clean, I'd have assumed wrong.

In fact, the whole outbuilding smelled off, like a sickening mix of noxious cleaners and damp stone. "You don't sleep in here, do you?" I had to ask it—I had a feeling I'd be breaking back in here and I didn't want any surprises when I did.

"Rats sleep in here. I look like a rat to you?"

"Of course not," I muttered. *It's only your teeth that are rodentlike.*

So, me and Mr. Dynamic weren't going to be fast friends. But scanning his shelves sure consoled me. All those boxes, aerosol cans, and canisters bearing unrecognizable foreign brand names—some kind of molding material was sure to be among them. And besides, there were worse things than spending the afternoon crawling behind Fournier's desk, swabbing spilled coffee. Who knew what secrets I might stumble across down there?

It was time to get started. I approached the shelf. "Where's the carpet cleaner?"

"No." He said it as though he were scolding a bad dog.

Uh . . . okay. "No?"

He sneered at me. "Girls clean lavatories."

I dug my nails into the mop handle, deciding that *Mr. Forward Thinker* better watch his back—I'd proven myself a whiz at long, sticked household items. "Is that so?"

Temper, I reminded myself. This guy was white noise, just a blip on my radar. I already had a bright and shining objective.

He shouldered past me, his hand going straight for a specific key chain among all the others on the wall. I got just a brief glimpse, and it sent my mind reeling. The key fob was a figure eight—one half was the ring holding the keys, but the other half was solid, with a triangle etched in its center.

That was the symbol—the symbol on the gate. Could it really be this easy? Was it just an emblem, or could this thing unlock the tunnel? It seemed preposterous, but why not? Service people had to enter the castle somehow.

As he turned for the door, I said, "Wait." I braved a step closer, thinking fast. "Are those the keys to the lavatories? If you point me in the right direction, I can go ahead and get started." I held out my hand, trying not to shake.

He snatched it out of my reach. "Girls don't get keys."

Of course not. Forcing a smile, I glanced at the workbench and pretended to marvel at his collection of keys. "It's amazing how you went right to the correct one." I looked back at the key chain in his hand, taking in as many details as I could in the dim shed. The infinity symbol looked the same size as the one on the padlock. The only difference was the triangle—this one was flat, neither protruding from nor indented in the metal. The whole thing was old and rusty looking, like he'd just dug it up from where it'd been buried in the dirt for about a hundred years. There were only two keys on it. "I mean, there aren't even that many keys on there."

He stared at the ring in his hand as though it were the stupidest thing in the world—after *me*, of course. "Them's passingkeys" was all he said, and then his cheek twitched. A real conversationalist, this one.

I leaned against my mop. He seemed anxious to leave, but I wasn't budging. "I beg your pardon?"

He grunted, then finally, grudgingly repeated, "Passingkeys." He'd said it louder, as though that might clarify matters.

I stepped even closer, approaching as slowly as I would a rabid dog. But it was worth the risk. Who knew there'd be such bounty in the janitor's shed? Forget a cast of the medallion. If I could somehow make a copy of *this*, I'd be golden. "Passingkey? Is that like a skeleton key?"

He snatched his hand back, his eyes suddenly hard, suspicious in a way that genuinely alarmed me. "You're nosy."

It was time for Drew Plan B: Relying on the Ignorant Assumptions of Others.

People saw a diminutive blonde and assumed the worst. Sometimes it served me to embrace it and simply become the cliché, which, just then, meant I began to babble like an airhead. "Oh, I'm not nosy," I said, pasting a big smile on my face. "I just really loved my Phenomena class. You know Phenomena? That was where we learned how to pick locks. We learned about tumblers and padlocks and bump keys but this sort of lever lock key that you have is new to me, and . . . *Hey, look* . . ." I squinted my eyes, meanwhile noting every detail with a precision that would've surprised this jerk. The infinity symbol seemed an exact replica in size and shape to the one on the sea gate. The keys themselves were weathered bronze, one with two teeth at the end of a thin haft, the other bearing just a single, thick bit. They were a standard size, matching my room key. Matching *Alcántara's* keys. I made all kinds of mental notes to consider later. "Wow, that is so cool." I pointed. "The loopy part at the top of that one even looks like a little skull. Oh, neat, I just got it. Do you get it? *Skeleton* key . . . *skull?* Do you see it? There at the top? It's like a teensy tiny—"

He turned abruptly for the door. "I got no time for this, girl. Chatter like a magpie on your own time."

I gave his back a great big grin. *Make time for* this, *jerkface.*

By the time midnight rolled around, my mood was more subdued. Before I could sneak back into the janitor's grim little hideaway, I needed to wait until Frost was asleep. Which, unfortunately, gave me way too much time to think.

In the wee hours like this, my anger at Carden always turned to dread. He'd been gone too long. I needed to confront the possibility that something had happened to him, something awful. He should've reappeared by now—to feed, at the very least. In my heart of hearts, I knew he'd have been here if he could . . . which meant some force was preventing him.

It was unbearable to contemplate. So much easier to remain angry.

I eased my mind, imagining how it would be if he *were* here. He'd tell me his funny stories and take my mind off my fear. Because I was afraid—this was a giant risk I was taking.

When I finally ventured out, the night was moonless. I knew firsthand how there were way too many things that saw better than I did in the pitch-darkness, but I assured myself I wasn't even really off the path—I was smack-dab in the middle of the quad. Which, when I thought about it, was scarier than anything.

I'd have to be quick, and wasn't that just the understatement of the year. But I had no choice. I'd shadowed that dumb man all day, and never once had he parted from his key chain. So much for him thinking it was stupid. I'd tried everything, even spilling an entire canister of Comet in the toilet. Then, claiming the need for more, I'd asked to borrow his keys to get back in the shed for supplies, and still he'd guarded them jealously, like the fate of the world depended on them. That, more than anything, told me I was on the right track. That his key ring might be my solution.

I squatted in front of the shed door for a closer look at the dead bolt. I'd cased the place well enough to know exactly what to expect and which tools to bring to break into his grim little hideaway. If I'd had a tension wrench, this thing would've been a piece of cake, but of course, there was no such thing in the rudimentary lock-picking kit we'd been assigned—the vampires weren't going to make it *that* easy on us. I'd have to get enough torque by using my file. Plus, I'd saved a can from the dining hall and folded a strip of aluminum into something narrow enough to fit in the keyhole but still sturdy enough to lever the pins.

I got to work.

My hands were raw, and I smelled like Borax, Windex, Ajax, and whatever other x-caliber toxicity I'd been exposed to all day, but it'd been worth it. It was hard going in the darkness, but finally I decided just to give in to it and shut my eyes, picking the lock by feel and instinct alone. Sure enough, the mechanism gave with a soft click.

Thank you, Judge, I thought, with a pang for my beloved-but-now-dead Phenomena teacher.

I cracked the door open as narrowly as possible, terrified the hinges might squeak if I swung it open all the way. I was worried about any makeshift traps, too—setting an alarm constructed of precariously stacked cans seemed like just the sort of thing the sourpuss maintenance man might do.

My heart punched at my chest. There'd be no Carden to save me if I got caught. Though the worst punishment would come from Ronan. I'd disappointed him once before, when they'd discovered my illicit iPod, and the look he'd given me had razed me. I didn't want to see that expression ever again.

Ever so slowly, I slipped inside, carefully placing a foot, waiting, sliding the other foot forward, waiting, and so on until I was inside. No squeaks, no traps.

I let myself take a quick moment to calm my heartbeat and

open my senses to the night. Nothing heard me. Nobody was coming. I was safe.

Originally, I'd wanted to get close to the janitor in order to get my hands on moldable materials, but in the end, that was the one element that'd been easiest to procure—especially as there wasn't going to be any extreme cliffside castings in my future. When the janitor lit a candle inside his shed, he'd given me the answer I needed. Wax. Duh.

I went straight to the wall of keys. In the blackness of the shed, it was a mass of metal—dangerously *noisy* metal—but I'd memorized well the approximate location of that one key ring. Shutting my eyes once more, I swept my fingers lightly along until I touched it, that strange infinity shape protruding from the wall differently from the others.

I took it from its hook, cringing at the tinkling sound made by the surrounding keys. I stood frozen, heart pounding, waiting to be caught. But still, no one came.

I worked quickly from there. It was easy to get ahold of candles in this place—the vamps loved all things antiquated—and earlier I'd melted one into a smooth puddle. I quickly warmed it, praying the smell of matches didn't summon any of the many creatures on this island with hypersensitive noses.

My first attempt was uneven, and finally I decided it'd be best to press the fob itself as flatly as possible into the wax, without the keys in the way, but they were proving remarkably tricky to pull from the ring. I fiddled with the thing, my panic rising with each passing minute. Finally, I just gave it a good twist . . . but rather than the keys sliding off, something else happened. Something else entirely.

With a soft click, the triangle popped out from the fob.

I stared in disbelief. Then I burst into action, warming the wax in my palms, rolling it into a ball, winding it around the triangle, taking an exact impression.

Later, I'd whittle the ends of several stakes into the same shape. Hopefully one of them would work and be a perfect fit for that strange triangular hole. I'd use the end of a stake to open that padlock. Open the gate.

This was it. It was becoming real.

I'd do this. I was breaking into the castle.

I wondered if I'd ever come out again.

CHAPTER THIRTY-TWO

I needed to see Ronan. I wanted to say good-bye. To thank him. And maybe there was a part of me that hoped someone cared enough to see what I was doing and stop me. I longed to feel some connection with somebody before I went off pursuing certain death. I wanted someone who wasn't Vampire to know what'd happened to me. I wanted to feel—or pretend to feel— that somebody gave a damn about my fate.

I didn't want to just disappear.

Because I had no illusions: I knew well that mine was a suicide mission.

Ronan had said he was off to the village, and so I set off for the village, too. I moved quickly, keeping to the coast. If caught, I'd claim ignorance. Claim I thought my newfound Initiate status protected me. And who knew—maybe it did. My skin crawled, recalling Ronan's words, how my status as Alcántara's greatest amusement protected me, too. I shoved away the thought.

Sundays were generally quiet, and I snuck off at dawn, heading farther north than I'd ever gone. Would I find Ronan? See him among his people? Would there be family who resembled him? Some cousin with his green eyes?

Once I was close enough, I headed inland, perching on a rock, surveying the valley below. Several cottages were huddled into a small settlement. They all looked the same—squat, rough-looking things, constructed of dingy stone connected by sloppy seams of mortar, once white, now weathered to a mossy greenish gray. Every roof was thatched, curving down on either side, close enough to the ground to touch. I tried to picture Ronan moving among them—he'd have to hunch while standing inside.

What struck me first was the quiet. It was a ghost town. Nobody was around. It wasn't the picture of what I imagined a quaint village to be—there were no laughing children, no gossiping women, no bustle to be seen at all.

I went on alert. This place had a weird vibe. A hostile vibe. And of course it did—I'd be pretty hostile, too, if forced to live in service to a bunch of old vampires.

I thought with a smirk how that was exactly my situation. *Servile, hostile:* check and check.

I scooted down the far side of the hill for a closer look, moving as stealthily as I could. It went unspoken that vampires and villagers didn't mingle, but how would these people view *me*? Lately, it felt like every time I went out alone, I was attacked. I was sure I could deal with a few regular humans, but I'd prefer to avoid a mob if I could.

I began to question this whole endeavor, but still, I waited. I'd wanted a glimpse of Ronan, but now my curiosity consumed me. I wanted to see someone, anyone. Who were these people? Would they be mostly like Tom: a realist who was wary but friendly? Or would they be like that janitor? Fearful. Hateful. Suspicious.

My eyes were drawn to movement just below me, behind one of the cottages on the perimeter. I waited until I saw it again—fabric fluttering. I scooted sideways, craning my head until I was able to peer behind the building. And finally, I saw a person, a woman, moving slowly and methodically, hanging laundry out to dry.

I edged down, keeping low and out of sight—unless, of course, there was someone looking out the window, in which case, I was totally busted. But nobody spotted me.

I reached the ground, inching my way closer, careful not to tangle myself in the thorny hedges growing along the side of the cottage.

I stole a peek. She was old, with weathered skin that'd been so thinned by the years, it seemed to sag from her bones. Row after row of mud-brown cloaks billowed in the breeze, and she worked her way down the line, reaching in her basket, pulling out a cloak, pinning it up, stepping over, reaching down, and so on. Each robe was the same color, the same size, with the same long hood drooping down the back. They looked like something Druids might've worn.

She hummed as she worked, and it was such a normal thing, it gave me courage to show myself. I carefully peeked out from a wall of hedges. "Excuse me . . . hi?"

Her wizened face burst into cartoonishly wide-eyed shock, her nearly lipless and mostly toothless mouth forming a gaping black hole. She looked like a witch carved from a dried apple.

I put up my hands in the universal gesture of *Relax; it's cool*, but unfortunately she wasn't acquainted with universal gestures, because she shrieked the kind of shriek generally associated with haunted house tours.

Crap. I put a finger to my mouth, desperately motioning for her to be quiet. "Sorry, sorry. It's okay." I stepped closer. "I'm sorry I scared you. I was—"

"Oot nooo." She waved at me, shooing me like an animal, repeating, "Oot. Oot nooo."

Was that even English? I spoke slowly, just in case. "I don't mean any harm. I'm looking for—"

Frantic, she shook her head, looking like a madwoman. She seemed like she might shriek again, so I sped it up. The last thing I needed was for this woman to call for backup. I dared not tempt whatever shrieking might happen then.

"*Shh*, please don't scream. Do you know—" *Ronan*, I'd wanted to say, but I stopped myself at the last second. For all I knew, this woman adored the vampires. I couldn't get him in trouble. Going off half-cocked through the countryside was exactly what he'd warned me about. "Do you know the way back to the beach?" I asked, in the lamest topic swerve ever.

Staring at me like *I* was the nutty one, she stabbed her finger back toward where I'd come from. "Ye best oot nooo."

I best out now? Was that what she'd said? Apparently, teeth were for more than just chewing—they also really helped with the whole diction thing.

What a twisted, isolated world this was. I should've learned my lesson with the janitor—old didn't necessarily mean kindly. But now that I was here, I had to know more. I had to press it. I ducked between the robes to get closer. "Who are you?" I brushed my fingers over the brown fabric. "What are these?"

"Fer auld ones. Nae touchin'!" She waved her hands at me,

but her mania had toned down a notch. I was no longer a homicidal interloper, just a stray cat sniffing at her stuff. "Shoo!"

Old ones. Now we were talking. I took a tentative step forward. "The old ones? You mean the vampires?"

Her eyes grew wide, terror making the irises expand till her gaze was all watery red and pale blue. The vampires, then.

Again, I touched one of the robes—the texture was coarse, like burlap—and she snatched it from me. "Antonsmas," she shouted. "Antonsmas oonly. Dinna touch."

Antonsmas. That was one of the names Ronan had given to the festival.

I heard men's voices in the distance. Sound would carry across this valley—how far away were they? I spoke quickly. "They wear these for the festival?"

"Shoo," she hissed. Panic had seized her again but, tellingly, she quieted her voice to a frantic whisper. "Go, you. Away," she pleaded. "Right away."

I heard the voices again. The clatter of tools. A faraway slamming door.

I didn't know what I'd been thinking. I'd never spot Ronan here, and if I did, would he even claim to recognize me? For all I knew, the men in town all had shotguns and dined on girl flesh. Later, I'd be sad I hadn't gotten to see him once more, but I couldn't get killed before I'd even begun.

And so I shooed.

But as I wove back through the maze of robes, one happened to make its way into my bag. It would be my ticket inside the castle.

CHAPTER THIRTY-THREE

The day came. Antonsmas . . . Up Helly Aa . . . whatever they wanted to call it. I didn't care. It was my day. The day I'd break into the castle and stake Alcántara.

In a stroke of luck, Frost was nowhere to be seen as I left. Usually, she spent every free moment lurking at her desk and studying, followed by gloating about how much studying she was doing. Briefly, I wondered where on earth someone like her got to this time of day, but mostly I was just psyched. Her absence meant I didn't have to explain to anyone why I was heading out with my wetsuit on a bitter cold night, under a pitch-black moonless sky, with only an hour left till lights-out.

It was dicey moving around in the dark, when so many other creatures came out to play, but I couldn't risk being caught. For once, my main concern wasn't the guys—if Ronan was right, the vampires and Trainees would be busy in the keep, whereas I could think of a dozen Initiates who'd love nothing more than to tell on me for sneaking around like this . . . assuming they stopped pummeling me long enough to think about it.

I'd actually worn my wetsuit under my coat and congratulated myself on the stroke of genius. The neoprene material was thick and would keep me warmer than my catsuit, yet was also snug enough to move freely and climb in. And who knew? If I slipped, the thing might even protect me from superficial wounds. In my first year, I'd mended enough tears in my uniform not to underestimate that particular side benefit.

I'd already scoped out the best and least steep spot to make my descent. Now that I knew the exact location of the sea gate, I hoped to have an easier time navigating the hillside, picking my way across and down—with an emphasis on *down*. The tide was at its highest peak, and wetsuit or not, I had no intention of setting foot in that water. A freezing night swim in that black churning sea frightened me more than the vampires' keep did.

I shed my coat once I reached the cliff's edge, rolling it into a ball and stashing it by a rock. Would I survive the night to retrieve it, or would some nosy Acari eventually find it instead? Everyone could wave it around and celebrate how tenacious me had finally met my end.

I couldn't think that way. As low as I'd felt lately, I needed to be positive. To taste success. To imagine it as an inevitable thing.

This is for you, Emma.

And for me, too, I thought. I'd reclaim myself, no matter the risk. And the risk, I knew, was tremendous. It could very well be my last.

Sucking in a deep breath, I looked out into the vastness, taking in the night. The moon was just a tiny crescent hanging low in the sky, and water swept before me, rippling like black satin sheets tucked somewhere beyond the horizon. Ronan had once told me to embrace the darkness, and I saw now what he meant. I felt cloaked in it. One with it. The night was mine.

The darkness was far from complete, though, and it was due to more than merely my improved vision. It was the stars. Millions of them clung here at the edge of the world, spattered across the sky like paint flung from a brush. Magnificent, they stole my breath, as though I'd never even known stars before *Eyja næturinnar*. The island's one gift to me.

Or rather, one of its gifts. I would receive something more tonight, only it was something I'd steal: the truth. I would wrest the secret of this island if it took my dying breath to do it.

I was resolved. Time to do this thing.

I did a body check, wriggling my feet, feeling the stars tucked in my boots. I flexed my arms, testing the stakes I'd jammed up the sleeves of my wetsuit . . . stakes whose ends were carved like so many triangles.

The cloak I'd stolen was lashed across my chest like armor. I hoped it would be my armor in truth, disguising me enough to get into the castle unsuspected. I needed only enough time to find Alcántara. To take him by surprise. Stake him.

My night from there looked iffy, but I was okay with that. Because I'd be me until the end. Not Alcántara's creature. Not a dupe in service of vampires.

Starlight hummed on my back as I descended. Confidence and resolve guided my hands and feet. I found holds so easily, it felt like magic. *Thank you, Carden*. He'd taught me about climbing. Me, his dove with wings of fire.

The thought was a blade, quick and deep, there and rejected just as quickly. I'd be even more than what he'd believed possible—I'd have a heart of fire, too.

I came to a thick shelf of brush. I knew the gate was concealed just below. I shimmied around and down, and then I was there. On the rock plateau.

The porch, I thought with a smile.

I was so close now, and oddly, my heartbeat was slow. My hearing was hollow, my vision focused to a narrow point. This was it, and I was calm.

I pulled the gloves from my hands, wadded them up, and shoved them inside my suit. Twining my fingers around the bars of the gate, I leaned close and held still, holding my breath, opening to the universe to feel if anyone was near. But the tunnel was dark and silent.

It was time to break in.

I had five crude stakes in varying lengths and sizes; two hadn't been thick enough to carve into a triangle, but I had three possible fits. This gate and its lock were a mystery to me—if one of the stakes actually slid into place, whatever happened next would just have to be a surprise. At this point, I *hoped* there'd be a surprise. The thought of climbing back up that hill, defeated again, was too much to bear.

I inserted the first triangle and gave it a jiggle. Too small. I told myself no big deal and went to the next one. But the angle on that one was slightly too obtuse. I could use one of my stars to whittle it to size, but I didn't want to waste the time if I didn't have to. I willed myself to be calm as I tried the next and final one. It slid in perfectly.

I waited. But nothing happened.

I wiggled the end of the stake. Turned it. I pushed down, pulled up, but still nothing. Panic began to crackle up my back, numbing my fingers and ratcheting up my heartbeat. I felt around the triangle. The fit was snug, but it was in there. I pried and twisted, and all it did was give me a splinter.

My panic began to bleed out into despair. Was this it? I tried to tell myself it was only a temporary setback, that I'd just have to go back to the drawing board. But such things were easy to say and hard to believe.

Despair hardened into frustration. Was I destined to keep failing like this? How was it the damned vampires still managed to get the best of me when they weren't even around?

Frustration sharpened into anger.

"Dammit." I slammed the side of my fist onto the butt of the stake. "Damn you." Then I hit it again, harder. I'd curse all I wanted now—I didn't care. I cursed and hit. "Damn damn damn all of—"

There was a sharp click.

"Crap!" I jumped about a foot in the air as the medallion sprang apart.

And then I giggled. Putting a hand to my pounding chest, I peered closer. "Holy crap." I'd done it. The outer casing had been spring-loaded, and when I pounded the stake, the infinity had split in two, popping open and revealing the inner workings of the lock.

Tentatively, I tried twisting the stake again, and this time the triangle turned easily. The ancient tumbler clicked. The gate cracked open.

I sat for a shocked moment, listening to the crashing of the waves and the silence of the beckoning tunnel. I smiled. And then I scrambled in.

The tunnel was dank, like something that'd been chiseled through the mountain centuries ago. The sulfurous smell was even stronger inside. I'd smelled it once before, fighting Lilac beside a hot spring deep underground. How extensive were these caverns? It was a disturbing thought.

I resheathed my stakes and scrabbled forward. Soon the tunnel expanded into something tall enough to stand in hunched over, then eventually to stand up straight.

I slipped on my cloak, shoving two of the stakes in the pockets, just in case. I readjusted the wetsuit underneath, tugging the legs back into place. The outfit might've been ideal for climbing in the freezing wind, but it was starting to bum me out now. Even so, it remained the best choice. I'd nabbed an extra shooter of blood at lunch and had rubbed some on my body in hopes of masking my scent, and what the blood didn't mask, I hoped this pesky wetsuit would. Months of salt water had given it a briny odor—enough, I hoped, to hide what I was certain was the unmistakable smell of girl.

Because surely we had scents, right? After all, the vampires were predators, and we girls their prey. The not knowing lodged a spike of resentment in my heart. Why hadn't Carden explained such things to me? Why wasn't he here now? I'd once come to his aid, in a dank tunnel not unlike this one.

Then it struck me—that other tunnel had been unlike this in a *very fundamental way*: This tunnel wasn't pitch black.

Crap. I immediately darted to the side, clinging against the cold stone. I'd been so focused on my stupid clothes, and the difference between starlight and this ambient light was so subtle, I hadn't considered it. But ambient light meant there was electricity, or at least torches, somewhere nearby.

Light meant people.

I edged forward, every sense so attuned to my surroundings, I began to imagine sights and sounds that weren't there. I gave my head a shake. *Can't lose my grip now.*

Soon the torches appeared, hung in occasional sconces along the tunnel walls. Just as it got too dark to see, the flickering halo of a distant torch would become visible.

The first time a tunnel branched off the main one, it gave me pause, but in my gut I had the sense of the castle's location and I followed its pull. Was it the vampires calling me? The thought was too disturbing to entertain for long.

As I progressed, more and more smaller tunnels branched off the main one, and the maze of passages was getting complicated. I hid in dark crevices as I went, stopping frequently to make sure I had my bearings and that nobody was around.

I also tried desperately not to think of Carden. In these, what felt like my final moments, all my anger and resentment dissolved, and I just felt sad and alone. I really, really missed him. I wished I could've seen him one last time. I wished I could've known where he'd gone. Why.

The curve of the tunnel ahead threw sound at me, and I heard footsteps and the *whip-whip* of torches. A solemn procession walked by. Terrified, I held my breath and waited till they were well past to exhale. I sucked in a breath and something twinged at my nose. Incense. I waited a full minute after they'd passed before I followed.

But then voices echoed to me, coming from another tunnel.

I froze. More people. They might've been rounding the next corner or hundreds of yards away. The sound bounced off the rock, impossible to tell how close.

I strained my ears, making sense of individual speakers. Individual words. I placed one of the voices. It was so familiar to me, as familiar as any other on this rock.

It was Alcántara.

CHAPTER THIRTY-FOUR

Alcántara was speaking with someone. Slowly, I slid a stake into my hand. I parted my feet, imagining myself connected to the tunnel. I was a part of this mountain. A creature of the dark. I *was* the mountain. I relaxed my legs, felt the bounce in my knees. I was power *and* strength. I'd been born for this moment.

Could it be this easy? Might I take him unaware? I'd kill Alcántara, and though his companion might turn around and kill me, *he'd* be destroyed.

I'd have avenged Emma. Avenged Yasuo.

I strained to make sense of the conversation. The volume didn't vary, so I took the risk that they'd stopped moving. I edged closer, to the lip of a branching tunnel. And then I halted, my every muscle seizing in place.

Alcántara was speaking with a woman.

I strained further, expecting to make out the familiar voice of a Guidon or a Watcher I might know, but what I heard instead shocked me. It was deference . . . in *Alcántara's* voice. He was speaking with a woman he feared.

There was talk of the list. Of the arrivals. It was hard to understand. They spoke English, but hers was heavily accented.

I braved a few steps closer. My knuckles hurt from the grip on my stake.

One of them shifted, and her voice suddenly bounced off the rocks, thrown to me as though aimed directly at my ears.

"You failed me, Hugo."

"You have my most humble apologies, Mistress Sonja."

Oh God. My legs wobbled. I leaned against the tunnel wall for support. *Sonja?*

"Why did you deliver the girl you did?" she demanded. Was this actually *the* Sonja speaking? Could that even be possible? *Sonja, ruler of vampires.* Had that meant Sonja herself had been Vampire? Did Sonja rule the vampires still?

Alcántara cleared his throat. He was nervous. I tuned in closely, replaying in my head what I'd already heard. He'd delivered a girl. . . . She hadn't been the right one. I shuddered, considering just how many girls were at his disposal. How many had he "delivered" in his lifetime, and to what ends? "The girl's friend was as dangerous to—"

"Spare me your excuses," she snapped. "I told you I need the golden one. How is it possible you lost control of such a simple scenario? *Two girls enter*, you said. *Only one will leave.*"

A bitter chill shot through my veins, settling like ice in the pit of my stomach. *Two girls enter; only one will leave.* . . . That could refer to none other than my fight with Emma. I had blond hair— was I the golden one?

"I believed the other girl would suffice," he said in a disturbingly meek tone. Had he been trying to help me? And what did that do to my plan? My goal hadn't just been revenge—it'd been to discover the truth. Would I kill Alcántara with so many questions left unanswered? I lowered my stake arm, knowing I wouldn't.

"That mealy farm child?" *Farm child*—she had to mean Emma. By bringing Emma to the castle instead of me, had Alcántara actually been *protecting* me? I remembered his creepy, cold kiss. Was his intent to keep me from harm or merely keep me for himself? "Tell me what I need with such a creature."

So what happened to my friend? What happened to girls they didn't need?

"You have my humblest apologies, mistress, if I have inconvenienced you with my most foolish error." Alcántara's deference frightened me. Because if he was protecting me from her, it didn't bode well for my situation.

"As well you have inconvenienced me, Hugo. Such a vulgar child she is. I cannot use her."

I clapped a hand to my mouth to stop my gasp. *Cannot* use her. Not *couldn't* use her. Present tense.

Could Emma be *alive*? Still alive, here in the castle?

I didn't have time to contemplate. Noises echoed down the tunnel toward me. A group of people were headed my way. Quickly, I pulled the hood of my robe low over my face. The fabric scratched at me and tickled my nose. I held my breath.

More sounds, closer now. Voices, young ones. Trainees. I concentrated, but the acoustics were just too warped, bouncing through such a vast warren of tunnels, that I couldn't make sense of how many were coming or from where.

I curved my shoulders, hoping my height would seem

merely like bad posture. I clung to the shadows, making like I was busy attending something in my hands. Maybe they'd look right past me.

I needn't have worried so much. When they did pass, it wasn't in my tunnel from behind, but rather they crossed in front of me, moving down an intersecting passage ahead. They didn't see me in the shadows. In fact, they were weaving as though drunk.

The boy in the lead carried a torch, illuminating the procession enough for me to make out details. They all wore the same brown cloak I did—thank you, washerwoman, for the tip—but in addition, each wore an elaborate mask. There was one with tiger stripes. One was so pale, it almost glowed, bearing a long, beaklike nose. Another was plumed with fluffy, emerald-green feathers. One that sparkled with gems and plump, rosy cheeks. Each was different and no less gaudy than the last.

A few of the boys carried censers hanging from chains. The bronze globes swayed with each step, sending smoke wafting. A wall of incense hit me, and my reaction was instant—it was a sudden rush in my brain, a loopy, muzzy sensation that passed as the boys did.

What the hell was in that smoke?

I hunched a little more and, covering my nose with my hood, I followed. A boy at the end was straggling. He paused, putting his hands on his knees to catch his breath, but his friends didn't notice. When the tunnel rounded out of sight, I came up behind him. Struck him hard on the temple with the butt of my stake. He dropped.

I pulled him to the edge of the tunnel and leaned him against the wall, drawing his hood low over his face. He'd look like he'd simply passed out. I slid off his mask, relieved when I didn't recognize him. Somehow, pretending to be a stranger felt like less of a risk. Silly, I knew, but I couldn't in a million years put on Rob's mask and pretend to be him; nor did I want my stolen mask to put me anywhere near his circle of friends.

I didn't recognize the guy, but who would I recognize? Was Yasuo here? All the vampires? Where was Carden on this night? It was a traditional celebration, after all.

There was no time for thoughts like that, and so I donned the mask and pressed on. I was now a gray mourning dove, with high cheekbones and tiny pinprick holes for eyes. A dove in mourning— it was a fitting theme and fueled my courage as I followed the echoes of the procession ahead of me.

The tunnel grew lighter. I was getting close to the castle now.

When I passed a cluster of boys sprawled on the ground, leaning against the wall of the tunnel, looking completely blotto, it hit home how the original owner of my mask wouldn't be missed. Nor did I think anyone would recognize his mask on me. I doubted anyone was thinking or seeing clearly with all this smoke.

I slowed my steps as I caught up to the Trainees. I wasn't afraid now. My presence didn't seem to matter—they were reeling, drunk or high or whatever it was that smoke was doing to them.

And what was that smoke doing to *me*? I breathed as shallowly as I could, but still I sensed the havoc it was wreaking on my senses. How it was making me brave. I tried to keep my wits about me, reminding myself this was bravado, not true bravery.

I could've argued with myself all I wanted, but still, the smoke was doing its work. It deposited me into a dream where I watched myself moving through the scene around me as though through a kaleidoscope. Sensations assaulted me. Flickering lights, smells, and sounds, getting louder now. Shouting, drumming. I walked toward it.

This was dangerous. I stopped and shook my head clear. Why was I here?

Truth, I remembered. I was here to find the truth.

I bent as though to tie my shoe. The smoke was thinner close to the ground, and I sucked in several cleansing breaths.

When I stood, my head was clearer, and I followed a knot of boys into a brightly lit room. *The castle.* I'd made it.

The contrast between rough-hewn stone caverns and wainscoted walls astounded me. The room was small, like a sitting room, but despite its modest size, candelabra were all around. There were chairs upholstered in gemstone colors. Enormous paintings in gilt frames.

It'd do no good for someone to stop me and talk, so I passed through the room and kept going. I moved with purpose. I breathed shallowly through my teeth now, squatting every now and then to clear my head. It helped, but didn't completely eradicate the woozy feeling.

A handful of boys made their way up a winding staircase. Pulling my hood low, I followed. I needed to see more. To take in as much of this world as I could.

Following the crowd, I found myself in a large ballroom. The ceiling was high, elaborate chandeliers replacing the candelabra. The noise was overpowering.

There were dozens of boys now, though in their creepy masks and flowing cloaks, they seemed like men, menacing, gathered in one place and yet not together, each lost to his own raving.

I scanned the room, searching for a familiar silhouette. Who did I know here? Part of me was terrified I'd spot Carden, and for once I was grateful he was nowhere to be found. I didn't know if I could've dealt with the sight of him, because seeing these boys in this strange, secret setting was more disturbing than I would've guessed.

The smoke was doubly thick in here, muddling my judgment, and there was no longer room to squat and catch my breath. I fought to keep a clear head. Fires roared all around, robbing the room of its air. I tried not to cough from the stench of incense that clouded the room.

Rhythmic drumming reverberated in my head, and my pulse rose to answer. *My heart* . . . Suddenly it was all I was aware of. Pounding in my chest. Punching against my lungs. Making it even harder to get enough oxygen.

I pressed through the crowd, desperate to find some space. Some oxygen. I wove my way through the bodies and suddenly met with cool air. An opening, along the edge of the room. I sucked in a shaky breath.

Something called to me, but I stood too close to the wall. I craned my neck up to see.

Weapons. The entire wall was covered with them. This was a collection of Acari weaponry.

I swayed and braced a hand on the wall to steady myself. Staggering forward, I scanned weapon after weapon. The collection was endless. Vast. Too vast, too much like hunting trophies hung for display, only instead of animal heads, these were relics of girls long dead.

Tiny details gutted me. The frayed leather on the end of a knife hilt. Smudges of dirt on a quiver. There were throwing stars up there, too, and that was the sight that shot clarity into my brain.

I bolted back the way I'd come. I had to get out of there, swerving around guys, weaving through the crowd. Those weapons, the smoke . . . I was beyond claustrophobic, beyond panicked. I was fevered. I ran into a body, spun around, lurched forward, slammed into something. Furniture. With a quick glance, I dismissed it. An ornamental table.

Then I did a double take. A hodgepodge of weapons had been dropped unceremoniously on its surface. But one stood out from the rest: Emma's Buck knife.

CHAPTER THIRTY-FIVE

M y throat convulsed, swallowing bile. I'd recognize
that serrated blade anywhere. How I'd mocked my
friend about it . . . I'd call her Billy Ray, joke about squirrel
dinners.

Oh, Em. Was she here, alive, in some sort of hideous limbo?

My stomach churned violently, needing to repel its contents. I swallowed again, choking down the burning fluids. *Not
now. Not safe.* I gathered my nerves. I wanted to crumple there
and then. I wanted to scream. To run. But I'd do none of those
things. Because more than anything now, I wanted to fight.
Emma wasn't truly dead. How could she be when her weapon
wasn't yet hung on the wall? Hope was ablaze in my chest.

Yasuo had said she couldn't be alive. That she was gone. He'd
crowed about her heart. He was haunted, but was it by something
he'd seen or something he knew he'd be forced to see?

Hope was momentarily crushed by a dawning horror: Acari
were entering the room. They were filtering in, just a few of

them, some recognizable as ones who'd disappeared. These were girls—like Emma—whom I'd presumed dead. Each wore a white robe, and they stumbled slowly, lurching as though drugged. I scanned the room, frantically searching for my friend, but she wasn't among them. I believed I'd have felt her if she were.

I'd assumed she was gone. Everyone had. But if she weren't . . .

Could it be true? Emma, separated from her weapon. It didn't bode well. But I couldn't let it pass. If she truly were alive, I could rescue her. I *would* rescue her.

I could look right now. I was here. When would I get a better opportunity?

I realized I was striding back into the crowd when I stopped myself. *No.* Not now. Now, more than ever, I needed to stop the recklessness. It wasn't just my life at risk anymore; it was Emma's. If I were going to rescue her, it'd take more than just me running through the keep wearing a stolen mask and cloak.

Sure, if I found her, I could probably get both of us out alive. These boys were drugged out of their minds. I could steal another cloak, carry her out if I had to. But then what? Where could I take her?

No, this would take planning. It'd take help. I'd need a boat, a destination.

I'd helped a friend escape before. I had no doubts I could do it again.

A figure popped from the crowd, catching my eye. His was a familiar walk. There was a familiar set to his shoulders. I edged closer. He'd been affected by the smoke, and his movements were broad, sloppy. He adjusted his mask. *Josh.*

His presence shocked me. Though why should it? *All* the guys were here.

I spun in place, taking in the crowd. They were swaying, boisterous, moving to the drumming, growing louder. My head spun with smoke, but cutting through it all was the sharp stab of betrayal, sobering me.

Josh. He was one of them.

Betrayed. Duped. Used. Shamed. Emotions reeled through me, shrill alarms sounding in my head, clearing the smoke from my senses.

I focused, watching, suddenly sharper than ever. This creepy museum of Acari weaponry, an unmistakable Buck knife among them. I had to get out of there. But not before I made a vow.

I'll come back for you, Emma.

I wended my way back through the crowd. I needed a door. Was it because I was regaining my senses, or was the chaos and revelry intensifying? I spotted Josh again, and I ducked behind a group of boys who I was certain weren't familiar to me. He was at the head of a pack, other Trainees trailing him like dogs. He was acting the loudest. The rowdiest.

It disgusted me. Who was he? How had he fooled me all this time?

I thought back to the days he'd been friendly with Lilac. Back then, I'd believed I couldn't trust him. I should've kept my resolve.

I couldn't watch him anymore. I had to escape. Suddenly, this was a roomful of wolves, and I was prey, hiding in plain sight. I'd entered the castle thinking this a suicide mission, but now more than ever, I needed to live.

I strode through the door and stopped short. This wasn't the one that led back to the staircase. Instead, I found myself standing in a vast dining room. At its center was a massive table of black wood, thick and scarred with age, like something Beowulf might've dined upon.

Only instead of a meal laid atop the table, there was a girl.

She was alive.

It was Frost.

CHAPTER THIRTY-SIX

⸻

Bodies jostled behind me. *Crap.* I'd started something. Guys were on my heels, following me in. Sheep, all of them.

The drumming was even louder now. I glanced from my roommate to the incoming tide of Trainees. Could I help her? I had to help someone, to do something. To take some action and assert my own humanity.

A hand shoved at my back, someone eagerly pushing past. Another hand, grabbing my arm, shoving me aside. They were filing in, focused only on getting nearer to the table.

To Frost.

She wore a long white robe and looked oddly serene for someone who was tied to a table. A small platform stood near her head, draped with a plush crimson cloth. A dagger rested on top, as did Frost's weapon—that distinctive halberd that could be hers and hers alone.

Pity and sadness swamped me. Why was she so calm? Why

wasn't she fighting? Had she been drugged? Brainwashed? Or did Frost actually believe this was some great honor?

It'd be just like my stupid vamp-loving roommate to believe she was being rewarded. She'd embraced the vampires, giving them her all—her faith, her efforts, her zeal. It was tragic that this girl who'd imagined herself the vampires' pet would, in the end, be so completely undone by them. And I had no doubts, she was about to be completely undone. If that dagger was any indication, it'd be in the most horrific of ways.

Poor Frost. Would anyone miss her? She'd had no friends. She'd suffered the torments of that boy—Marlin, was it?—she'd suffered in silence, believing it was right. That it was her place. The island had brainwashed her, and it was pathetic and tragic both.

Just as I was being brainwashed, a tiny, traitorous voice said in the back of my head. The only difference between Frost and me was that I was putting up more of a fight. Killing to keep myself alive was one thing, but killing out of spite was another thing entirely. It had to stop.

"Come, boys." The voice resounded through the cavernous dining room, startling me from my thoughts. It was the woman who'd been speaking with Alcántara—I recognized her voice instantly. *Sonja.*

Was *this* what the Spanish vampire had been protecting me from? Would I have been trussed on a table for a bunch of Trainees to ogle? And what would happen if I were caught now?

"Come," she said again, beckoning. Something about her voice mesmerized me.

I found myself wanting to go to her and stopped. Under my

mask, I'd broken into a sweat. It took great effort not to glance her way. Because I wanted to look . . . how I longed to look, to catch just one glimpse. To see her.

The guys, though, they didn't fight it. They swarmed her. I'd cursed them as they'd come in the room, but I was thankful now, hidden in the crush of bodies.

"Gather to me as we celebrate with this night of fire and life." Something in that powerful voice resonated, calling to me. But I forced myself to stare blindly forward. I couldn't catch her eye. There was no leaving now—I was stuck here. "Be here, with me," she ordered. "Celebrate with me." Did she sense that not all eyes were upon her? Her voice got richer, deeper, as she intoned, *"Look upon me."*

I couldn't fight it any longer. My eyes were drawn to her—I couldn't not look. My eyes drank her in. She was not at all what I'd expected. She was magnetic. Breathtaking.

She was also a petite, white-haired girl, looking no older than fourteen.

I knew not to trust my eyes. This Sonja had been born hundreds of years ago. I felt it. Felt her power. It thrummed through the room. This was the one who wanted me, delivered by Alcántara like I was a take-out meal. This was Sonja, who'd carved the runes. Sonja, ruler of vampires.

Did that mean *she* was Vampire? Could women *be* vampires?

Her robe was a deep crimson, made of a fabric so fine, firelight danced across it, rippling along her body like she was made of the fire itself. She was irresistible. A lodestone at the front of the room. She was the pulse of the keep.

"Who among you knows the misericordia?" She raised her arms, and her sleeves fell back, revealing pale, thin arms and a dagger clutched in her hand. "Behold." She held a dagger aloft. It was long and thin, its blade a delicate thing. "Behold the blade."

I beheld, all right. I also beheld dozens of Trainees shuffling into the room, blocking off my exit as they did.

The guys began to chant, sonorous and rhythmic, in time with the drums. The sounds coalesced, their meaning becoming clear. *Sonja.*

Panic swelled in me as boys' bodies jostled me. I stood tall. Tried to project an air of guy-ness.

They chanted for her, and I had to bite my tongue not to be swept in. The smoke was affecting me again, and I panted in several quick breaths. But it was Sonja's hypnotic power that was the greatest threat of all. I focused on the strange disconnect between that deep intoning voice and her diminutive child's body. It helped me regain some of my wits.

"Misericordia," she repeated, and the room fell instantly silent. "It comes from *misereri*, to pity. And *cordis*." She touched a hand to her breast. "The heart." She paused long enough in the silent room that I began to freak out someone might hear my own galloping pulse. "This is the giver of mercy," she said finally, easing the dagger back down. With every movement, firelight caught and shimmered along the fine blade. "It was used by knights of old to give a quick and merciful death to their foes."

She extended Frost's hands up to the top of the table, then ran her fingers down my roommate's arm slowly, almost sensually. "The misericordia delivers one final gift," she purred. "A good death."

A good death . . . what a stupid Viking thing to say.

She gazed at the misericordia. "This blade is fine enough to pierce armor. Precise enough to pierce the heart at a single stroke."

Or to stake vampires, I thought savagely.

I hung back as much as I could, terrified now. I couldn't stay. But I couldn't leave either. I was utterly enthralled, desperately curious. And anyway, leaving would draw too much attention. I could only hope this ritual didn't involve removing one's mask, because then I'd really be toast.

"This very blade was the weapon of the first Initiate," Sonja continued. "The first Acari fought with this. Died by this. She gave her heart so that you could have an immortal body."

An immortal body, but what of the soul? Did the vampires sacrifice that in addition to innocent girls?

Sonja placed the tip of the blade at Frost's armpit and rolled her eyes back in her head. She began to chant, repeating an Icelandic word I recognized. *Epli . . . epli . . . epli . . .*

Apple.

A conversation shot into my head—ironically, it was an argument I'd had with Frost. Ever since she'd seen the runes I'd transcribed—the runes *she'd* accused of being incorrect—she'd taken every opportunity to mock me about them.

"A girl ruling vampires," she'd jeered. "As if."

"What do you mean *as if*? Who *wouldn't* want to be Vampire?"

Her expression was pure scorn. "As if women could have such power."

That set my hackles up. Why couldn't women be powerful? "There were powerful goddesses in your precious *Poetic Edda*," I said. "Like . . . like Idun." I'd remembered the name then—it was fresh in my mind from a chapter we'd just covered in Dag's class. Idun was a goddess in the Norse pantheon, who'd kept apples and was eternally youthful.

"Actually, Idun"—she'd used an elaborate accent to pronounce it the correct *Iðunn*—"appears primarily in the *Prose Edda*, not the *Poetic*."

"Whatever, *Audra*."

And on we'd went . . .

Was this ritual about Idun? For all I knew, the goddess was alive and well, running around Valhalla—seeing Sonja had made the most impossible notion possible.

"*Epli . . . epli . . . epli . . .*" they chanted, and it must've struck a chord with Frost, too, because I saw a fleeting moment of panic in her eyes. There and gone.

"Are you ready, dear Acari?" Sonja traced a tender finger down Frost's cheek, and my roommate didn't move. She looked paralyzed, but whether by fear, hypnosis, or the cloying smoke, I didn't know. "Are you ready for your good death?"

Apparently, Sonja didn't care about her answer, because she turned her attention back to the crowd. "Women are the givers of immortality. Beginning with the goddess Idun, whose apple granted eternal life."

Bingo.

Sonja looked so peaceful, so calm, so *triumphant*. . . . I could tell something very bad was about to happen. I held utterly still, holding my breath, clenching my teeth till my jaw throbbed.

"You must thank this young woman for her sacrifice," she said. "Come, partake of the young Initiate. It is through the apple of her flesh that you will experience Idun's deathless power."

And then she plunged her blade into Frost. *Oh God, oh God.* I wanted desperately to look away, but couldn't.

"Consume," she shouted. "Consume and know immortality."

Her face bloomed into the most magnificent smile as she thrust deeper still. My roommate seized once, her body arching and stiffening on the table, before sagging into death.

"Epli," Sonja was chanting, over and over, and the Trainees' voices rose to match hers. The drums pounded wildly now. "Celebrate, dear children. Celebrate this night upon which you ascend to the next level. Thank this girl for her gift."

A chorus of male voices rose around me.

She turned her loving attention to Frost's chest and— *Oh God, her heart.* I was desperate to look away, to shut out this ghoulish scene, but was too terrified of what the consequences might be. She was going to do something to Frost's heart. Her voice cried above the din, "Thank Idun for her immortality."

I could tell from the riotous chants of the boys that something was happening. I realized I'd shut my eyes tightly beneath my mask, and I forced myself to look. I couldn't be caught now.

Sonja swayed in place, hands raised. The drums were pounding, smoke choking the room. Trainees were passing something from hand to hand, each taking a moment to take a taste.

Oh God. Oh no . . . It was Frost's heart.

They passed it along, each boy tasting in a haze of ecstasy. I saw Josh take his turn, saw the rapture on his face. He held it longer than anyone.

Nausea punched me in the gut. Spit pooled in my mouth, revulsion washing over me in violent waves. My body rebelled, wanting to expel the contents of my stomach, to repel everything about this. I had to swallow and swallow again, choking back my bile. *This* was how the boys became vampires. How vampires became immortal.

Except for Yasuo. Yasuo wasn't surviving the transition. I doubted he was even here tonight. He'd spoken of Emma's heart. *Her heart.* Of course Yasuo was turning Draug. Did he know he'd be forced to hold his girlfriend's heart in his hands? Or was she already gone?

A Ferris wheel spun in my brain, making me woozy, blurring my vision. I was sick. Confused. Hysteria clawed at me, desperate to be unleashed. A thin, rational thread was all that held me together, while the rest of me had snapped, wanting only to fall to the ground and curl into a ball, weeping and trembling.

I fought it. I had to save Emma from this. Had to save *everyone* from this.

I backed up until my hand touched the wall, clutching at the cold, damp stone to hold myself upright. I panted through my teeth. Deeper than this horror was the visceral, animal instinct that I couldn't be caught. I couldn't betray my presence.

The madness in the room reached a fever pitch. Miraculously, I managed to edge away.

I stayed away from the "apple." It repelled me. And it was easy enough to avoid—the boys were too doped up on smoke and Idun's immortality to notice me shifting through the crowd.

Sonja, though . . . I imagined I felt *her* eyes on my back. But she made her grand exit, and the boys filed out behind her.

I wanted to run, to shoulder my way through the crowd and be the first out the door, but I made myself wait. Finally, everyone was gone.

All that was left was Frost, on the table, alone in death as in life. Her eyes were wide open, and I couldn't help it. My feet stuttered beneath me, walking toward her. I had to shut those eyes. I had to do one kindness for this girl.

Her skin was already cold when I touched a hand to her forehead. Closed her eyes. "Bye, Audra."

All my talk of power. I had no power. These were vampires. How could I ever kill them? Forget power.

And forget Alcántara, too. Al was small-time. Some greater force was at work.

But then I saw it. Sonja's dagger. The misericordia. It gleamed, wiped clean and placed adoringly on its velvet-cushioned platter.

Who was Sonja? What did this all mean? I'd thought she was my heroine, but—oh God—she wasn't my Wonder Woman at all. She was at the root of all this. Ruling with an iron fist.

I'd thought much about the nature of strength. Of power. Standing there, utterly disempowered, I realized: Such things didn't exist in a vacuum. Strength was meaningless without something against which it could be measured. There was a yin to every yang. Power wasn't power until it was tested. Which meant, if there were such creatures as these fighting for dominance, then who were they fighting against? If there was a force this evil, surely somewhere there existed a good just as formidable threatening it.

I was tired of being strong. But I had no choice. I'd be strong a little longer. For Emma. I wouldn't give these vampires power. I'd take it. And it would start here.

I stared at the misericordia. If it could make vampires, then maybe it could destroy them, too.

I didn't pause. I took it.

And then I ran. The smoke had cleared, and with it, my thoughts. My instincts burst alive with renewed intensity. My body was an explosion of muscle and adrenaline. I raced back down the stairs, arms pumping, until I reached the tunnel; then I bounded down passages, guided only by my gut. I was heedless of danger. Heedless of anything but the need to flee. I'd have clawed all the way out of my skin if I could.

I tore off the robe as I ran. Ignoring my injuries, ignoring the elements, the cold and the wind and the darkness, ignoring the very real possibility that I was about to hurtle toward certain death, I leapt from the sea gate and plunged into the waves below.

CHAPTER THIRTY-SEVEN

Waves dark as midnight sucked at my legs. The freezing water churned, brutal slaps at the back of my head. Caught in the breakers, I couldn't get my bearings. The surf wasn't so very deep, but it was violent, tearing my feet out from under me, slamming my face into the rocky sand, holding me down. Waves rolled over me. I couldn't tell up from down. Churning, churning, I stole a breath, then was sucked back under, pounded some more.

Survive. I had to survive. I gripped that blade harder, my hand frozen into a claw clutching the misericordia like a lifeline.

Rolling in the breakers, I turned the last of my energy inward. My own fear would kill me, not these waves. I imagined my panic was a balloon . . . and then I let it go. I could swim. I *would* swim.

I went limp, let my body spin underwater, trying to sense the angle of the riptide. Rocks punched my ribs. Caught my ankle.

My knee slammed hard onto rocky sand. Feeling the bottom beneath my feet, my reaction was instinctive, instant. I jack-knifed, kicking up out of the water, bursting as high over the waves as I could, diving sideways. My arms windmilled. I managed to begin a crawl stroke across the riptide.

I made it to shore. Lumbered up the beach. I had to get out of there. Far from the castle.

Calm down. Calm down. Calm down.

Hysteria would kill me. I lengthened my stride, slowing down. I slowed and deepened my breaths.

The knife. I had to protect the knife. I stopped, unzipped my wetsuit enough to slide the dagger in, nestled along my rib cage. Trembling, it took me forever to manage that simple task.

I was alive, though. Maybe Emma was, too.

But Sonja . . . she was immense power. Pure evil.

I had her blade. Would she sense it missing? I had to hide it. Had to act normal. I sucked in a deep breath, held it, blew it out slowly through my teeth.

I'd return to the dorm. Tomorrow, I'd make a fuss about Frost's absence. I'd feign shock, surprise.

In the past hours, my world had tilted sharply. Everything I'd thought I understood about the island was wrong. Emma—I had to believe she was alive. Josh couldn't be trusted. And Alcántara, what of him? Was he friend? Foe?

I'd felt so alone, but was that true? There was always Ronan. Would I see him soon?

My dorm came into view, a hulking shadow in the darkness. A single bulb was lit in the foyer. It was enough to illuminate the person waiting for me.

I *wasn't* alone. It *was* Ronan, sitting on the front stoop.

"Ronan," I exclaimed, so unutterably relieved. I took the stairs two at a time, ready to throw myself into his arms.

But then he stood, hands held stiffly behind him. He looked nervous. "Acari Drew," he said formally.

I stuttered to a halt. My world had just shattered, and now this. Was I losing my mind? How long had I been gone? How much time had I spent in the castle? Suddenly everything, even my own sanity, was thrown into doubt. "What's going on?" I asked dumbly.

Another figure emerged from the shadows. "Och, my wee dove."

Carden. Carden was back.

My mouth opened, but I was unable to make a sound. I realized I was shivering violently, emotions buffeting me more savagely than any surf.

Carden turned to Ronan. Had he sensed the emotion between us? My urge to go to Ronan for comfort? I expected him to lay into the Tracer, but instead the vampire approached him, clasped his hand. Carden put a brotherly arm around Ronan's shoulders. "Thank you," he said. "Thank you for guarding her. It was much to ask, and you have my gratitude."

The ground jolted beneath me. *Thank you for guarding her.*

I'd wondered why Ronan kept showing up, all those times he was concerned for my safety. But he hadn't been there because he wanted to be. It was because Carden had asked him.

My knees gave way. But Carden was suddenly there, catching me. I shoved him away, steadying my own self. "You asked Ronan to *babysit* me?"

"I knew I'd be away for a time," Carden said gently.

"So you had Ronan babysit me," I repeated flatly. I stared at the Tracer, but he didn't—couldn't?—meet my gaze. I'd thought I knew him, but after seeing Josh at that ritual, how could I think I knew anybody?

He'd been there for me because Carden had asked him to be. Because if anything had happened to me under his watch, he'd have been in a world of hurt.

Look at me, Ronan. What about our almost-kiss? Because I hadn't imagined *that,* had I? I could only guess what would've happened to Ronan if something had happened *with* Ronan.

"I dared not leave you to face danger alone," Carden said gently.

I spun on him. "You were the one who left in the first place. No, check that. You took off . . . in the night . . . without telling me."

"I didn't know until—"

"You had enough time to ask Ronan to mind me. You put me in his care. What am I to you, a child?" I felt Ronan disappearing into the shadows—of course, he'd want to sit out on the lovers' quarrel. "Bye, *Tracer* Ronan," I shot out, putting a cold edge to the formal term of address. "It's been real."

Carden took my arm. "Come, *mo chridhe.* You are upset."

I made myself flinch away, wanting to lash out. "You bet I'm upset." I was furious. After the horrors of that ritual, I felt lucky to be alive, and here was Carden, nonchalant as ever with his affections. And the really crap part about the whole thing was that I was angry mostly because I was *embarrassed.* Because seeing him now, I realized how much I'd missed him when he clearly hadn't even cared enough to say good-bye. "Do you *want* to be with me, or did you come back because you had to?"

"I long to be with you." His voice was low and mellow, and it rippled over me like warm flowing waters.

"Then why weren't you? I *needed* you, and you bailed. I lost Emma, I lost Yasuo, and you . . . you just vanished. You weren't here when I needed you most."

"There was something you needed more. If you let me—"

"Cryptic much? You're just thirsty." I stormed inside. He could follow me or not.

He followed. "Are you *not* thirsty?" he asked, and he actually sounded baffled.

I stopped short. "Is that it? Did you come back because you craved me? Do you even like me?"

"I came back because you're mine." He stepped closer, his body pressing against me as he cupped my cheeks in his hands. "I came back because I love you."

My throat clenched. He'd called me *love* before, but he'd never said he loved me. Could it be true? I peered hard into his eyes. He was looking so sad, so confused.

I couldn't trust it. I stepped back, headed to my dorm room. "Why'd you even leave in the first place? After all we shared, all we did . . ." I tapered off, sudden chagrin choking me. It was so hard not to be insecure about the times we'd been together physically—had I done something wrong? Some rookie error? Did I kiss weird? *What?*

He stopped me when we reached my door, putting a fingertip to my chin. "You are angry."

I cut my eyes away, fumbling with my keys. "You think?"

"I will explain everything. But first you must forgive me."

"Must I?" I stormed into the room, shivering like crazy now. "You should go. I need to change."

"I cannot bear this, Annelise. Please look at me."

I couldn't. And yet looking at him was all I wanted to do. To look at him. To curl in to him. I was so cold. I'd missed him so much. This close, my blood sang to his. My every sense longed for him. I fought it. "It's just the stupid bond. That's the only reason you came back." I made myself meet his eyes and refused to believe the bewilderment I saw there. "You couldn't take it anymore. You had to come back when you got too thirsty."

He looked pained. From his thirst or from my words? "I thirst for you, yes. But your company is what I missed most."

Hadn't I always credited his honesty as one of the traits I admired most? He readily admitted his thirst *and* to missing me. He could've made up an elaborate lie. Had he really left for a reason? "I thought you wanted to break up with me."

"Never," he said, his voice hoarse.

"Then why'd you go?"

"I will explain everything. But it's been so long. And to have you so close . . ." He leaned down, touching his forehead to mine. "Please, love. You're shivering. Let me hold you."

All I wanted was to curl in to him. I knew how much I'd missed him, but now that he'd come back, I felt how much I *needed* him. That tug deep in my belly, pulling me toward him like I couldn't do anything but be by his side. But I forced myself to be strong. Hadn't I proven to myself how strong I was? How powerful?

"No." I forced out the word.

"Just a single kiss. Then I promise, I will do as you ask."

"It's not that easy. I needed you, Carden."

"I asked Ronan to keep an eye on you. Was he not attentive?"

The words crushed me anew. Ronan had been there for me,

but not truly. It was a swell of emotions, too confusing to con-sider. "Ronan was fine. But I needed *you*. You were gone for so long."

"Time flows differently for me. I was gone not a moment longer than was necessary. Trust me when I tell you, you are all I've thought about. Being apart from you . . . it was as though a limb had been torn from me." He slid his arms around me, and warmth spread through me, soothing me.

How I wanted to believe him. I wanted everything to be okay again. "You should've thought of that before you disappeared."

"I thought only of you when I left," he said. "I left *for* you."

"What does that mean?"

"Please, love." He sounded so . . . broken. "Just touch me back. Just once. And then I will tell you everything."

Before I knew it, before I could help it, I was in his arms. He was kissing me, and relief so profound swept through me. Rippled across my skin. Carden felt like home.

And it made me angry. I'd fought so hard to be strong, and just one look, one word, and I was weak again, huddled in his arms. He felt so good. He *was* so good, and so dashing and easy and handsome. Surely girls flung themselves at him wherever he went.

I pushed him away, trying to keep hold of the anger. "Where were you, anyway? Were you with another woman?"

"Aye." The word was raw, as though torn from him.

That one syllable shattered me.

But then . . . then the world stopped as he spoke again:

"I went in search of another woman, but not as you think, dear one. I found her. I found your mother."

Like her heroine, **Veronica Wolff** braved an all-girls school, traveled to faraway places, and studied lots of languages. She was not, however, ever trained as an assassin (or so she claims). In real life, she's most often found on a beach or in the mountains of northern California, but you can always find her online.

CONNECT ONLINE

veronicawolff.com